CHASER

Chaser, Book One

Rick R. Reed

A NineStar Press Publication

Published by NineStar Press
P.O. Box 91792,
Albuquerque, New Mexico, 87199 USA.
www.ninestarpress.com

Chaser

Printed in the USA
NineStar Edition
February, 2020

Print ISBN: 978-1-951880-50-7

Also available in eBook, ISBN: 978-1-951880-49-1

Warning: This book contains sexually explicit content, which may only be suitable for mature readers.

For Bruce, who has always been just the right size—
for me.

Part One

Chapter One

"I like fat men."

"You like big butts?"

"I cannot lie."

Caden and his therapist laughed together over the song reference, both old enough to remember Sir Mix-A-Lot's 1992 rap hit "Baby Got Back." Camille D'Amico reined in her laughter abruptly, pushing her tortoiseshell glasses back up on her nose and fussing with her frizzy halo of brown hair. She adopted a serious expression. "So you're attracted to heavier men. Is that a problem?"

"Not really a problem, I guess. It's just that I wonder why. I mean, look at me."

Caden stood up, turned around slowly, and sat back down in the comfortable overstuffed chair facing Camille. He knew what he was displaying—a very trim, tight five-foot-eleven frame upon which not even an ounce of fat rested. In the dictionary, if one looked up the word "lean," there was Caden's picture, the perfect illustration. He rubbed his hands over his black buzz cut and then brought one hand down to the stubble of his just-coming-in beard. Not only was he very fit, he was a very handsome thirty-year-old man.

"What?" Camille asked. "You think you're too good for a guy with a few extra pounds on his frame? Think you're slumming if you take a walk on the fat side?"

Caden shook his head and put up his palms in self-defense. "No, no, that's not it at all. I don't think I'm better, not by any stretch. I'm just wondering why, lately espccially, I've been drawn to heavier men."

"Is this something new for you?"

"Not really, but it's only something I've been acting on in the past few months. I have this friend, Bobby, who I usually go out with and he's, well, he can be kind of superficial..." Caden's voice trailed off as he thought of his gorgeous friend, who looked a lot like the porn star, Dawson, with a trim build, cut abs, closely shorn auburn hair, and luminous gray eyes. The difference between Bobby and Dawson was that Bobby was much choosier than Dawson, although perhaps no less promiscuous—no mean feat when one considered one of Dawson's films was entitled *Dawson's 50-Load Weekend.* Anyway, this session was supposed to be about Caden, not Bobby. "And he always gives me a hard time about wanting to meet, as I said, heavier men."

"And this Bobby's opinion is important to you?"

"He's my best friend."

"Important enough that you would alter going after what you really want for him?"

Camille's question stopped him short. He'd never really thought of it that way. Why *did* it matter what Bobby thought? So what if he didn't approve of the bearded redhead he met online and invited over last week? And what business was it of Bobby's if he liked to peruse the profiles at footballplayerbuild.com?

Obviously, it bothered him enough to bring it up here today with Camille, whom he had been seeing for the past three weeks. His visits to her were his thirtieth birthday present to himself. He hoped to figure out why, at age thirty, he had yet to find a relationship that lasted more than three dates.

He had begun wondering if there was something intrinsically wrong with him. He was a good catch—at least that's what his mother told him—but on paper, he did look good. No one could argue with that. He was handsome, having inherited his mother's Sicilian olive complexion, black hair, and eyes that ranged from amber to green. His nose was strong, patrician, some might say (his mom again, anyway). He wasn't a bodybuilder, but years of running four to six miles four to six days a week, along with summertime lakefront bike rides, had given him a good, solid build.

And it wasn't just in the looks department where he thought he had a lot to offer. He had a good head on his shoulders. *That* he got from his late father, who had been a fully tenured professor of English literature at Northwestern University in Evanston before passing away unexpectedly one morning in the bathroom of a heart attack. That same head on his shoulders had given him, if not a stellar job, a solidly respectable and reliable one as a copywriter at a medical association in downtown Chicago. He had been there since graduating from Northwestern nine years ago, starting out as an editorial assistant on one of their trade journals.

So why did he feel the need to try to apply the same standards Bobby applied to his own dates, standards that could be summed up by Bobby with the initials FG, which stood for "fucking gorgeous"? If a man was not FG, so Bobby's rationale went, he was not worth fucking.

Sometimes Caden wondered why he had Bobby as a best friend. But he could be hilarious at times, and he could be a lot of fun. Caden on his own in a bar was a wallflower, but with Bobby, some of his charm and charisma, the devil-may-care attitude, rubbed off on Caden.

Plus, going out with Bobby usually meant he would hook up with one of Bobby's FG prospects' fucking gorgeous friends. Because, as Bobby always said, "The hot ones travel in packs."

Caden shook his head and looked at the therapist, who was sitting patiently, waiting. "What did you ask me again?"

"I asked you if Bobby's opinion was more important to you than getting what you want." Camille cocked her head.

"No, no, of course not." He answered too quickly.

"You know," Camille said, "I'm like what's in your own head. There's no need in here to try and come up with what you think is the right answer. No need to censor yourself. Do I need to remind you there's no judgment here?"

"No."

"So, I won't ask you about Bobby's opinion again, but I do want you to think about your answer."

"Why?"

"Because you brought up your attraction to heavy men for a reason." Camille shrugged. "It doesn't matter so much what the reason is, so much as it matters what *you* think about it. Look, people are attracted to other people for all sorts of reasons, and there's no right or wrong way to be attracted. Take my mother—please!" Camille laughed. "Ever since my father passed away a few years ago, she's been all about younger men. And I am not talking forties and fifties here. I'm talking about much younger, your age, Caden, and even in their twenties. Mom's sixty, but she's a knockout."

"Cougar?" Caden asked.

"Use that word around her and you might get your eyes scratched out. Anyway, my point is that it's what she likes, and even though I did question it at first, especially when she was having me meet guys who were younger than I was, it wasn't my call to make. Attraction is subjective—totally."

"You're right."

Camille laughed. "I'm not looking for affirmation. I just want to understand why you chose to bring up this particular attraction with your therapist."

And Caden realized he'd like to know the reason himself. If he could only get a handle on it, a love handle, if you will. He shook his head, censoring his inner Kathy Griffin.

The therapy session failed to illuminate the rationale for Caden's attraction, and he left Camille's office with homework not on why he was attracted to heavy guys, but why he felt that mattered.

It didn't matter, did it?

Chapter Two

Bobby slid next to Caden, who was standing next to the wall on a crowded Friday night at Sidetrack. The huge video bar, the jewel among dozens of gay bars clustered along Halsted Street and the epicenter of the gay community's nightlife in Chicago, was the first stop on their weekly Friday night pub crawl.

"There you go." Bobby thrust a bottle of Bud Light into Caden's hand and smiled at him.

"Thanks." Bobby took a swig of the beer and wondered if putting in a couple of extra miles in the morning during his lakefront run would be enough to rid him of the calories. This was his third beer.

Sidetrack was lively this Friday night at the tail end of autumn. Bobby and Caden stood on a riser overlooking the main bar. Several screens of various sizes throughout the place were predictably playing the video for Lady Gaga's "Born This Way," a song that like "I Will Survive" was guaranteed a long and healthy life in gay establishments. Above the pounding beat was the music of male conversation, ice clinking in glasses, and the occasional burst of laughter.

A man edged by them on his way to the bar. He could have been a model for Abercrombie and Fitch—a perfectly chiseled face with just a touch of five o'clock shadow, warm brown eyes, and a build that was headed toward that of professional wrestler John Cena. He was outfitted in a leather bomber jacket (too warm for the night, but it looked hot in every respect), a pair of faded green cargo pants, and a form-fitting white T-shirt that Caden supposed had to have been at least 50 percent spandex. It showed off his massive pecs to good advantage.

"Hey, how's it goin'?" Bobby asked, his voice a full register deeper than his regular tone.

The guy stopped and eyed Bobby up and down. Caden witnessed the approval—no, make that lust—in the guy's eyes. "Great." He flashed a smile that revealed perfect teeth so white they put Caden in mind of Tic Tacs. "Just on my way to get a drink. You gonna be here for a while?"

"Why don't you come back after you get your whistle wetted and find out?"

The guy laughed as though Bobby was the new David Sedaris and said he would do just that.

Caden turned to Bobby. "So does this mean I will soon be on my own again?" He glanced down at his watch. "It's only nine. I thought I'd have you to myself for a little while longer."

"Oh, don't be such a Klingon, Caden. You know the law of the jungle—if one of us finds a man, all bets are off. Right?"

"Right." Caden took another swig of his beer, knowing already the predictable outcome of the evening. He wondered why he chose to go out with Bobby since he almost always ended up going home alone. That was, if Caden's romance du jour did not have a buddy for him to hook up with. Caden wasn't even sure he was in the mood for that, anyway.

"Besides," Bobby said, "I don't know if the guy will even come back. And if he does, who knows if it'll go anywhere. He could be a complete idiot, or supremely self-centered, looking as hot as he does, or—God forbid—a Republican." All three, according to Bobby, were causes for dismissal, yet somehow defined pecs and a killer smile always seemed to trump Bobby's so-called standards.

Caden returned to scanning the mostly male crowd (there were a few "Graces" here and there, out with their "Wills") and watching Gaga and trying to determine the secret of her mysterious allure. The woman probably looked like a real plain Jane when she woke up in the morning, but her obvious slavish devotion to wigs and haute couture bordering on costumes (as Caden had learned as a seasoned viewer of *Project Runway*) elevated her to something irresistible to look at, at once ethereal and gritty.

Bobby whispered in his ear. "See anything you like? Any prospects on the horizon?"

Bobby did have his eye on one guy, down on the lower level at one of the high-topped tables, talking with a couple of friends. He stood out because he was not built like most of the guys here, who were, to a man, either too skinny or too pumped up to register on his attraction meter.

This guy seemed comfortable in his own skin, and Caden liked the way he threw back his head and laughed when one of his buddies said something funny. Unlike most of the other guys in Sidetrack that night, he did not show any signs that he was conscious of his appearance. Caden liked that he wore comfortable clothes, a cotton sweater of faded blue-gray, and a simple pair of carpenter pants, most likely Carhartt. He peered over the rail and saw the guy's feet were encased in work boots. *Ah. A blue-collar man. A working guy. Just my type.* Caden also liked his tousled blond hair, which revealed fetching layers of color that went from almost brown, to wheat, to pale blond, to nearly platinum, yet revealed no indication, Caden thought, of the attentions of a hairdresser. And what put him on the "edge of glory" was the crowning touch: a thick beard, not manicured into tortured geometric lines.

And he was blessedly overweight. Not fat. But a bit of gut protruded, and his thighs, in denim, looked like tree trunks. When he turned around, he revealed an ass of ample proportions, the kind Caden could just imagine as two perfect, creamy-white spheres made for grasping and pulling apart.

"Is it hot in here?" Caden shouted in Bobby's ear. He took a gulp of beer and fanned his hand in front of his face.

Bobby came back with, "No. But from the way you're gazing dreamily into the crowd, I am betting you've spied some man candy who's making your temperature rise, if not something else." Playfully, Bobby grabbed Caden's crotch, testing. Caden slapped his hand away. Bobby was his best friend and had been for years, perhaps due to the fact that neither of them had ever crossed the line that would allow one to enjoy the other on sexual terms. "Come on, you can tell Daddy. Which one is it?" Bobby gazed out at the crowd. "The black guy that looks a bit like Ty Diggs? Or maybe that shaved head at the bar, with the ass that looks like you could rest a tray on it?"

"Nah." Caden looked at the object of his attraction once more, suddenly wishing Bobby's Abercrombie stud would return, if only to free him up to at least make eyes at the blond. "There's no one. Just checking things out." Caden thought of his therapist, Camille, and wondered what she would have to say about Caden's inability to admit who he was really lusting after.

Again, why would it matter what Bobby thought?

His ruminations were brought to a screeching halt when the Abercrombie guy returned with what looked like a glass of Scotch, neat, in his beefy paw. Ah. It's just for show, Caden thought disapprovingly.

"Told you I'd come back," he said to Bobby, pointedly ignoring Caden. "I'm Dreyfus. And you are?"

Dreyfus? Seriously? Caden stifled an urge to chuckle. He leaned over to Bobby and spoke into his ear. "I'm gonna hit the bathroom. I'll be back in five minutes, and I'll want a full report."

Caden weaved through the crowd, which seemed to have grown exponentially since he and Bobby had arrived. He practically had to shove and elbow his way to the john. The restless sea of bodies, constantly shifting, offered no clear path.

The three beers pressed urgently as he finally made his way inside the high-tech confines of the main floor men's room. Caden imagined his bladder as a balloon ready to pop.

With relief, he sidled up to the long trough urinal, and with no pretensions or shyness, hauled himself out of his jeans and let free the stream that had been threatening to erupt since he left Bobby standing along the wall. Surprisingly, he was alone. He sighed with relief, bracing himself with one hand on the wall above him and, with the other, hosing the stainless steel urinal. He closed his eyes with the pleasure of the simple release.

Perhaps because his eyes were shut and he was so completely absorbed in the simple act of urination, he didn't hear someone else enter the restroom.

"Life's simple pleasures are the best, huh?"

The deep voice jerked Caden's eyes open. Startled, he turned toward the voice, dick still in hand and still working out those last few dribbles.

"Whoa! Didn't come in here for a golden shower, for Christ's sake."

"Sorry!" Caden said, breathless with shame and embarrassment. He turned back to the urinal and shook himself off. Staring hard at the wall, he felt his face burning.

Of all people to come into the bathroom at just that moment, it *had* to be the object of his affection—the beefy blond. What a lovely first impression nearly pissing on another human being makes! Caden imagined if the guy saw him again around town, he would forever be "that guy who almost pissed on me at Sidetrack. And it wasn't even a kinky thing!"

But Caden, in spite of all his mortification, was still enough of a gay man to use the opportunity to check out the blond's equipment. *Wasn't that how it always was with gay men? A building could be burning down around you, you could be on the deck of a sinking ship, on an airplane hurtling toward earth, in the midst of a natural disaster—earthquake, tornado, or hurricane—and you'd still, if fate offered it, grab a gander at another guy's dick.*

Why, it's only natural!

So he looked. And was somewhat calmed by what he saw, because Beefy Blond's endowment matched the rest of him in eye and libido-pleasing pulchritude. It was not porn star huge nor beer can thick, but it was of ample size and girth, with a healthy purple helmet head, out of which issued a lovely golden stream. Yes, Caden's momentary embarrassment was fading fast, replaced by an urge, inappropriate and perhaps legally actionable, to reach over and give that lovely cock a gentle pat or caress.

"Dude. You're staring."

And the embarrassment was back. Caden looked everywhere but into the eyes of Beefy Blond, who, he was sure, was either disgusted or amused, neither of which boded well for their future together as a couple.

Caden hurried out, trailed by the voice of the blond, yelling, "I didn't mind!"

Two other guys were entering the bathroom as Caden exited, chattering to one another about the latest episode of *The Walking Dead.* Had it not been for them, Caden might have gone back in and apologized to the guy, tried to put things right so they might have a chance to talk.

That is, if the man wanted to talk to a guy who nearly sprayed him and then ogled his cock, barely able to keep the drool in his mouth.

Hey, maybe he was flattered.

Yeah, right.

Caden thought, if Bobby was willing, now might be a good time to beat a hasty retreat, cross the street, and go on over to Roscoe's. He didn't know if he could bear to see Beefy Blond again, bear to see what was sure to be a smirk branded across his handsome, bearded face.

When he returned to the spot where he and Bobby had stood, though, Bobby and his new friend Dreyfus appeared to have taken a powder. Disbelieving, Caden scanned the crowd, looking for some sign of Dreyfus's distressed leather jacket or Bobby's bright-red hoodie.

No luck.

Shit. He wouldn't have just left me here, would he? Without even waiting to tell me what was up, to say goodnight? Caden rolled his eyes. *This is Bobby you're talking about here. Bobby with a fucking gorgeous guy.* That combination ruled out common courtesy or, for that matter, even common sense.

Caden made his way up near the entrance, where there was a little more room, and texted Bobby with a single punctuation mark: "*?*"

He waited for a few minutes, eyeing a group of guys who looked barely old enough to be out of New Trier High School entering the bar. Guffawing loudly, they were already on their way to full-on drunkery. The guy on the door checked their IDs with a little flashlight and let them pass, apparently satisfied that they were over twenty-one, although to Caden's thirty-year-old eyes, none of them looked a day over eighteen.

His phone made that little sound he could never describe but always recognized as a text arriving. He glanced down at his phone.

"Law of the jungle, buddy. Have a good night. Talk to you in the morning."

Caden pushed his way out of the bar, disappointed at the turn the evening had taken. Outside, there was a party atmosphere on Halsted as scores of gay men made their way up and down the brightly lit, rainbow-pylon-lined avenue, all pumped up, the promise of a new weekend before them.

Anything could happen.

So why, suddenly, did Caden feel so left out? It was as though an invisible wall separated him from the Friday-night revelers. He felt alone, abandoned, and stupid. Not only had his best friend left him while he was in the bathroom, he had made a complete ass of himself in front of the one man out of a couple hundred or so he had felt attracted to.

This wasn't the first time Bobby had pulled a stunt like this, and Caden knew that it certainly would not be the last.

So why do you put up with it? Don't you deserve better? Caden wandered north on Halsted, asking himself questions he had asked a hundred times or more on previous nights just like this one.

I don't know. He can be sweet sometimes. Caring. Underneath that thin veneer of superficiality was a person who was actually loyal. *Really?* Dependable. *Seriously? Yes, yes, I know it sounds unbelievable, but it's true.* Caden thought of the many times that Bobby had cheered him up when things didn't work out with yet another guy. He had even made like Caden's mom and cooked him chicken soup when he came down with a cold.

Caden's first impulse was just to go home. He knew a couple guys waited there for him, and he could hop into bed with them and have a very sweet and satisfying three-way.

Their names were Ben and Jerry.

He could put on one of his collection of tearjerkers, eat Chunky Monkey, and feel sorry for himself. What would be good tonight? Lana Turner in *Imitation of Life*, maybe? Or no, Barbara Stanwyck in *Stella*?

Caden couldn't think of a more pathetic image than one of himself in bed, alone, on a Friday night before eleven, eating ice cream and watching an old movie. He might as well put a gun to his head and pull the trigger if that was all the life he had.

No, damn it, he would not be that pathetic loser! He would get some of what Bobby was probably getting right now (which, if he knew Bobby, involved his legs being flung acrobatically over some guy's muscle-bound shoulders).

Determined, Caden headed north. Little Jim's was only a few steps away. It was a low-key kind of place, definitely not the province of posers and twinks, and tonight, Caden wanted to find himself a real man. Besides, if there were no hot prospects, the bar always had hot porn going on their screens, and he could at least file away some fodder for a liaison with Mr. Thumb and his four sons later that night.

But...as God was his witness, there would be man flesh on the table tonight.

Chapter Three

Little Jim's was perhaps the only bar on Halsted that had been untouched by gentrification. The Lakeview neighborhood around it, rehabbed by gays, couples or singles, was now occupied mostly by straight people, yuppie couples, and their offspring. The bars too had changed, becoming more like Sidetrack or Hydrate, with high-tech adornments and occupied by crowds that leaned toward younger and more clean cut.

Yet Little Jim's, on the corner of Cornelia, had remained the same. You wouldn't find any microbrews or fancy European drafts here. You'd be pushing your luck too if you dared ask for something like an appletini or even a Cosmo at the bar. Even though the ban on smoking in bars in Chicago had been in effect for several years now, the walls seemed to retain a nicotine cast, and Caden was certain, if he inhaled deeply, he could still smell the scores of cigarettes that had once been consumed on the premises.

The crowd too was as unpretentious as the bar. There were no pretty boys here, no Abercrombie couture, and no twinks. Here, heavier men, men who were over forty, and those whom God or a gym membership had not blessed with perfect masculine forms could feel at ease.

The latter, Caden supposed, was why he landed at Little Jim's and not some other watering hole. In the back of his mind, he thought if there was a bar that Beefy Blond would end up in, it might be Little Jim's.

Well, a guy could dream, right?

There were a couple of stools open at the bar, and Caden snagged one. It afforded not only a view of the bartender (a good-looking Daddy type who put him in mind of the actor Sam Elliott) but also of one of the video monitors, which was currently playing a lovely heartwarming scene: a tattooed guy with a shaved head and handlebar moustache was suspended in a leather sling. Multiple guys were making use of his alluring hole—too many to count, really, but the guy in the sling seemed to be taking on all comers, so to speak, with hearty abandon and good will. Why, Caden even imagined the guy would be smiling if he wasn't getting his mouth stuffed full of cock in every shape, size, and color. And even though the sound was muted, Caden imagined that all the tops were whispering romantic endearments to the bottom, pledging loyalty and devotion, implying a lifetime of happiness awaited them, right after the next guy's crack at his crack.

"Hot video, huh?"

Caden gave a little start at the voice beside him. He looked up from his beer to see a very cute guy about his own age leaning against the wall and boring into his eyes with chocolate brown ones. Caden was a little disappointed to see there was no real meat on the man. An up and down viewing revealed a trim build that probably weighed in at about 160 on what Caden would guess was about a five ten frame. The guy had short curly brown hair, a little lighter than his eyes, was clean shaven, and had a nice smile that revealed a little gap in his two front teeth. In other words, he was quite ordinary looking, and Caden surmised he might not have noticed the guy had he not spoken to him. Even his clothes did nothing to make him stand out from the rest of the crowd—a black-and-green plaid shirt topped off a pair of simple Levis.

"Yeah, I guess," Caden responded to his question about the video. "Although I'd have to say I prefer a little more romance. What's going on there doesn't leave much room for that, does it?"

"No. And that's exactly why it's hot." The guy shivered. "Just kind of gets me all worked up, thinking of taking on one guy after the other like that." He grinned. "Mind if I sit down?"

Caden wasn't sure if he did mind, though he didn't want to be rude. But if this guy was into gangbangs and slings, he wasn't sure there was much hope for the two of them. How could two ever be enough? "Sure, go ahead." The guy sat down and slid his draft beer toward him, taking a pull off the mug.

"Hey, Chuck, how 'bout another shot?"

The bartender looked up from the glass he was drying. "Jack again?"

"You got it." He turned toward Caden and asked, "You want anything?"

Caden noticed the smell of alcohol fairly poured off the guy. "Nah, I'm good."

"I'm Matt." He stuck out his hand and shook Caden's. He had a nice, firm grip.

"Caden."

"Really? That's an unusual name."

"I come from an unusual mother. She probably read it in one of her romance novels when she was pregnant."

Matt paid the bartender for the shot.

Caden asked, "So you like that sort of thing? Ever done it?" Caden was curious and maybe a little intrigued. Although he did like a good Chunky Monkey, his leanings were definitely, almost strictly, in the realm of the vanilla.

Matt laughed. "God, no. Never been that lucky." He looked over toward the mirror hanging above the bar for a moment. "That kind of shit really is more in fantasy land, you know? I don't even know if I had the opportunity, I'd really actually go through it. Not unless I wanted to be wearing Depends by the time I'm forty!" He chuckled. "But it does look hot."

Caden glanced around the bar and realized that Matt here was probably his best prospect for the night. He also realized he didn't want to go home alone tonight. He couldn't bear the thought of having Bobby call him the next day, waxing erotic about his hot night with that Dreyfus character, and he would have nothing to come back with. Caden mentally shrugged. Matt here, although not his dream date, could do nicely. He wasn't beefy or blond, but he had his charms.

Caden just hoped he wasn't *too* drunk.

The two men spent the next hour or so talking about the things two strangers talk about when they've just met in a bar—where each worked (Matt did underwriting reports for a large insurance company downtown), what each liked and didn't like about their respective jobs, where they had gone to school, if they were from Chicago originally, what TV shows they followed, and how they kept in shape.

During the course of their conversation, the movie changed from the gangbang spectacular to a vintage Joe Gage porno from the 1970s, *LA Tool and Die*, of which both men approved—they both loved the hirsute guys on display and the freewheeling pursuit of pleasure. "Ah, those were the days!" Matt had sighed. Also, during the course of their conversation, Matt managed to down several more shots of Jack followed quickly by equal numbers of draft Michelob. Caden wondered how the guy could stand up, yet Matt's eyes remained clear and his words—mostly—unslurred.

When they were reduced at last to staring at the video monitor over the bar, their legs surreptitiously touching and their breath coming just a little bit quicker, Caden was not surprised in the least to be propositioned.

Caden shivered as he felt Matt's wet breath in his ear, shrugging up one shoulder because it tickled.

"Wanna come by my house? I live just a couple blocks away on Cornelia."

The proposition came along with an aromatherapy of alcohol fumes on Matt's part and a cloud of second thoughts on Caden's. He knew, from what little conversation they had shared, that the pair of them had little in common. He also realized that the hour was growing late, the beefy blond had not appeared as he had hoped in Little Jim's, and Bobby had left hours ago with his FG man of the night, about which, he was sure, he would hear endless details the next day.

Caden could stagger home with Matt, have quick, probably unsatisfying sex, exchange phone numbers that would never be called, and have perhaps a headache and an STD to show for it in the morning.

The choice was an easy one. Caden turned to Matt, smiled, and said, "Sure. You about ready?"

"I am *so* ready, handsome. Let's go."

*

Matt's apartment on Cornelia was in a charmless four-story building Caden would have dated from the 1970s. It was basically a big box with a parking garage underneath. Briefly, he wondered what the architects were thinking when they put up these monstrosities. About the only charitable thing that could be said about them was that they lived up to their intended function—providing a home. But they looked so hideous, especially next to the elegant greystones and vintage apartment buildings also dotting the neighborhood.

The lobby was more of the same midcentury blandness—a bank of bronze-colored mailboxes on one wall, faux marble tile on the walls, stained beige carpeting on the floor, and a gilt-adorned chandelier with dusty teardrop crystals and strands of cobwebs running between its upright electric candles, about a third of which had burned out.

"Nice place," Caden said, trying to put some conviction behind the words. Tacky or not, this was still someone's home. Besides, he had not followed Matt back here to check out his building's décor.

The two boarded the elevator, which was tiny, rattling and shimmying all the way to the fourth floor. Caden pretended to admire the gold-leaf wallpaper and smoked gold-vein mirror tiles as they arose, just so he wouldn't have to look at Matt's clenched-teeth, drunken grin.

It took a couple of tries for Matt to match key to keyhole at his front door. Caden waited politely, thinking how Matt smelled like a cross between a distillery and a brewery. It wasn't exactly an arousing combo, yet he made no attempt to leave. *You can, you know. You can just walk away. You could say something honest like, "Sorry, man, I'm just not into this" or even lie and say you aren't feeling so hot or the old chestnut about realizing you have to get up really early in the morning. Why go through with this when, right now, you're feeling hardly any attraction? Out of politeness?*

Matt turned and grinned at him when he got the door open. Caden noticed the light sheen of sweat on his face. *You can leave now before he pukes all over himself, or worse, you.*

"Come on in," Matt said, and Caden continued to be amazed at the clarity of his new friend's words. It was like the signs of drunkenness were present in every other aspect save this one. Indeed, they had walked home looking like lovers, with their arms wrapped around the other's waist. The truth was that this was Caden's way of ensuring his friend did not stagger, or worse, fall down, as they made their way back to Matt's apartment.

Go on, say it. Just tell him you'll take a pass and you're heading home. In spite of his inner dialogue, Caden felt powerless to do anything other than follow the guy inside. Whether it was out of an absurd sense of decorum or that he was simply horny and any cock would do didn't really matter, because Caden knew he was going to go through with this as much as he knew he would regret it tomorrow.

Maybe if I get things over with really fast…

The apartment was utilitarian and very, very small, even for a studio. Matt revealed himself to have neither the alleged gay propensity for decorating nor neatness. One wall was taken up by a big picture window, through which the illumination from a streetlight showed through vinyl mini blinds. Beneath it was positioned a futon, still wearing its smashing outfit of striped sheets and a wadded up plaid comforter. For throw pillows, there were two actual bed pillows crouching at one end. The coffee table in front of it could have come out of central casting for "bachelor pad." Its faux oak surface was hardly visible beneath the Giordano's pizza boxes and numerous empty

Michelob bottles and cans of Diet Coke. Wads of clothes occupied a lot of the floor space, and Caden took in Matt's sad attempt at decorating—a Herb Ritts poster, unframed, tacked to the wall with pushpins.

A dead spider plant languished on the windowsill.

"Come on in and sit down," Matt urged. "You want something to drink? I'm gonna get a beer."

Caden wandered the few feet it would take to get to the couch and sat gingerly on it. A profusion of crumbs adorned the futon's surface. *Maybe we could just blow each other real quick, and I can be out of here in fifteen minutes—or less. That is, if I can get it up, or if he can...*

Matt raised his eyebrows from across the room, where he stood poised at the smallest refrigerator Caden had seen outside of a dorm room. "Well? Beer?"

"Nah. I think I've had enough." *And so have you*, he thought, but didn't say.

Matt opened his beer, flinging the cap into the sink, and sat on the couch next to Caden. Caden turned his head, watching as Matt took a big swallow and thinking Matt's next move would be to kiss him. After all, they both knew why he was here, right? Caden settled back into the futon, trying to ignore the crunching sound and the stiffness of the sheets beneath him.

Why does this futon smell like Old Spice? he wondered.

He spread his legs and let his head loll back, thinking he might be looking very seductive, especially to a drunk stranger at about one o'clock in the morning. He waited for the feel of Matt's lips on his own. In no time, they would be tugging at each other's zipper. Cocks would be produced, sucked, drained, and Caden could be mercifully on his way.

How blissfully romantic!

Except that's not what happened. Caden opened his eyes to see Matt crouched on the floor beneath what appeared to be a forty-two-inch plasma screen TV, loading up the Blu-ray player beneath it. The TV was the only thing that looked new—and clean—in the entire apartment. Caden guessed Matt was putting in some mood-setting porn, and although the prospect was tawdry and sleazy, he was all for anything that would accelerate the inevitable.

He longed for the comfort of his own clean sheets.

He undid the top button of his jeans and lowered his zipper to about half-mast. He was pleased to feel he was actually getting a little aroused at the thought of new porn and the prospect of Matt's drunken lips on his cock.

Matt joined him back on the futon, his shoulders touching Caden's. Casually, Caden let his left hand slide onto Matt's thigh and let it rest there while Matt aimed a remote at the opposite wall.

Imagine Caden's surprise when what came up on the screen was not the latest offering from Hot Desert Knights, Catalina, or Treasure Island Media, but that 1980s Christmas classic *Scrooged*, starring Mr. Bill Murray. While Caden had seen the movie and certainly found it an amusing take on Dickens' *A Christmas Carol*, it just seemed, well, weird, that a trick would put it on now. For one thing, it was October, so the movie was clearly inappropriate.

For another, who the hell put on a Christmas comedy to heat things up with a trick?

Am I really here? Is this really happening? Caden wondered as he watched the opening images of the film before glancing down at his own hand, lying hotly on Matt's blue-jeaned thigh.

It was then he heard the snore. He looked up to see Matt's handsome face in repose, mouth open and drooling, his head lolling on the back edge of the futon.

Really? You've fallen asleep on me? Seriously? This is what I trekked over here for? Scrooged *and a sleeping alcoholic? This is what my life has become?*

Caden flashed on an image of Bobby in bed with the muscular and drop-dead gorgeous Dreyfus. Bobby was probably in ecstasy, sliding down on what had to be at least a ten-inch cock, thick as a baby's forearm. Caden wondered how he'd ever have the nerve to tell his friend about tonight's adventure.

Caden leaned forward. "Dude, wake up. Don't you wanna play? I thought we were gonna get into some nasty sex." He squeezed the ample bulge between Matt's thighs to no result, other than Matt slumping over dramatically onto the pillows at one end of the couch. The beer bottle Matt had heretofore clutched expertly in his drunken paw dropped to the carpeted floor with a thud, spraying foam on the already stained carpet.

Caden refastened his belt and rezipped his pants. Getting lucky tonight was looking more and more out of the question.

Ya think?

He got up from the futon, crossed the room, and pulled a wad of paper towels from the rack suspended over the sink. A cockroach skittered madly among the dirty dishes piled there. "Fella, you're about the only one showing a little life in this hovel. Good for you!"

Caden recrossed the room, squatted down at Matt's feet, and blotted up the spilled beer. He then removed Matt's shoes and covered him with the comforter. Through all of this, Matt did nothing other than snore and once, charmingly, fart.

Caden paused at the door. "Good night, my sweet prince. It's been amazing."

Bill Murray screamed at one of his employees just as Caden closed the door on this latest chapter of his scintillating and romantic life.

Chapter Four

Outside, the night had turned colder. Caden made his way along the streets of Lakeview, aka Boystown, heading first west and then north to get to the L stop at Addison, by Wrigley Field.

He hadn't noticed it before, but a full moon had risen, and its silvery opalescence cast a shimmering glow on the streets, especially the darker areas and alleys, which looked like sets from some 1940s film noir. Wind sent fallen leaves skittering along the sidewalk. The evening he had left just a short while ago and that had seemed full of revelry now seemed lonely and desolate, just like his mood.

Maybe that full moon is the reason my evening went in such crazy directions. Scrooged? That's gotta be a first! I wonder if that form of entertainment has worked for him in the past.

Caden hurried along the streets, now gone quiet at a little after two, wishing he had worn something warmer than his jean jacket. By the time he had ascended the escalator at the L stop, he was shivering. He gazed down at Addison, watching as cabs headed east and west and here and there, as fellow travelers scurried, heading home or to the next party. Caden noticed that most of the people on the street were young men about his own age. He wondered if they were all, like him, searching for something elusive, something that maybe didn't exist.

Oh, get hold of yourself, sister! Enough with the morbid thoughts. You're just exhausted, a little drunk, your balls are a little blue, and you need to get home and get a good night's sleep. Morning will bring a nice three or four mile run, a strong cup of coffee, and a couple poached eggs. Those things will have you thinking right again.

Caden peered down the tracks and saw the headlight from an approaching northbound train. The sight of the light, moving closer, made him feel relieved. He started to put the bad night behind him as he thought of getting on the train and riding it for fifteen minutes or so to his stop at Bryn Mawr. A short walk east would bring him to his own little studio apartment (clean, neat, and tastefully decorated, unlike some fellas he knew!), where the idea of his bed was very appealing, if only for the promise of slumber it offered. *And clean sheets, don't forget clean sheets.*

Caden boarded the train. Just before its doors were about to close with their familiar gong sound, someone rushed along the platform and hopped into the car behind him.

Breathless, Beefy Blond surveyed the car, presumably looking for a seat. Caden wondered why, because he, a homeless man fast asleep in the rear of the car, and a couple of guys he pegged as Loyola University students were the only ones occupying the train car. The blond's gaze lit upon Caden, but if he recognized him, he gave no indication. This was both a relief and a disappointment.

Caden watched as the guy sat near the middle of the car and realized he suddenly was no longer tired. In fact, he felt downright energized. Caden turned in his seat to peer at Beefy Blond, who stared out the window as the train lurched forward.

You are not thinking of talking to him, are you? It's late! Caden glanced down at his watch, which revealed that it was two thirty in the morning. *Besides, you all but humiliated yourself with him back in the men's room at Sidetrack. I doubt very much he'd appreciate being accosted by you and, in fact, might even be a little frightened by it.*

The homeless man began singing softly to himself at the rear of the car. The tune sounded very much like the Peggy Lee classic "Fever." Caden shook his head, marveling at city life.

But if you don't make a move and try to talk to him, you may never have this chance again. After all, this city is full of millions of people. Odds are good that your paths may never, ever cross again, even if he is a gay man and even if he did put in an appearance at a bar you frequent. Weren't you and Bobby always saying how the cool thing about Chicago was you could go out and run into an entirely new crowd every time? Where did all these homos come from, anyway? Schaumburg? But you digress! This is fate that he boarded the same car that you did at this hour. Can't you see that?

Go. Talk. To. Him.

Caden stared out the window at the backs of apartment buildings flying by, thinking he didn't have long. The station at Wilson was coming up in seconds. *What if he got off there? Your opportunity would vanish.*

Caden angled himself in his seat so he sat sideways, legs across two seats, back against the window, Asics-clad feet dangling. This also allowed him to admire the object of his affection—no, lust—without being obvious.

The guy could have been custom-built for him. Caden's breath came a little faster as he surveyed the landscape of the man before him, a man who would fit very well in the linebacker mold, or the Wisconsin farm-boy mold. Hale and hearty. And yes, a bit chubby.

Caden loved that in a man. He didn't know why. But what the hell did it matter?

The announcement sounded for the next stop, and Caden thought if he didn't make his move now, he never would. He had let doubt and fear get the best of him in the past and only had the ashes of regret to show for it. He had nothing to lose and everything to gain, if only he would deign to speak to the man.

Caden propelled himself up and out of his seat. He didn't know what he would say but figured when the guy looked up at him, (he was confident) he would think of something. Forward momentum, putting one foot in front of the other, and acting as if was often enough—the simple stuff that made dreams come true.

Caden stopped by the guy's seat, and for a moment, Beefy Blond did not notice him standing there, so absorbed was he in the landscape of darkened apartment buildings and lights from neon and sodium vapor outside his window. When he finally did turn his head to look, just as the train pulled into the Wilson station, Caden's heart skipped a beat. Their eyes really did connect, and Caden thought he had never seen more soulful eyes than the ones examining him curiously at this very moment. They were a rich, deep brown, so dark one could barely discern where the pupil ended and the iris began. They made a lovely and stunning contrast with the pale wheat of his hair, different from the usual blue-eyed, blond combination.

Caden was so taken, so dumbstruck, he said the first thing that popped into his head. "If I promise not to piss on you, can I sit here?"

The guy chuckled and scooted over. Caden felt his face burning. *Did I just say that? Was that really my opening line? Jesus Christ!*

"Go ahead, sit."

"You remember me?" Caden sat hurriedly, hoping the man would simply forget his opening salvo, lame and weird as it was.

"Of course I do. I just didn't recognize you with your penis back in your pants."

Caden turned to look at him, mouth agape. Was he being tossed *attitude* at nearly three o'clock in the morning? Had he made a mistake? He was about to grin sheepishly and wander back to his seat at the front of the car, head hung low, when the guy laughed.

Caden looked back at him, appreciating the laughter, deep, full-bodied, and completely out of place on this nearly deserted L train car. Caden joined him, tentatively at first and then louder and harder with great relief.

The guy spoke, "I was just giving you a hard time. Relax." He gazed at the window for a moment again, then turned back to Caden. "I'm Kevin."

Kevin. Such a solid, no-nonsense, manly sounding name. Not Luke or Josh or Jake. Just plain old Kevin. Caden liked that. He suddenly wished his name was something similar, wishing he was a Bob or a Bill, or a Billy Bob. He stuck out his hand and said, "Caden."

Kevin's big paw fairly enveloped Caden's, his grip firm and bordering on bone crushing, but there were no complaints from Caden's corner.

They were silent for the next few minutes as the train glided out of the station. Caden's stop was coming up in only a few minutes, and he wondered how he could best maximize this opportunity without seeming pushy. Should he thrust his number into Kevin's hand? Should he attempt goo-goo eyes? A hand whispering suggestively across his own, or even Kevin's, crotch? *Yeah, that will win you points for subtlety and being suave as all get-out.*

"Long night?" Kevin was looking at him again, and it relieved him for the moment of pondering how best to make his move.

"Oh, God. You wouldn't believe it if I told you. Almost pissing on you at Sidetrack was the least of it."

"Hey, I might have liked that. You never gave me a chance, hightailing it out of there like a cat with a firecracker up its ass." *Now there was an image.* Is that how Kevin saw him? And did he like, er, watersports? Cute as he was, that would be a deal breaker.

"I'm kidding," Kevin said. "Do you always take everything so literally?"

"Only when the comments are coming from extremely hot guys." Caden grinned. *Did I just say that? Well, at least my cards are out on the table. If there were any doubt I was interested, that comment would have erased them.*

"Why thank you, Caden. You're not so bad yourself." Kevin pushed his shoulder against Caden's, awakening his other head, farther south. Amazing what a simple touch could do...

Kevin continued, "You were telling me you had a particularly bad—or at least long—night?"

"Oh yeah." Caden launched into his story about Matt. By the end of it, Kevin had tears in his eyes from laughing so hard. Kevin's laughter made Caden see the humor in the evening, and he no longer felt so bad about it. He could even stop questioning his appeal because a guy fell asleep on him.

Caden realized his stop was next. He hadn't paid much attention to the stops between Wilson and Bryn Mawr—he was so entranced and absorbed in getting to know Kevin better.

But if he got off the train at the next stop, how would he ever have a chance to continue their conversation—and maybe more? "My stop is next," he blurted out, hoping the pronouncement would spur Kevin into action. *You are almost passive-aggressive, you dope. Why do you have to wait for him to make a move?*

"Bryn Mawr. I'm in Rogers Park myself, get off at Jarvis."

"Love that neighborhood." Caden raised his voice to make himself heard over the sound of the announcement of his stop, which was momentary. *Good Lord, what should I do?*

"I'd say let's go have a drink somewhere, but most places around me are closed by now." Kevin's brown-eyed gaze bored into him.

Caden was about to suggest he would take a rain check and that he would love to have the chance another time. *Maybe tomorrow night? Or brunch on Sunday?*

"I do have a refrigerator full of Stella back home."

Caden heard the reference to Stella in a refrigerator and was immediately chilled, envisioning a comely lass stuffed into a refrigerator, duct tape across her mouth, frost icing her blue, blue skin. Was this guy a serial killer? It would be just his luck.

"Maybe I should have specified. Stella Artois, the lager from Belgium. Very, very tasty." Kevin rubbed his sizable gut. "She's my girl, and I like her a wee bit too much." He chuckled.

All too soon, they were pulling into the Bryn Mawr station. "This is my stop," Caden said, a little frantically.

"Well, it seems you have two choices, buddy. Get off here or stay on with me until Jarvis, then come on over and enjoy a Stella with me...and maybe listen to a little music. I have a new Etta James CD I just bought."

"Is she still recording?"

"Well, no. She died recently. Didn't you hear? But this was her last CD. It's called *The Dreamer,* and it's amazing."

The doors closed, and the train headed on its relentless path northward.

"I guess that means you're coming home with me, then?"

"I guess so." For the first time that night, Caden relaxed, mentally saying a little prayer. *Thank you, God.*

Chapter Five

The two were quiet on their walk back to Kevin's apartment. He lived a block north of the L stop at Jarvis, on Fargo. The cool air and the quiet—no one was out on the streets—imbued the mood with anticipation.

Caden wondered if he was doing the right thing. He could see already from his very limited contact that he liked this guy. Not only was he his physical ideal, everything about him indicated he had brains and a sense of humor too. That trifecta was something Caden had yet to encounter in his romantic life, and he wondered if he was moving too fast by going home with Kevin when they had just met only minutes ago. On the train. At nearly three o'clock in the morning.

What does that say about me? That I cruise the L, looking for pickups? Well, even if it does, the same could be said for Kevin, right? Yet you came up to him. He was just looking out the window, minding his own business.

Will you quit it with the self-doubt? He wouldn't have invited you home if he thought you were a sleazebag.

Or maybe he would. Maybe that's exactly why? Hey, Kevin, how do you spell easy?

As they passed under the L tracks and turned left to continue westward to Kevin's building on Fargo, Caden wondered if maybe, out of respect for what could be the blossom of a new relationship, something good, something he had longed for, something he thought he might never find, he should be taking things slower. "If you want to be treated like a lady, act like one," his mother was always telling his sister, but Caden thought she was looking out the corner of her eye at him when she made this pronouncement.

But did Mom have a point? Caden wondered. Would it have been better to have just given Kevin his number (and hope the guy would reciprocate in kind)? Would he have seemed more respectable, more in the league of someone to consider for the long term, if he had given him his number, smiled, and said, "I'm glad I had the chance to bump into you and redeem myself. I'll call you, and maybe we can do coffee or a drink soon."

Isn't that what respectable guys did?

Ah, to hell with respectable guys! Caden glanced out the corner of his eye at Kevin's beard, his strong jawline, his full, almost pouting lips and had to wonder where the value was in playing it respectable. Especially when one considered the prospect of being able to actually touch, kiss, lick, and fondle the object of his desire—immediately.

Delayed gratification, Caden thought, was not all it was cracked up to be.

"Caden? We're here." Kevin's voice interrupted Caden's internal monologue.

"You seemed a thousand miles away. What were you thinking about?"

Caden wasn't ready to confess his thoughts, so he just smiled and said, "Nothing."

"It didn't look like nothing to me. Sure you're not having second thoughts?"

Here's your chance to do the respectable thing, Caden. You can give him your warmest smile and say, "You're really special, and that's why—for the first time—I'd like to take things slow. Would you mind terribly if we set up a date? Go out like normal people—for dinner and a movie, maybe?" Wouldn't that be a nice thing to say? Caden was certain Kevin would think more of him for it, so it was all good.

"Who me? Second thoughts? No way, man. You promised me Stella."

*

Kevin's apartment was a study in masculinity. A one-bedroom in a red-brick vintage six-flat, the place reeked of warmth and comfort and had absolutely no touches of Martha Stewart. Kevin's place was minimal, but everything inside seemed to define who he was, from the warmly glowing hardwood floors, to the distressed leather couch, to the coffee table with its collection of textbooks (Caden would have to check them out later to see what they were all about), to the computer desk in one corner of the dining room with his laptop sitting open on top of it. The place was neat, but not fussily so. The only adornments were some botanical prints of various leaves on the walls. Bamboo grew out of a couple of glass vases on the windowsill, and a ficus tree, thriving, occupied the space next to a door that looked as though it might lead out to a balcony.

"Nice place," Caden said.

"Thanks. I like it. Been here for four years. It's got a great balcony and even a backyard, which keeps the thought of getting a dog at the back of my mind all the time. I love dogs! The only drawback is it's right next to the L, as you probably noticed when we walked up."

As if on cue, an L train rumbled by, its roar almost deafening.

Kevin grinned. "You get used to it." He turned and said over his shoulder. "Let me get you that beer. Grab a seat."

Kevin disappeared, and in moments, Caden heard kitchen sounds—the fridge opening, the relieved sigh of beer bottles being opened, a drawer opening and closing, water running briefly. Caden sat, peering at the books. They were all about animals and veterinary medicine.

Ah, he's a nurturing type too. Don't screw this up!

Kevin returned with the beer and handed Caden one. He squatted in front of his stereo and popped in the CD they had talked about on the train. In moments, Miss Etta James was providing very smooth and smoky background music. Caden wanted to close his eyes and just listen.

The music, the quiet outside, save for the occasional L train, turned the evening decidedly romantic. Before, it was tentative with the promise of the erotic—a hook-up, a one-nighter—but now the night seemed wrapped in a different kind of veil, one that promised something more substantial.

Suddenly, Caden felt shy and could sense Kevin did too. It would have been easier, Caden thought, without the beers, the chitchat, and the music. If they had just started ripping clothes off each other the moment Kevin threw the deadbolt on his door, Caden could have handled that. Why was it so much more difficult and scary connecting with someone on an emotional, rather than a physical level? Perhaps that was another question to throw out to his therapist. If she'd ever answer—that damned woman always forced him to answer his own questions!

He watched Kevin's throat contract and release as he swallowed his beer, thinking how he'd so love to kiss that scruffy neck, to feel the stubble and the warmth beneath his lips and tongue.

Although Caden never thought the question a smooth one, something compelled him to ask it now. "Mind if I kiss you?"

Kevin turned to him and smiled, setting the beer down on the coffee table in front of him. "Nah," he said softly and held out his arms.

Caden leaned over, feeling his heart rate increase about tenfold the closer he got to Kevin, and tentatively touched his lips to Kevin's. His beard tickled, and Caden wanted to laugh, but he suppressed it because what he wanted even more was to mash his lips into Kevin's, part Kevin's lips with his tongue, and explore the inside of his mouth, which tasted sweet from the beer, a taste Caden might dub the essence of Kevin.

Kevin's arms moved around him, pulled him closer, enveloped him, as their kiss grew in heat and passion. Caden realized he had longed to do just this since the moment he had spied Kevin laughing with his friends at Sidetrack. He surrendered to the kiss, reaching up to run his fingers through Kevin's thick hair and then letting them tumble down to the beard. He pulled his lips away, and since his fingers were still close to Kevin's mouth, Kevin sucked them in. Their eyes met as he did this, and Caden felt something like an electric jolt pass through him. The connection of their eyes made him feel several things all at once—passion that was reflected in the steel girder rising between his legs, to be sure, but also a flood of warmth and caring that Caden recognized as irrational and mysterious—and entirely welcome.

Caden moved a bit awkwardly, to climb onto Kevin's lap, to straddle him, their faces connected in a renewed kiss, one even more heated—if possible—than the first. Caden ground his ass downward on the hard bulge he felt straining for release (in more than one way!) in Kevin's jeans. He rocked back and forth on his lap, sucking Kevin's tongue, his breath quickening, almost delirious with desire.

Kevin pulled away to gasp. "You keep that up, boy, and there's gonna be a mess to clean up in my shorts. I mean it!" He pushed Caden back, staring intently at him. "Stop."

Caden could practically feel Kevin's entire body pulsing and felt on the verge of orgasm himself. He wondered if he should just go ahead and finish things, to dry hump Kevin, riding him like a prize stallion, and to hell with a pair of briefs filled with come.

Kevin, though, had a cooler head. He kept his hand tenderly but firmly on Caden's chest and said, "We need to go into the bedroom, finish this like adults. We'll appreciate it more if we take our time. Right?"

Caden groaned, feeling the bulge of Kevin's erection pressing against the crack of his ass, hardly able to think. "I don't know," he whimpered.

"Right?" Kevin repeated.

Caden turned away from that beautiful, manly face for a moment, staring into the darkness pressing against the glass of the balcony door so he could collect himself, rein in his desire just a bit, dial down the moment because "Of course you're right."

Kevin gently slid Caden off his lap and rose. Caden took in the sight of this glorious man—his beefy form so solid, so made for groping, grasping, and tasting—and wanted to laugh with joy. He eyed the erection tenting the front of Kevin's loose-fitting pants and thought if he didn't see that dick naked very soon—like within the next few seconds—he would faint or his heart would surely give out or he'd simply stop breathing.

Kevin was holding his hand out. "Come on."

Caden took his hand and followed Kevin into the bedroom. Kevin let go of his hand to light a pillar candle on the dresser. The candle's flickering glow revealed an old four-poster bed with a plaid comforter and dark wood furniture. On the wall were some paintings that looked as though they had been salvaged from a thrift store, but charming nonetheless, all of them large dogs—spaniels, perhaps—tearing through autumnal woods.

Kevin pulled the comforter back to reveal plain white sheets. He sat on the edge of the bed. "You go first. I want to watch you undress. Please."

Caden had no qualms about complying. Though his instinct was to rip his clothes off as fast as he could, he suppressed it, because he wanted to make this moment last. It was, after all, the very first time he would reveal his body to Kevin, and that moment would never come again. So he slowly pulled his shirt over his head, taking the time to run his hands over his lean torso and to tweak his own nipples, grinning slyly at Kevin all the while. He bent to untie and remove his shoes and socks, trying to maintain a semblance of grace and balance and nearly succeeding. They both laughed as he stumbled. And then it came time to undo the buttons on his jeans, which he did one by one, pausing after opening each. His cock, sheathed in the cotton boxers he wore, sprang eagerly out of the opening. Obviously, *it* had not gotten the memo about going slowly.

Caden hitched his hands in the waistband of his jeans and shorts. Tugging them down inch by inch, he revealed more and more. Kevin gasped when Caden's cock rose up out of his dark pubic hair. "Nice," he said softly.

Caden had never felt more turned on. Or more appreciated. He wriggled finally out of the jeans, kicked them to the side, and stood naked before Kevin. His dick rose up so hard it was just about pulsing. Precome dripped from its head to puddle on the floor, and even Caden was surprised at how copious the clear liquid was.

"God, you're perfect," Kevin said, his voice full of undisguised desire and admiration. "Man, what I wouldn't give to have a body just like yours."

Caden wanted to tell him that was the last thing on earth he wanted, but stayed quiet, saying only, "Your turn."

Kevin stood up, close enough that Caden could feel the heat from his breath. "You're a tough act to follow, buddy. Maybe I should blow out that candle?"

"Don't you dare. I've been waiting all night just to see you naked."

"I hope you want to do more than see. But be warned—I need to lose a few pounds."

"Oh, would you just shut up and take your clothes off before I have to rip them off you?"

Kevin laughed and began to undress, revealing a body that was, to Caden, as perfect as it could be. Solid. Manly. Covered in fine pale brown fur. A firm belly, massive thighs, and at last, a solid, thick, and uncut dick rising up from an unshaved nest of sandy curls. Caden thought if he could just die now, with the image of Kevin naked before him imprinted on his brain, he would die a happy man.

But death was not to be, at least not a death in the literal sense. *Maybe the "little death" they write about in books*, Caden thought...

Kevin moved to embrace Caden, taking him in his arms so hard their bodies mashed together and Caden gasped, the air rushing out of him in a great whoosh. But Caden was not complaining. The heat of their bodies pressed so close together was akin to a line of silken electricity coursing through Caden. Their heat doubled, and for long minutes, Caden nearly lost conscious thought, wrapped up as he was in the supreme feel of flesh against flesh. Kevin's heart pounded against his chest. Caden smelled the tang of his sweat and reveled in the roughness of his body hair chafing against Caden's own smooth skin.

It was magic.

And then Kevin was kissing him, his lips teasing, his tongue darting in, then biting first his upper lip, then his lower. The bites were gentle at first, then not so much.

Caden thought if he didn't find some support for his legs soon, he would collapse right there on the hardwood floor—his pulse was racing so fast.

"I can't wait," Kevin whispered.

"Huh?" was Caden's snappy comeback.

"I wanted to do all this foreplay, this big buildup, lick you from head to toe, finger your ass, eat your ass, suck your dick, take each of your balls in my mouth slowly, one by one, but—I can't wait."

"You talk much more like that and I don't know if *I* can wait."

Kevin's next words were urgent. "I need to fuck you. Now. Turn around."

Caden had read Shakespeare's sonnets, the love poetry of the Brownings, but none of them could compare to Kevin's simple declaration. Caden turned around, still standing, lowering his chest to the bed so his ass rose up, sure that he was giving Kevin a sight that was nothing short of tantalizing.

Caden listened as he heard Kevin rooting through the nightstand drawer, feeling a chill on his naked body as Kevin left him momentarily. Then there was the familiar sound of a condom being ripped open—then the cold shock of a dollop of lube being smeared into his ass crack.

"I'm sorry. I just need you so much."

Caden had lost the power of speech. He knew about need. Right now, his entire body felt like one big vessel, waiting to be filled by Kevin. He wriggled his ass, impatient, and knew the entry need not be gentle.

He was that ready.

But Kevin did take the time to kneel, drawing Caden's cheeks apart. He must have liked what he saw because Caden heard him suck in a breath. "Good God," Kevin said. He slid a finger, then two inside, gently massaging, working them in deeper and deeper.

"You don't have to do that," Caden said. "I want you so much. Just fuck it." He spit out the last three words, hungry, knowing he sounded filthy, slutty, and certain he was striking just the right chord.

Kevin pushed down on his shoulders, raising his ass even higher, and Caden sighed as he felt Kevin position his cock at his crack.

"Go," Caden whimpered.

And Kevin did, grabbing his hips and pushing in gently. Mentally, Caden both thanked and cursed him for his consideration. He pushed back against the cock, wanting it in all the way, as fast as it could get there, hitting his prostate, filling him with the perfectly lovely sensation of being full—of Kevin.

"Just fuck me. Hard."

"You sure?"

Caden peered over his shoulder, smiling his answer. His ass responded too, squeezing down hard on the half of Kevin's dick already inside.

The holds were unbarred, and Kevin fucked Caden ruthlessly, hips slapping against Caden's ass as he buried himself deep inside, then pulling out almost all the way to the tip, and then slamming back in. Mercilessly. It was what Caden wanted, and he couldn't quiet the groans, grunts, and cries of pleasure that escaped his lips without thought. He pushed back feverishly, wanting to devour Kevin's cock with his ass, reaching back to pull him in deeper by his thighs, switching to grope between his legs for Kevin's hairy, swinging balls, which were already tightening.

"I want to fuck you forever. I want to do a million different positions," Kevin panted, "but you're too fuckin' hot. I can't take much more, man. I'm gonna come."

Caden squeezed his eyes shut tight, burying his face in the bed. He heard Kevin cry out as he slammed deeply into him. There was a little pain there, at that moment, but Caden wouldn't have erased it for anything. Bliss was the only word he could think of to describe what he felt as Kevin emptied himself inside him, his entire body bucking and quivering.

They stayed joined for a long time after the climax, Kevin resting his hairy body on Caden's back, their sweat connecting them like glue.

Finally, Caden felt Kevin's dick begin to soften, and then with regret, felt him wrap his hand around the base and pull out slowly.

Breathing hard, Kevin fell back on the bed in front of him, his big hairy body glazed with perspiration. His penis, with a drop of come poised at its tip, lolled heavily along one thigh. "That was incredible. I'm sorry I came so fast."

"Don't you apologize for a thing. You're right. It was amazing, and I wouldn't change a minute of it." Caden's knee touched the side of the bed, which was wet. He moved back and looked down to see he had come all over the side of the mattress and box spring.

Caden laughed. "Got a towel? I'm afraid I made something of a mess." He grinned. "I didn't even know I came!"

Kevin growled, rolling over to reach for the shelf beneath the nightstand. He handed Caden a white hand towel. "Here you go. And next time, I want you to know when you come."

"Oh, I wasn't complaining. But I'm glad to hear there'll be a next time."

"I sure as hell hope there will be."

Caden knelt and began blotting up his semen as best he could, both embarrassed and delighted. "You can count on it. Maybe even within the next ten minutes or so." Caden grinned at Kevin.

Kevin scooted over so he was in a more conventional position on the bed, the pillow behind his head, big legs splayed out before him, making room for Caden. "I can tell you're going to a force to be reckoned with. But I need some rest. My poor old heart needs to get itself back down to something resembling a normal beat." He patted the bed next to him. "Come on. Think you can sleep?"

"With you? No problem." Caden scooted onto the bed, fitting his body against Kevin's and resting his head on his shoulder.

Kevin stroked his hair. "You're sweaty. You wanna shower?"

"Nah. Let's just go to sleep."

And they did, like a pair of lovers who had been together for a long, long time.

Chapter Six

Caden let his head rest against the cold glass of the L window. The rocking motion of the train was almost enough to put him to sleep, but he knew he wouldn't sleep—deeply—until he got back to his own place. Even though words like "drained" and "exhausted" applied, he was too euphoric for sleep.

Outside, the landscape whizzing by was illuminated by the gray dark of an almost wintry morning. It was a little after nine, and Caden had just had the most remarkable night of his life.

He'd fallen in love.

Face still to the window, barely taking in the sights of buildings hurtling by and here and there a glimpse of Lake Michigan, whose waters looked so still they were like a mirror, Caden recalled the last few hours with bliss.

They had made love two more times, once again after their first time, when Caden awakened to find Kevin's warm mouth on his cock, expertly laving the sensitive flesh until Caden exploded in his mouth. He tried warning him to stop, but Kevin wouldn't let go until he drained every drop.

When he had finished and the early gray of dawn was lightening the room, he looked up at Caden with a smile and asked, "Did you feel yourself come *that* time?"

"Oh yeah. God, yes."

And Caden had responded in kind—physically.

They had slept again after that, for an hour or so. When they awakened, the sunlight, a milky pearlescent white, filled the room. This time, Caden had awakened in a spoon, with Kevin's arms around him, his chest pressed into his back. Caden had grinned sleepily as he felt Kevin's erection pressing against his backside. Still groggy, he had wished they lived in a time when it would have been safe for them to just maneuver their bodies beneath the body-warmed bedclothes so Kevin would simply slide inside, but they were cautious and sensible enough to grab a condom.

This time was slower, more tender, starting out side by side and then, finally, with Caden on his back, his legs on Kevin's broad shoulders, Kevin moved slowly inside him, building up to a climax both of them would feel. Caden had loved the engagement of their eyes as they fucked—that almost magical connection that eloquently spoke more than words ever could.

When they finished, Kevin had gone into the kitchen. "I'll let you catch your breath," he had said. Caden had lain there, feeling contented and wondering how his world had improved so markedly in just a few hours. He was so glad he had not listened to the angel on his shoulder the night before, the one who had told him to just give Kevin his number, to go slowly.

Caden awoke once more to the smell of bacon frying and coffee brewing and realized he was ravenous. The two shared breakfast on Kevin's couch, eggs and bacon in the nude, with Kevin's steam heat radiator clanking.

It had been perfection. Caden hadn't wanted to leave, but even though it was Saturday, Kevin had to work. He worked the front desk at a Rogers Park veterinary clinic, and the place opened at eight.

"Go ahead and shower, read the paper, have some more coffee. Just flip the lock on the doorknob when you leave." Kevin looked like a doctor in his pale blue scrubs, standing at the door. They had kissed goodbye, just like a live-in couple, and Caden had wished Kevin a good day.

Kevin had said, "I want to see you again. I'm not in the habit of picking up guys off the L late at night, but I'm glad I did. Will you see me again?"

"Just try to keep me away," Caden had responded.

Even though Kevin had invited him to stay—and Caden loved that he trusted him enough to do that—Caden wanted to get home to his own place. Yes, the night had been wonderful, magical even, but he didn't feel quite right alone in Kevin's apartment after he was gone.

So now, he rode the train, heading home, wearing a cat-that-ate-the-canary grin that he didn't care who saw.

*

Farther south, Bobby awoke alone. He lay in bed, taking in his perfect bedroom, with its Room and Board minimalist contemporary furnishings—the platform bed with leather headboard, the sleek cherry dresser with its brushed aluminum pulls, the framed Keith Haring and David Hockney prints, the forty-two-inch plasma screen mounted on the wall, opposite the bed—and felt dissatisfied. Yes, he had this great condo in the Lakeview neighborhood. Yes, he had a view of Lake Michigan from his east-facing windows and a view of downtown from the south-facing ones. Yes, he had a good job as a marketing executive for a pharmaceutical company in the western suburbs, to which he drove in a late-model Lexus every day.

But what he really wanted was someone to wake up next to.

Lord knows he tried to find someone. Night after night after night! If he wasn't picking up someone in the bars, he was hooking up online. He had accounts on Manhunt, Adam for Adam, and Men4SexNow. He even ventured regularly into the murky and uncharted waters of Craigslist.

And he had standards—which even he was shocked to find were almost always met. No one over forty. No one overweight. Nobody effeminate. Even in the shorthand of the Internet, Bobby always ensured his tricks were hot, in shape, educated, and even made good money.

Bobby rolled over and looked at himself in the mirror hanging next to his bed. Sometimes he wondered if it was there as much for this kind of gazing as it was for the time when he had a visitor over, watching himself get fucked in a multitude of positions.

But he needed those standards because he was a catch. He admired his reddish brown hair, with the curls cut short, but not so short they vanished. Gray eyes that had been called, on more than one occasion, piercing. He threw back his high-count linen sheets and goose-down comforter to reveal a body made for modeling or high-end porn—defined, bulging where it needed to be, tanned, and toned. Hell, he even had the eight-inch dick *for real* that almost everyone online boasted of having.

Why should he settle?

But why had he never met *the one*? He had a parade of gorgeous men in and out of his designer apartment night after night (and sometimes day after day), yet with none of them had he felt any connection beyond the momentary rush of attraction and the heat of lust. Those things were all well and good, but when they always came—and had come for years—with no real emotional connection, well, Bobby simply felt his heart was as empty as his bed last night.

Dreyfus, the guy he had met at Sidetrack, was a prime example. They had been unable to keep their hands off each other as they headed home in the cab. Desire had risen in the back seat like a fire growing out of control, despite the rueful eyes of the cabbie in his rearview mirror.

Bobby had caught the disapproving deep-brown eyes a couple of times, but he didn't care. He'd throw the guy a twenty-dollar tip for his trouble. Meanwhile, the two of them made out like horny teenagers after the prom, kissing, groping, mashing themselves against the other as though such action would fuse them into one person.

By the time the cab pulled up in front of Bobby's high-rise at Lakeshore and Addison, he had felt almost delirious with lust. He had paid the cabbie, who roared off in a snit, and grabbed Dreyfus by the hand, pulling him into the mirrored and marble-tiled lobby, where he was eyed with amusement by the doorman. Bobby wondered if their erections were that obvious.

"Evening, Pete," Bobby said as he yanked Dreyfus toward the bank of elevators. Not that the guy needed any pulling—he radiated the same level of desire as Bobby.

Once inside his apartment, Bobby didn't bother with social formalities like offering Dreyfus a drink or even turning on lights. No, he simply slammed him up against the front door, which he had the presence of mind to lock, and began ripping off his clothes.

Dreyfus moaned all the while, allowing himself to be undressed.

Bobby tried to take his time, and when he at last yanked the Calvin Klein black briefs down to Dreyfus's knees, he was not prepared for what he found.

He had read somewhere about a condition known as "micropenis" and wondered if here it was, staring him in the face, eye to eye. There was no doubt the little devil was excited. The tiny cock pointed straight up at Dreyfus's perfect six-pack, waxed as clean and smooth as a baby's bottom, if that tot had an ass fashioned from cast iron.

But the penis, and Bobby suppressed, during the course of an uncomfortable minute, an urge to laugh, looked like a baby's finger. He wanted to peer up at Dreyfus's panting face and ask, "Really?" Maybe if he did so, the man would reveal his real cock—one that could be compared to something equestrian, one that matched the rest of his perfection.

But Bobby kept his own counsel.

Dreyfus, on the other hand, was not so quiet. "Suck it, bitch. You know you want it. Suck my big dick, boy."

And Bobby did, not from any desire to perform fellatio, but because he needed to keep his mouth occupied so he wouldn't collapse in hysterical giggles. The porn movie chatter *so* did not match the decidedly un-porn-movie dick.

It was so pink it was almost fuchsia.

So Bobby sucked, feeling more like he had gotten hold of a Vienna sausage rather than a kielbasa.

"Yeah, that's it. Take it all, boy, every fuckin' inch."

Take it all? Seriously? And just how much was "every fuckin' inch" anyway? Three? Four?

Dreyfus grabbed the back of Bobby's head and savagely fucked his face. Or at least it would have been savage, if Bobby had felt he was being orally penetrated by something larger than a baby carrot. No worries about gagging tonight!

To be courteous, Bobby went through the rest of the encounter politely, giving no indication of his disappointment. He even managed to get and stay hard, a feat he was worried about because he knew himself well enough to know that the term "size queen" applied to him.

Dreyfus fancied himself a rough top and probably believed he threw a vicious fuck into his connection for the night, as he pounded Bobby's ass first with Bobby obligingly on his back, then on all fours, and, finally, standing in front of the mirror. He could barely feel anything, but the guy was going on, with exhortations like "Take it!" and "Feel me rape that tight ass" and "Let me nail you hard, you little fucker," as if he was blissfully unaware of his own shortcomings.

The whole time, Dreyfus did not once meet Bobby's eyes, but only stared into the mirror, a vision Bobby imagined was Dreyfus in his own self-directed, self-loving porno.

Bobby did give the guy credit; he had some control. It took him at least ten minutes of furious pounding (which felt, really, as though the dick was only sandwiched between his ass cheeks, rather than through his ring of muscle) before he cried out that he was coming. What he actually said was "Can you feel my babies inside you, bitch?"

Um, no. Number one because you are using—laughably—the Magnum extra-large condom you brought with you, and two, because I don't think you've fully penetrated me.

Once he came, he was all business, rushing off to the en suite bathroom to clean himself up. He was out the door with a hurried "Thanks! See you around!" within one more ten-minute period.

Prince Charming!

Bobby was not disappointed to see him go.

He waited for the slam of the door and then jacked off to a movie called *Manfuck Manifesto* that featured handsome guys with sizable endowments getting relentlessly, obsessively nasty. Yet, even as he lay panting in a pool of sweat and his own come, he still felt unsatisfied.

He went to sleep hugging the pillow next to him.

At least now, by morning's dull light, he could call his friend Caden and commiserate with him. Caden would understand—Bobby's best friend seldom got lucky himself, and when he did, the results were usually disappointing.

It would be good to give his misery some company.

They could console each other over the phone and then make plans for a little Michigan Avenue shopping, followed up by lunch and Bloody Marys.

Bobby rolled over and brought up Caden's listing on his iPhone and pressed the screen to connect.

*

Just as Caden was closing his front door, his phone began playing its Bobby-specified ringtone, "I Know What Boys Like," originally sung by The Waitresses.

Good Lord, do I really want to answer this? Do I really want to sit and listen to him gloat about his steaming hot night with Dreyfus or some other dude he picked up? Do I really need to hear tales of huge cocks, geysers of come, all delivered with dirty-talking adeptness by a guy—or guys—who were fucking gorgeous?

Caden pressed Accept as he headed into his own apartment, kicking the door shut behind him. All he wanted to do was sleep and sleep and sleep—for hours, until the noonday sun roused him and called him out for being a miserable lazybones, a reprobate who had spent all night fucking a stranger he had met on the L. Shameless.

Caden grinned at the thought of Kevin—his smile, his large and comforting hairy body—and thought he, himself, was not such a reprobate, because what happened last night, he was pretty sure, was the opening pages of a real, true-life love story and not some romance novel by the likes of Josh Lanyon or ZA Maxfield.

Why the hell had he answered the phone? Why didn't he just strip off his clothes, ignore the ringtone, and collapse into bed, letting visions of last night lull him off into a blissful slumber?

Because Bobby was, after all, his friend.

"Hey, what's up?"

"Just getting in?" Bobby asked, a hint of devilish knowing in his tone.

Caden knew he was kidding, knew his friend was certain he was more likely just getting up after a long night alone. Why? Because in Bobby's world, he was the only one meeting gorgeous guys; he was the only one getting laid. Caden's lips and tongue were both poised to prove his friend wrong, but then something held him back—an image of Kevin, setting a plate of eggs, bacon, and toast before him with an eager smile—one that was as delighted to be feeding him breakfast as Kevin had been to feed him his cock.

And suddenly, unsure of his motivation, Caden responded by saying, "Yeah, right."

"Didn't you get lucky after I left you last night?"

As much as it would have given him a perverse sense of pleasure to lay out all the steamy details for his friend, Caden wanted to keep what had transpired the night before all to himself. He called it selfish. "Ah, you know me. I wandered around Boystown for a little while, did a little flirting, ended up in Little Jim's—"

"Little Jim's? Yuck. But go on."

"Nothing really to tell. I was home by midnight and in bed by one. Same old, same old. But I have a bone to pick with you."

"Oh yeah?"

"Yes. You could have at least said goodbye before you cut out on me while I was in the bathroom. What kind of shit is that?"

"Sorry. I had just met my perfect Mr. Right Now, and we needed to get the hell out of there and back to my place, striking while the iron was hot. Or the cock!" Bobby laughed. "You know the law of the jungle."

Caden shook his head, sat on the edge of his bed and began getting undressed, starting with his shoes and socks. He didn't really want to hear it but asked anyway, "So was he hot?"

"Oh. My. God."

"I guess that's a yes." Caden put the phone on speaker and stripped down to his boxers. He pulled the blind on his one window and slid under his comforter. "So do tell."

"Biggest fucking dick I have ever had in my life. I mean, I do not know how I am going to walk for, like, the next week. That guy had ten inches, at the very least. And he knew how to use it!" Bobby laughed. "The soreness I am feeling today—all over, because he threw me in so many different positions I lost count—was all worth it, man. Totally fucking hot. And you saw him. Gorgeous!" Bobby sang the last word out.

Normally, Caden would have been jealous, or rubbing his own erection while Bobby talked, imagining himself in his best friend's place. But this morning, he felt a curious disconnection, almost as though he felt sorry for Bobby. Because, even though Bobby had had a night as hot as Caden's own, somehow he doubted Bobby had forged the same emotional connection.

To prove his own point, Caden asked, "So are you going to see this guy again?" Caden already knew the answer. In spite of Bobby's parade of gorgeous fuckers, one seldom played an encore. They even joked about it, saying Bobby had more than his share of SDTs, which, in their parlance, meant "seldom dated twice."

"I don't know," Bobby responded. "He was hot and all—really—and he had that monster cock, but we just didn't connect on a personal level."

Caden nodded, murmuring, "Mm-hmm." He had heard this song so many times before, he wasn't sure what he would do if Bobby actually mentioned a second date or that he really felt something for one of his many conquests, other than lust.

"That's too bad," said Caden. He was glad now, for an altogether different reason, he hadn't mentioned Kevin. It would only have made Bobby feel worse to know his friend had met someone special the night before.

"Yeah, well, there's always tonight!"

It made Caden sad to hear the faux excitement in Bobby's voice. The optimism seemed so forced; it was as though Bobby had given up on believing it himself. He was about to tell him that it could happen, that there were worthwhile men out there, if only he kept trying, but before he could say the words, Bobby was asking him: "So? Lunch today?"

Caden looked at the clock on his nightstand. It was already past ten. "Late lunch. Two be okay?"

"Two is always better than one!" Bobby laughed.

"Right. I'll swing by your place and call you from the lobby. We can walk and find a place."

"See you later, tater."

"Bye."

Caden hung up the phone, having never felt so tired. He was asleep within minutes.

*

The phone on his nightstand ringing woke Caden within an hour. Groggily, he picked it up and peered at the display.

Mom.

Oh Lord. Just put your head under the pillow. Throw the phone across the room. You need sleep.

Caden pressed Accept. Even though his mother was almost five hundred miles away, in Western Pennsylvania, Caden had the eerie feeling she'd know if ignored her call.

"Hi, Mom."

"What were you doin'? Sleeping?"

And there's my proof—she can see me. God, I hope she couldn't see me last night. Caden grinned.

"Oh, just resting my eyes."

"Bull. It's almost noon. You're young. You should be up and enjoying your Saturday."

"I enjoy sleeping."

"Incorrigible. So, what's new? You don't call. You don't write. Don't you love your mother?" She laughed to show she was kidding. Caden knew, though, she was not.

"Everything's good. Work is good. I'm eating right, getting lots of rest. Nothing really special going on." Caden sat up more in bed, knowing that sleep had been forfeited until at least that night.

"You meet anyone special?"

It was uncanny. How did she know? She didn't, but Caden was a good boy: he could never lie to his mother.

"Well, actually, maybe I did." Caden couldn't, no matter how hard he tried, suppress the ear-to-ear grin spreading across his face.

"Really? Is she cute? Has she been blessed by the pope?" This last question was his mother's way of asking if his new love interest was Catholic.

"What do you mean, 'she,' Ma? Do we have to go through the whole coming out thing again? Are you getting a touch of Alzheimer's?"

"Just kidding. A mother can dream." She paused. "Kidding again. I love you just the way you are, son. I wouldn't change a thing. If I did, you wouldn't be you."

"That's right."

"So who's the lucky man who caught the eye of my boy? How did you meet?"

Caden had a good relationship with his mother. In spite of the distance between them, he talked to her several times a week on the phone, and had even hoped she'd get herself a computer so they could one day chat via email, Skype, or Facebook. But such technology, for right now, seemed beyond his Italian mother's grasp.

Nonetheless, in spite of an open, honest—and, yes—affirming relationship between mother and son, Caden doubted he could simply say, "Yeah, we met on the L, and he took me back to his place and fucked me six ways to Sunday."

At heart, his mother was a good Catholic girl, a widow who spent her Sunday mornings at Mass at St. Aloysius and Sunday evenings at the local Sons of Italy club playing bingo. She would probably have a brain hemorrhage if her son dared to utter such a bald and crude line.

For all Caden knew, his mother still thought he was a virgin.

"We met at a bar. He caught my attention from across the room, and when I ran into him in the bathroom, I sort of struck up a conversation."

"In the bathroom? Are you kidding me?"

"Well, I just said 'hi.' I didn't talk to him until later. I bumped into him on the L when we were both on our way home." Caden proceeded to give his mother a sanitized version of their meeting, the one where he gave Kevin his number and told him he hoped they could get together soon.

"So do you have a date set up?"

"Not yet. I'm waiting to see if he calls me." That, at least, was the truth. Kevin *would* call him, wouldn't he? Caden recalled the look of hunger in Kevin's eyes when he kissed him goodbye, a look eclipsed only by Kevin's delight—or so Caden thought—at their having met. Of course he'd call. Why wouldn't he? They'd had an amazing time.

But the little pessimist always lurking somewhere in his subconscious, wearing black clothes and a frown, reminded him: *You've been sure about guys in the past. Guys you thought were wonderful. Guys you thought you made a real connection with, and they never called. You always wondered why.* Kevin could be just like them.

Oh, shut up.

"Well, take your mother's advice. If he doesn't call within a day or two, give him a call. Don't be shy. God gave you a mouth, so use it."

Caden suppressed a chuckle at how his dirty mind took his mother's last remark. "Oh, I'll use it. I won't be shy."

"Good. I've always told you that shy people get nowhere." His mother paused for a moment. "So what's his name? What's he look like?"

And Caden told her, yet he omitted the fact that Kevin was a little on the heavier side, maybe a bit pleasingly plump. Again, he didn't know why.

The pair hung up on Caden's promise to call his mom midweek, when they could discuss his plans for returning to Summitville for Thanksgiving. He didn't think too much, at the time, of his mother's final words—"I haven't been feeling too good lately"—because his mother was a regular complainer with enough ailments to make a hypochondriac jealous. Most of these ailments came and went as it suited his mother's need for sympathy and attention. When he asked her if she'd been to the doctor, he got the expected answer: she said she hadn't, and that was all par for the course.

He'd see her at Thanksgiving.

*

There was only one way Caden would feel ready, awake, and alive for meeting up with Bobby for lunch.

Running.

Running was his escape, his sanctuary, the only time he could truly be alone with his thoughts, while he pushed his body past what he believed it could do. Instead of making him feel even more tired, as he did right now, he knew if he got out there and ran, it would energize him, make him feel right again.

He supposed he was a little addicted.

He quickly donned a pair of running tights, a sweat-wicking T-shirt, a fleece pullover, and his Asics. He did a few stretches, using his wall to brace himself. But he didn't stretch as much as he should have; he knew that, but he was too impatient to get outside.

One of the reasons Caden had chosen his studio on Kenmore Avenue in the Edgewater neighborhood was its close proximity to the Lakefront Trail. The trail ran all the way from Northwestern University in Evanston through downtown and beyond, all the way, he guessed, into Hyde Park, although Caden was not that much of a distance runner. On one side of the trail, the city with its high-rises rose up, on the other, the vast ever-changing expanse of Lake Michigan.

Today, its waters had shifted since he had left Kevin's apartment earlier. Now, the grayish-blue water roiled, throwing up big waves, white caps as they crashed into the shore.

Caden kept his breathing even as he made his way south, to the bridge over Lake Shore Drive, where he would turn around and come back up the other side, near Fullerton. It was a good five or six miles, and Caden could do it in under an hour.

As he ran, he thought about Kevin, wondering what he was doing, how his day at work was going and, most importantly, if he was thinking of him. Caden knew he had fallen for the guy because, try as he might, he could think of nothing else as he ran. No matter where he forced his mind, whether it be his hometown in Summitville, PA, his work at the professional association downtown, his last trick before Kevin, or what he should have for dinner that night, he always came back to Kevin. He always returned to the memory of their perfect night and morning together. His mind always showed him Kevin's—to him—perfect body, big enough to lose himself in, comforting in its girth, its solidity.

Kevin wasn't fat. He was solid. Beefy. Manly.

Caden slowed his pace to a trot, then a walk, as he realized he had almost completed his course. The miles had gone by unnoticed.

"Thank you, Kevin," he whispered, his breath coming out in a puff of steam.

Caden had probably had just burned about six hundred calories.

Chapter Seven

"Do you want to put Bella on the scale? So we can get a weight?" Kevin instructed the Chihuahua's owner to put the fawn-colored dog on the steel platform of the digital device. Bella was reluctant and barely registered, but finally they got the skittish pooch to hold still long enough to get a reading.

"Four pounds! She's up a little from last time. The tech will be out in a minute to take Bella back to get her toenails trimmed, and then Dr. Semple will see her." Kevin watched as the Chihuahua's owner, a middle-aged woman desperately trying to hold on to a Carrie Bradshaw vibe in her big flowing skirt, sparkly top, and designer heels, found a seat in the waiting area.

"Everyone's checked in, for now," he said to Prunella, his front-desk cohort for the day. Saturday was always a short day at Rogers Park Pet Clinic on Devon.

"I love Saturdays. I thought I would hate working them, but it's a bit more low-key."

"Careful you don't jinx us," Kevin said, out of the corner of his mouth. Even though the waiting room was currently full of low-trauma patients who only needed shots or well visits, there was always the potential for emergencies. "Remember the St. Bernard puppy who swallowed the rope and rubber chew toy a couple weeks ago?"

"Oh God! Don't remind me!"

The St. Bernard in question had to have the toy removed surgically, and the front desk staff was left to deal with the hysterical tears of the owner. Fortunately, all turned out well for both owner and dog.

"Well, we'll just pray the day stays its course and we're out of here by one, as usual."

"Big plans for the evening?" Prunella raised an eyebrow at him and then went back to sorting patient files that needed to be checked and sorted.

"Maybe," Kevin responded coyly.

Kevin, truth be told, liked Saturdays best in the clinic because it was the only time his and Prunella's schedules overlapped. He had become fast friends with the woman, a gal who was large in every respect—mouth, heart, soul, and body. Her kind streak was only surpassed by her sarcasm and weary worldview. She could be abrupt, bordering on rude, but there probably wasn't a person in the clinic—veterinarians, vet techs, and receptionists— who cared more about each and every animal that came in. He had seen her crying outside an exam room on more than one occasion when an animal was put down. At such moments, she would always tell him, through her tears, "If you let anyone know you saw me crying, I will have to neuter you. I mean it!"

Her secret was safe.

Kevin often wished he could get Prunella to come out with him to the bars. With her bigger-than-life presence, her shock of spiky red hair, and her piercing green eyes she kept tamed behind horn rims, she fit the profile perfectly as the dreaded fag hag.

Except she wasn't. Prunella had little time outside work for Kevin simply because she was so in love with her husband, Lenny, a shy, balding man who obviously worshipped her, and their menagerie of animals, including two bull mastiffs, a Maine Coon cat, and several parakeets. They all lived quite happily, or so Kevin believed, in a sprawling brick ranch in the western suburb of Skokie.

"Well, I *hope* to have big plans for tonight."

"Do tell."

Kevin held up a finger indicating that she should hang on while he took a call. He deftly brought up Annie Shace's Siamese cat, Pretty Soon, on the screen, noted that she was a "fractious" cat and that she was due for her annual exam. He located an appointment time for Annie and Pretty Soon and returned to the waiting Prunella.

"You have met a man, haven't you? I can smell a new man at five hundred paces. What's going on?"

More than any of his gay male friends, Prunella had become his principal confidante in matters of the heart, and as sad as he was to see Caden leave that morning, he was just as eager to get to work so he could fill Prunella in on the details of his good luck.

"Last night was big," Kevin said and laughed. He scooted his stool over closer to Prunella. "Do you believe in love at first sight?"

"I believe in lust at first sight."

"Well, there was that too. But I think this guy has more promise than just a roll in the hay."

"And I assume you've already rolled him."

Kevin looked up at Prunella shyly, batting his eyelashes, and whispered, "Three times."

"First sight? You just met this guy and you already boinked him three times? Lord have mercy." Prunella waved a hand in front of her ample bosom. "You gay boys have all the fun. I swear. I'm lucky if I get a monthly backrub from Lenny. Go on, tell me all about it. I can live vicariously through you."

"Now, you know it's been a long dry spell for me—"

"Honey, it sounds like it was pouring last night."

"And this morning." Kevin winked. He told Prunella everything and did not spare any details. By the time he was finished, his face had gone bright red and his jeans were tight in the crotch.

"He sounds perfect. At least in the bedroom department."

"He *is* perfect. But he's a really nice guy too. I really have a feeling this could go somewhere. Which is why I need to get out of here today, so I can call him up and see if I can get a repeat performance, if not tonight, then tomorrow. There's only one problem..."

Prunella cocked her head. The phone rang again; she took the call, dealt with it, and got back to Kevin. "So what's the problem?"

"This." Kevin made a sweeping gesture to indicate his body.

"What? I don't see anything." Prunella laughed. "If I wasn't already spoken for, and if you didn't prefer sausage over pie, I'd do you. You're gorgeous. A big, gorgeous hunk of man."

"Big being the operative word." Kevin frowned.

"So you're a few pounds overweight. So what? Who isn't? This may be Chicago and the big city, but sugar, it's still the Midwest. We could *all* stand to lose a few."

Kevin didn't say anything for a moment. "There's one person who couldn't."

"The new guy?"

Kevin nodded. "The new guy is perfect. I told you. Lean, muscular, not an ounce of fat on him. He's a runner, for Christ's sake."

"Running?" Prunella pursed her lips. "Why on earth would anyone want to do that to themselves?"

"To have a gorgeous, worshipable bod," Kevin replied.

"Oh, being skinny is so overrated!" Prunella sighed. "I like a man who has a little somethin' to hold on to. Like you! Maybe this new fella feels the same. Did that ever occur to you?"

Kevin shook his head. He pondered Prunella's words as he checked in old Mrs. D'Angelo and her calico, Helen. Sure, it was possible Caden liked him just the way he was, but it was unlikely. Maybe in the world Prunella lived in, overweight men were acceptable, but she was only familiar with the gay world through him. She didn't know how the bars could be meat markets, where only the prime cuts were sought after and the less-than-desirable—at least on a gay scale—were routinely ignored or rejected, until last call. Kevin had been on the stinging side of this equation more than once, and it had crossed his mind that Caden had only hit on him on the L train because he was horny and Kevin was, well, *there*. After all, hadn't Caden told him he'd gone home with someone—presumably thin—who had fallen asleep on him?

That experience had probably left him with a case of blue balls. He had met Kevin briefly at Sidetrack, so he knew he was gay. It was probably a simple case of beggars can't be choosers—so he had come on to Kevin.

And Kevin was only too happy to have him.

But now he didn't feel so happy.

Caden probably wouldn't want to see him again tonight. Or ever, for that matter. He'd be like so many of the guys who drifted in and out of Kevin's life—after some good sex and the promise of something more substantial, they suddenly made themselves scarce, refusing to take his call or even answer an email.

Caden, with his good looks and lean body, would most likely be the same.

Who was Kevin trying to kid, anyway?

"Well, did it?" Prunella was eyeing him.

"Huh?"

She rolled her eyes. "Were you even listening to me? I *said* maybe this new guy likes what he sees. Maybe he likes a little meat on his man's bones. I know I do. Give me an ass I can hold on to, drive him in deeper, not some scrawny, flat thing!" Prunella shrieked with laughter. Several people in the waiting room looked up, and Kevin grinned at them, knowing his face had flushed red and hoping against hope they hadn't heard her comment.

He shook his head. "Impossible. Guys like Caden never go for guys like me."

"You're selling yourself short, my friend. Listen to Prunella." She scooted her stool closer to his. "You *are* gonna call him again, aren't you?"

"I don't know." Suddenly, Kevin didn't know if he wanted to deal with endless voice mail messages, which was what his self-esteem told him he'd get if he called Caden, especially so soon after their meeting.

Maybe if he waited a few days...

"Look, you know what they say about the lottery?"

"What?"

"You gotta play to win. You can call this guy, and maybe you're right, maybe he'll blow you off, and not in a good way, but maybe he won't. But there's only one way to find out."

"Yeah?"

"Call him, Dumbass. You never get anything in this life unless you try. Don't come crying to me about your shitty-ass man troubles and your poor, sad love life if you can't get off your own deliciously fat ass to pick up a phone." Prunella rolled her stool away from him and gave the smile of a nun to a young man who had just come in with a Bernese mountain dog puppy. "Aw, isn't he precious? This must be BoBo. First visit to the Rogers Park Clinic?"

The woman could turn on a dime. But Kevin knew she was right. He would call Caden. The worst that could happen was he wouldn't reach him. If that happened, he'd leave a message, wait a day or two, then call again. If there was no response after that, he'd leave the guy alone.

Why are you thinking this way? You really are the biggest loser, for cryin' out loud. Think positive. Caden may pick up your call on the first ring and be thrilled to hear from you and totally available tonight. Visualize it. It's yours...

Yeah, right. We'll see.

Whatever way he looked at things in the immediate future, one thing Kevin knew was that all this thinking had brought him to a conclusion. If he wanted a man like Caden, he would have to be his equal—in every respect.

Prunella interrupted his thoughts. "You want to go grab some lunch after work?"

"Sure. Okay."

"There's this new Southern cooking place that just opened over on Clark that I'm dying to try. It's like Paula Deen has set up shop in Chicago!" Prunella closed her eyes in an approximation of rapture. "Mmm—fried chicken, mac and cheese, biscuits with butter and honey." Her eyes popped open, and she regarded Kevin, looking almost a little dazed. "Doesn't that sound good?"

"I was thinking more along the lines of sushi."

"Sushi? Why would you want to do that to yourself?"

"It's lower in calories...*a lot* lower in calories. No carbs, very little fat."

"Lo-cal is overrated." Prunella looked around to make sure no one was looking and pushed her ample boobs together. "It takes a lot of calories to maintain these." She snickered.

"Come on, Prunella. For me?"

"Oh, all right. I do believe some of those rolls contain cream cheese, if I'm not mistaken."

And some do not. And I am counting on getting away from lunch with no more than three or four hundred calories spent.

The new me begins today.

Chapter Eight

Kevin stared at the screen on his iPhone for what seemed like an hour, but was in reality probably only a few minutes. He had entered the number Caden had given him before leaving that morning, and now it stared him in the face, taunting him, daring him to press the button that would send the call. Kevin mused that it was interesting that he had identified his new friend as only "Caden" since they had never gone so far as committing to last names. Sheesh, he knew what Caden's butthole tasted like but didn't know the guy's last name. Kevin could tell you the consistency, texture, and volume of the guy's come, but yet he couldn't tell you his last name.

What *was* this world coming to?

Will you just press the damn button? Remember what Prunella said about needing to play to win? The worst that can happen is he'll blow you off in a way that will make it obvious he doesn't want to see you again, like subtly mentioning he doesn't want to see you again. The second worst thing is that you'll get his voice mail. If that happens, you leave him a low-key, no pressure message about how much you enjoyed meeting him and your hope that you could hang out again sometime. And the best thing could happen too. He could pick up, be thrilled to hear from you, and will be just as eager to see you as you are to see him.

And what were the odds of *that* happening? Kevin set the phone down on his coffee table and went outside on his balcony to stare at the L tracks to the east (where a southbound train was, at this very moment, rumbling by, headed downtown) and Fargo Avenue below him. A couple of men, middle-aged, walked companionably west, with a Boston terrier puppy on a leash leading the way. Kevin surmised they were a couple and the puppy was a recent gift. He grew a little misty-eyed as he stared at them. They had no idea how much he envied them.

They looked as though they had what he wanted—a family.

And you are never going to find that if you're too fucking scared to make a phone call.

Kevin knew his inner voice was right. So why was it so hard to make this call? Was it simply the fear of rejection? It was true: as long as he didn't call Caden, there was still hope. The phone call could erase that.

So don't call him. Go in, sit down, turn on the TV, and veg out. When six or seven rolls around, do have the courage to pick up the phone and call your good friend Giordano and order delivery of a mushroom and cheese pizza, or maybe even a stuffed spinach if you're really feeling sorry for yourself, and enjoy a beer or three with the pizza. Fall asleep on the couch. Wake up in the middle of the night and crawl into bed, dropping your clothes on the floor before you do.

Repeat.

Kevin went back inside, and before he allowed his self-doubt to get the best of him, snatched up his phone, woke it, and pressed the button that would connect him to Caden.

Caden answered on the second ring. "Hi, Kevin!" he said cheerfully, and Kevin felt a wave of warmth that was an awful lot like joy course through him. He was happy for two reasons. The primary one, of course, was that Caden sounded, even in his greeting, genuinely glad to hear from him. The second reason was that Caden recognized who was calling, which meant he had entered Kevin's number into his cell and that boded well for the future. If Kevin was simply a one-nighter, he wouldn't have bothered. He probably would have just thrown his number away as he walked to the L. Kevin had seen other guys do that very thing as he watched them from his balcony.

But now was not the time to dwell on such memories.

He was connected to Caden. They were talking again.

"How was work?" Caden asked, and again Kevin flushed with warmth, because Caden remembered that small detail.

"Oh, same old. No emergency cases, so it was kind of a low-key day."

"That's good. So you're not worn out?"

"Well, a little." Kevin grinned. "But not from work."

Caden chuckled. "Me too. So..." Caden didn't say anything for a second, a second in which Kevin felt his pulse and heart rate increase. "So, if you're not too tired, I was wondering what your plans are for tonight."

"Oh gee, let me check my book."

"Okay."

"I'm kidding. I was contemplating a hot date with a pizza and a couple DVR'd episodes of *Glee*."

"I love that show! Too bad you already have plans, because I was hoping we could get together again. Maybe even—wait for it—have a proper date. Dinner at a place where we actually sit down to order. Imagine! But you already have plans. Wah-wah."

"Plans were made to be broken."

"I was hoping you'd say that. Pick you up early, say at five? That'll give us time to have a drink before we head out."

"I'll be ready." Kevin wondered—hoped—that Caden had more in mind than just a drink.

"See you then, sexy." Caden hung up.

Kevin sat down hard on the couch. He was a little weak in the knees.

*

After hanging up, Kevin made an executive decision—they would not go out for dinner. Restaurants were full of people, people who would be shocked and maybe even outraged if they kissed, fondled one another, or removed their clothes. They could end up in a jail cell at that police precinct on Irving Park Road.

Kevin simply didn't know if he could trust himself to keep his hands off Caden, regardless of the threat of imminent arrest.

Having dinner here would also accomplish something other than privacy and close proximity to the bedroom. Kevin could impress Caden with his culinary skills, which weren't bad, actually. Kevin had grown up around a father who loved to cook and passed that passion along to his son. Whenever Kevin thought of his dad, he thought of him sitting at the kitchen table, perusing a cookbook. Christmas gifts were always things like ladles, pots and pans, high-quality knives, and things that often went unused, like garlic presses, because Kevin's father preferred to do the cutting himself.

So Kevin was well-equipped to feed Caden's stomach as well as his heart and his libido.

Eating at home would also allow Kevin to control portions and contents. Restaurant meals could be nice, but they were often full of hidden calories, oversized portions, and generous use of fats and sugars.

If he was going to make a new start and lose weight by taking a different approach to food, there was no reason to screw that up on the very day he'd made his resolve. He'd already done well at his sushi lunch that afternoon with Prunella, eschewing the sushi rolls with their sticky rice and opting instead for miso soup and a few pieces of sashimi. Why, lunch was practically calorie-free, which was a fact Prunella harped on to no end.

But enough of thoughts of lunch! If he dwelled on that, his stomach might remind him it could use a little more in it—and he didn't need *that*, not when he needed to think about shrinking the size of it. What was the stomach, anyway? An organ? A gland?

Whatever. Caden would want Kevin's to be smaller, flatter, and if all went well, defined, just like Caden's own.

Kevin checked his back pocket to ensure he had his CTA pass and headed off for the L stop at Howard Street, where he would catch the Purple Line to Evanston and Whole Foods. He was thinking of some poached halibut filets in a spicy chili lime broth, an arugula salad with oranges and pine nuts, and a little lemon sorbet for dessert.

Of course, Caden would be the real dessert, served up on his bed, naked, stomach down, and a heart-healthy Honeycrisp apple in his mouth. Honey, indeed.

Kevin grinned as he closed the door and locked it behind him.

*

"You look good enough to eat," Kevin said as he opened the door to Caden. It was true, and Kevin suddenly wanted to abandon the dinner he had started in the kitchen. A big part of him told him to simply grab Caden and pull him into the bedroom, tearing off his faded jeans and Big Chicks T-shirt as he went. Hadn't he heard someone once make the very sensible pronouncement: life is short, eat dessert first? Even at his most sugar-tooth happy, Kevin could think of no sweeter dessert than Caden, who now stood smiling at him with a bottle of wine in one hand and a bouquet of lavender asters in the other.

Kevin wanted to freeze the moment in his mind forever.

"Are you just going to stand there? Or can I come in?" Caden smiled.

"Oh! Sorry!" Kevin felt heat rise to his cheeks and stepped back. "Please. Come in."

Caden swept by him, leaving in his wake the smell of soap and shampoo. Kevin liked that he didn't gild the lily, so to speak, by wearing cologne. Kevin preferred his men to smell like men—simple and clean was good enough for him. He also liked that Caden hadn't bothered to dress up. Of course, when you had a body like Caden's—with its flat stomach, broad shoulders, and long legs—you looked pretty good, no matter what you chose to wear. He handed Kevin the wine and flowers. Kevin glanced down and saw the wine was a nice Italian pinot grigio—his favorite. Was this guy for real? Or was Kevin making him up to quell his loneliness? Would he wake up only to find himself alone in his apartment, realizing that Caden was too perfect to be a real person?

Caden leaned in, brushing his lips across Kevin's, reassuring Kevin that he was, indeed, real.

How in the hell did I get so lucky? Kevin wondered. He also wondered why Caden had brought him hostess gifts, when the plan was to go out for dinner. At least he believed that's what Caden thought.

"Thank you for these. I love asters. But you didn't have to. How did you know I was making us dinner? You even brought the right wine for the meal." Kevin hurried into the kitchen to start the wine chilling in the fridge.

Caden followed him. He looked at the pan on the stove, already steaming and full of lime juice, chicken stock, and red chili paste. "I didn't. I thought we'd head out to that new Italian place on Sheridan. I hear they make a mean handmade fettuccini." Caden wandered over to the stove, peering down into the simmering poaching broth, and then moved to the counter, where Kevin had the halibut waiting on a plate. The arugula stood beside it in a glass bowl. Caden plucked a leaf out and ate it. "I didn't know. I brought the wine for when we came back."

"Oh, I hope you're not disappointed."

"Don't be stupid. Disappointed? Getting dinner made for me by a hunky man who I am already growing very attached to a disappointment? If that's the case, bring on the disappointment and heartache. I don't think I can get enough."

Before Kevin had a chance to count his blessings or let his self-esteem cloud his mind with questions like "How can such a total hottie be so into the likes of *me*?" Caden had crossed the kitchen and pulled him into his arms.

Caden kissed Kevin. Hard. His lips mashed against Kevin's, and his tongue forced Kevin's mouth open, probing, hungry, insistent. Kevin could feel Caden's erection pressing against him through the loose denim of his jeans. His own cock rose in response. They kissed while minutes passed. The stock simmering on the stove rose to match the passion simmering in both men.

Finally, they pulled away, breathless.

Caden said, "Life is short."

And Kevin, delighted, responded, "Eat dessert first." His voice was hoarse with passion. "Let me just turn off the flame." He did so.

Caden grabbed his hand, tugged him toward the bedroom, and said, "Only on the stove, man. Only on the stove."

"I think there's only one way another flame could get turned down," Kevin whispered.

"Let's get to work on that."

Dinner would not be served that night until *much* later.

*

They lay next to one another as twilight seeped into the room. Outside Kevin's big window, the sky was a brilliant orange near the horizon, filtering up into layers of lavender, gray, and finally cobalt blue. Caden, nestled into Kevin's chest, snored softly. Kevin smiled, gently petting Caden's dark hair, wondering how he had gotten so fortunate.

As recently as this same time last week, Kevin had been pretty much of the mind that he might never meet anyone special. Or if he did, it would only be after he lost twenty or thirty pounds. His line of reasoning went that the gay world was a superficial one, and oversized guys, pleasingly plump fellas, had no place there. He had only to get on any of the online hookup sites to see his beliefs confirmed. In a few seconds' worth of scrolling, he could always find someone saying something along the lines of "No one over forty," and even worse, "No fats or fems." It was cruel, especially since Kevin didn't consider himself "fat," even though he couldn't deny he needed to lose a few pounds. Why couldn't they just accentuate the positive, instead of calling out the negative?

It was heartless out there.

Kevin liked working with animals for just this reason; they often loved a person without question or judgment.

And now, here he was, with the kind of man he thought would have been completely out of his league asleep beside him, worn completely out and sleeping the slumber of the sated. Caden had fucked him ruthlessly, tenderly, and for a long time, staring into his eyes as he thrust. He told Kevin over and over how gorgeous he was, how he just couldn't get enough of him, how he wished he could stay inside him forever.

Kevin couldn't believe it, even though all the evidence around him pointed to the contrary. His image of himself as a chubby guy chilled him with clichés like "Just wait for the other shoe to drop, buddy" and "What's wrong with this picture?" That little wheedling, cruel voice inside told him that a hot, built, and *thin* guy like Caden couldn't possibly be falling for him. Caden had merely hit a dry spell, and Kevin was a ready vessel who happened to come along at just the right time.

As soon as the next Brad Pitt and Zac Efron look-alike appeared in one of the bars or even online, Caden would drop Kevin like a hot potato. A hot potato waiting to be mashed into submission and whipped into obedience with healthy dollops of cream and real butter...

Kevin laughed softly to himself, wondering if the dreams of such carb- and fat-laden forms of food would become more intense the more he denied himself their savory charms.

Kissing the top of Caden's head, he doubted it, as long as he had this man beside him.

As if he had read Kevin's thoughts, Caden stirred, lifting his head from Kevin's chest to look up at him. "Sorry. Didn't mean to fall asleep on you. Lord knows I should know how insulting that can be." He snickered. "But I was so satisfied and so filled with warmth that I just happily drifted off. You understand, don't you?"

"God, yes. I felt the same, but there was something sweet about lying here and watching the sky change colors as the sun set, listening to your breathing deepen as you fell asleep. In a way, it was like a dream." Kevin lazily worked his fingers through Caden's hair. It was on the tip of his lips, almost unbidden, to simply say "I love you," but propriety, common sense, and fear conspired to hold his tongue.

It was too soon.

Caden sat up in bed and leaned back against the headboard. Just the feel of their naked shoulders touching was enough to make Kevin hard again. Caden noticed the growing tent in the sheets below them and reached down to give the head of Kevin's cock a playful squeeze. "I am more than ready to flip," he said, referring to taking his turn as a bottom, "but I think we should have dinner first. You know, for our stamina. Plus, you went to all this trouble to make dinner. I need to see if you're as good in the kitchen as you are in the bedroom."

Kevin's lower head began to droop as it realized imminent physical connection was not on the menu.

Kevin swung his legs over the side of the bed, groped around on the floor for his clothes, and dressed in the dark. He was still shy about his body, even though, by now, Caden was quite well acquainted with every inch of it. And all indications seemed to be he liked what he saw. "You just lie there, doze some more if you want, and let me finish making dinner. I'll come get you when it's ready."

*

Caden settled back against the pillows and watched Kevin leave the room. He couldn't believe how his luck had suddenly changed. He had, quite literally, met the man of his dreams. Not only was Kevin his physical ideal and a tireless lover—apparently, he could cook too.

He would have to make sure he'd do whatever he could to hang on to this one. This one dished out sweet and sexy in equal measures, and that combination, Caden thought, was hard to come by.

Thinking that he might even doze off again, Caden pulled Kevin's plaid flannel comforter up tight around his neck. He was looking forward to a long night of good food and good sex with a guy who just might proudly wear that oft-dreamed-of label, "the one."

It was nice here, in Kevin's comfy home and bed. Caden could see them together here in this little apartment in the future. He imagined long walks along the lakefront, nights of passion on their balcony, maybe getting a puppy together. On this latter note, he knew it was something Kevin would want, even if they had never discussed it. After all, the man worked at a vet clinic and was studying to be a veterinary technician. Of course, he would want a dog.

But what breed? Caden closed his eyes, imagining the pair of them on a beach, and tried on various breeds for size—beagle, chow, boxer—but in the end, the clearest vision he had into the future saw them running on the sand and splashing through the surf with a mutt, something bordering on big, a Lab mix with some German Shepherd thrown in. Somehow Caden knew Kevin would want a rescue dog; that knowledge just seemed to fit the wonderful package that was Kevin.

Caden rolled onto his side, listening to Kevin in the kitchen, banging pots and pans around, whisking, all the while humming something soft and sultry in his deep voice. Sarah Vaughn, maybe? The melody sounded like "I've Got the World on a String," and the title fit his mood perfectly right at this moment, which Caden wished he could freeze, to ward off anything bad waiting for him in the future.

All of a sudden—or maybe not so suddenly—Caden got caught up in the grip of his own realization. He sucked in a breath.

My God, I am falling for this guy. I am not just in lust, although there's plenty of that. I am in love. In love— me. Imagine...

Caden turned on his back, smiling.

It was then his phone rang. He pulled a pillow over his head, not wanting to get out of the body-heated sheets to cross the room and pick up the cell he had left on Kevin's dresser.

Why was the universe conspiring against him to upset this moment of perfect peace and contentment? *You don't have to answer it, you know. Whoever's calling will leave a message, if it's important.*

Caden wanted to listen to that very reasonable voice telling him to not allow any high-tech disruptions to his evening, but he just couldn't. He at least had to see who was calling. Groaning, he hoisted himself up from the bed and walked to the dresser, glancing down at the phone's display, where one word shone up at him—Yvonne.

His sister. The two were separated by many things—years (she was nine years older than he), way of life (she had been married since she was just out of high school and had never worked outside the home), and interests (she leaned more toward reality TV and romance novels for entertainment, pastimes a sometimes snooty Caden deemed beneath him).

In spite of all this, the pair were blood. And Caden couldn't deny the love he felt for his big sister, who had always been there for him, even when he teased her mercilessly when he was a little boy. That same blood had forged an indescribable bond between them, and he couldn't deny it.

Yvonne rarely called him, and if she did, it was usually on his birthday or a holiday when he was unable to make it back home. Calling him on a Saturday night seemed odd, sending a prescient chill through him. Caden snatched up the phone.

"Sis?"

Before she even spoke a word, Caden knew something was wrong. He could tell by the way her breath sounded broken, as if she'd been crying.

"What is it?" Caden backed across the room and plopped down on the bed, with the eerie knowledge his life was about to change.

"It's Mom," Yvonne sobbed.

"What? Did something happen to her?"

Yvonne didn't say anything for several long moments. It was time enough for Caden to picture his sister, back in Pennsylvania, on the other end of the phone line. Their differences extended to their appearance as well—she was short where he was tall, plump where he was lean, blond where he was dark. He had always taken after their father (who had died of a heart attack at the tender age of forty-five and who provided impetus for Caden to keep up with his daily runs), and Yvonne their mother. Caden visualized her twisting a phone cord around her finger, though it was unlikely she even owned a corded phone anymore. Who did?

"Yvonne?" he prompted. "What about Mom?" He tried to hold in check the rising panic within him, the fear that his sister's next words would be "She's dead."

"Mom's sick," Yvonne finally said.

Caden immediately felt a small surge of relief course through him. "Sick" could be fixed, right? Sick could be a cold or the flu. Sick wasn't final.

"What is it?"

It was at this moment that he saw Kevin headed toward him, a big grin breaking up his bearded face as he held a pan proudly aloft. When Kevin saw what must have been obvious—Caden's concern—he retreated back to the kitchen.

"She has cancer." Yvonne said the words blandly, almost as though she were saying their mother had a pocketful of change or a lamp she wanted to sell on eBay. Caden knew his sister well enough to know that her lack of emotion was not because she didn't care, but because she did.

She was trying to hold herself together.

"Cancer?" Caden found it hard to swallow.

"Yeah. Lung cancer."

Caden barked out a short laugh. "Lung cancer? That's not possible. That woman never smoked a cigarette in her life. Remember how she used to get after Dad about his smoking? She hated it." And it was true. This was a woman who had once posted no smoking signs in their kitchen to force her husband outside to indulge his nasty habit.

"I know, but it's not always smokers who get lung cancer."

Caden paced the room without saying anything for several minutes. "How...how long?"

"How long does she have or how long have we known?"

"I don't know. Both."

"Well, she may have a long time, depending on how her treatment and the surgery go."

"Surgery? Why didn't anyone tell me about this before?"

"She didn't want to burden you. You know Mom." Yvonne started to cry again, just a little, and then regained control of herself. "We found out a couple weeks ago. She hadn't been feeling herself for a long time, but it was still like pulling teeth getting that woman to go see a doctor."

"Why are you calling me now?"

"Because she's being admitted tomorrow. They're going to remove a good part of her left lung in the hopes they can cut out most—if not all—of the cancer. Then, after she's better, we can look into her options—like chemo."

Caden pictured his mother alone in a hospital bed and bit his lip to hold back the sob that threatened to rise up and escape.

"You want me to come home?"

"Mom wants you to come home. Yes, I want you to. Me and Bill and the kids. We need to be together as a family. For her. For each other. Can you come tomorrow?"

"Of course," Caden said softly. "Of course. I'm at a friend's right now, but I'll head home and check out flights. I'll call you when I know when I'll be getting into Pittsburgh."

"I'll try to pick you up if the timing works out."

Caden nodded, then realized his sister could not see him. "Okay. Or I can just rent a car."

They said their goodbyes. There was no joy in the fact that a sibling reunion was imminent. Caden hung up, feeling numb.

Like a zombie, he walked into Kevin's kitchen, where Kevin was busy plating their food. In spite of how everything was arranged just so on the plates in an almost artful way, Caden had no appetite.

Kevin added a sprig of parsley to each plate. "We eat first with our eyes."

"I have to go," Caden announced without preamble.

Kevin glanced down at the perfect plates, disappointment etched on his face. That disappointment was quickly replaced—Caden was relieved to see—by concern. "Is everything okay?"

Caden just shook his head. "Not really. I'll be in touch, okay?"

"What is it, Caden?"

"It's my Mom. She's very sick." Caden couldn't bring himself—yet—to say the dreaded word: cancer.

"Oh, sweetheart, I'm so sorry. Is there anything I can do?"

Caden again shook his head. "I need to get home and book a flight."

"Okay. You want me to wrap your plate up for you? I have Tupperware."

"Nah. I'm not hungry."

Caden noticed how expectantly Kevin was looking at him and knew he was waiting for him to say something along the lines of "We can do this another time" or "I'll take a rain check," but Caden was simply too preoccupied with his own sadness and fear to allay Kevin's perceived needs.

He turned away, got dressed, and left.

Chapter Nine

Caden stared out the window as the plane descended into Pittsburgh International Airport. The day was at odds with his fearful mood about what awaited him. Outside, the sun shone brightly on a crisp autumn day. The rolling hills of Western Pennsylvania below him were alive with brilliant shades of vermillion, yellow, rust, and orange. Oblivious to Caden's worry, cars raced along concrete arteries, here far more spaced apart than on Chicago's crowded freeways.

He remembered leaving Chicago that morning. It now seemed a lifetime ago. It had been a weird exit. He had stepped out of his building preoccupied with getting a cab to the airport and even more preoccupied with what awaited him at the other end of his flight. He couldn't bear to see his mom, his rock, sick. Not this sick...

He had been surprised, no, maybe shocked was the better word, at seeing Kevin waiting outside for him. There was a surreal moment when he just stared at Kevin, leaning against a lamppost and watching the traffic course by.

Caden had approached him. "What are you doing here?"

Kevin smiled, and his grin looked, to Caden, sheepish, as if he had been caught doing something wrong. Kevin shrugged. "I felt bad for you, so I checked online when flights were leaving for Pittsburgh this morning and thought if I got lucky, I could catch you—say goodbye."

Caden felt a wave of heat rush through him. What a thoughtful guy! "That's really kind of you, Kevin." He put a hand on Kevin's chest and stared up into his eyes. "You didn't need to go to this trouble, especially when you could have easily missed me."

"I know. I know. But it was on my way to work."

"We both know that's not true. You work north of here."

Kevin grinned. "You got me." He scanned the cars passing by, one of which was a taxi, and turned back to Caden. "Listen, I know you're probably in a hurry, so I'll get to the point. I brought you a little something." He reached into his pocket.

Caden cocked his head. "A present?"

"No. Not a present. A loan." He pulled out a gold crucifix on a chain. "I want you to wear this while you're gone to remind you of me." He brought his face close to Caden's and whispered, "I don't want you to forget me."

"Oh, I think that's pretty unlikely," Caden said.

"Well, just to be sure." Kevin lifted himself up on tiptoe to put the chain over Caden's head and onto his neck. Caden touched it, feeling it against his skin.

"It feels warm, doesn't it?"

"Yeah, that's weird." The morning was chilly, fog-shrouded.

"It always feels warm. It belonged to my own mother. Don't take this the wrong way, but my dad gave it to me when my mom was killed in a car accident. I was twelve. I know that sounds bad, but really, I have always kept that close to me because I think, somehow, a piece of her stayed with that crucifix. She never took it off. That's why it always feels warm." Kevin swallowed, and Caden could tell it was a little hard for the man to speak. "I thought you should have it with what you're going through with your own mom. Maybe mine, a little part of her, anyway, can be there to give her strength and hope. To fight..." Kevin looked away, and Caden thought it was to hide the brightness in his eyes.

Caden touched the crucifix again. Hoarsely, he asked, "Are you sure you want to part with this?" Caden didn't know if he wanted the responsibility of the care of such a precious memento. But he had to admit—this was one of the sweetest gestures anyone had ever made to him.

"Yeah. I want it back, of course, but keep it with you for hope—and to remind you of me."

Another cab was coming up Kenmore, and Caden knew he needed to get going if he was going to make it to the airport on time. Impulsively, he pulled Kevin to him, gave him a quick but passionate kiss, and turned to hail the cab. He called over his shoulder, "That's just to hold you until I get back."

Kevin nodded and waved.

Now, he barely heard the flight attendant thanking them for choosing American and his recitation of the current temperature in Pittsburgh. "It's going to be bright, sunny, and unseasonably warm for the next three days! If Pittsburgh is your final destination—enjoy!" he said, too perky. Caden wanted to tell him to shut up.

When the plane was at last on the ground, Caden snatched his carry-on from the compartment above and his backpack from the seat below and knew he was good to go. He had no idea how long he'd be staying. He had given his boss at work a prediction of a week off, but he had no way of knowing what this trip would turn into, at least not until he'd seen his mom and had a better grasp on what was going on with her health. He texted Yvonne: *"On the ground and waiting to get off, see you outside baggage claim."*

As the passengers slowly moved forward, Yvonne texted him back: *"Outside. Circling."*

As he headed out through the airport, Caden was seized with a feeling that all of this was surreal. Every single time—save for one, when his father had passed—his arrival in this airport had signaled a homecoming, a good time ahead.

And now he didn't know what to expect.

What did Yvonne have planned? Would they go directly to the hospital to see Mom, who had been admitted that morning? Would she have brought her kids with her? The sullen teenage Matt and his wise-beyond-her-years sister Sidney? Or would she have left them at home with Bill? He hoped so. He wanted time alone with Yvonne, even though he was sure she'd have nothing new to tell him.

Outside, it was warm, almost balmy for late October. Caden took off his windbreaker and stuffed it into his backpack. He walked away from a young guy lighting a cigarette and gave him a dirty look over his shoulder.

Secondhand smoke, asshole; that's what probably got my mom. Enjoy your coffin nail. The words were almost on his lips to say, but Caden had the good sense to speak them only in his mind. It was none of his business, anyway.

He scanned the cars, looking for Yvonne's gold SUV, and saw it coming toward him. He was relieved to see his sister was alone.

She pulled over and flipped the hatch open. Caden hurried around to the back and lifted his bags inside. Yvonne emerged from the driver's side and came back to hug him. His sister felt solid, warm, smelling of strawberry-scented shampoo. In his arms, she felt even bigger, as though she had gained weight, and Caden closed his eyes, pulling her closer. Her soft breasts and pillowy body were a comfort.

She finally pulled away and held him at arm's length, eyeing him. "You're too skinny. We're gonna fatten you up while you're here. You look like a scarecrow."

"Thanks, sis. Wish I could say the same for you. Still a regular at the Donut Shack on Fourth?"

Yvonne shook her head, a wry smile making her eyes crinkle. This was the way brother and sister had always talked to one another, and there was no malice in it, only love. "They know me by name. They start getting a half-dozen glazed ready for me soon as I walk in the door. I would have brought you some, but I ate them all in the car."

Caden pulled his sister into another hug, burying his face in her neck so she wouldn't see him cry.

It was Yvonne who, again, broke their embrace. She was never as much of a hugger as Caden or his mother, in spite of their Italian heritage. "Come on, we need to get out of here before that cop over there gives me a ticket."

Caden looked back to see a cop car pulled over and the uniformed officer just getting out. He hopped in the passenger seat. "Where to?"

"I thought you'd want to see Mom first. She's expecting you. Maybe after that, we can go get some lunch."

"How is she?"

"You'll see."

Yvonne pulled away from the curb. She and Caden didn't talk.

*

Half an hour later, Yvonne pulled up in front of Summitville City Hospital at the main entrance. "You go on in. I'll park the car."

"Sis, I can come with you. It's not like it's raining or I can't walk." Suddenly, Caden was afraid to face his mother alone. He had never seen her sick before, and something with sharp nails was scratching to get out from inside his gut. He gnawed at a hangnail on his pinky. It wasn't that he didn't want to see her. He just didn't know what version of his mother awaited him in the old red-brick hospital on a bluff above the Ohio River.

"Go," Yvonne urged, making a shooing motion with her hand. "You and Mom should have a couple minutes alone, anyway. You're her son."

"I know *that*. It's just—"

"Go on, now. You're a big boy. I'll be in in a few minutes."

Caden couldn't argue, so he slid out of his seat in the SUV and trudged toward the double doors that would take him into the hospital. He turned suddenly to stop his sister and ask what room his mother was in, but she was already speeding away.

He could ask at the desk. He went inside.

*

His mother was asleep. Caden was taken aback, and he stuffed a fist in his mouth to stifle a sob. How dare Yvonne send him to see her by himself when she knew damn well what he would be facing.

His mother, like his sister, had always been a hearty woman; a big-boned gal was how she referred to herself with a laugh. And laughter was something that always surrounded his mother, whether she was laughing herself or inciting it in others.

This woman on the bed looked nothing like her. Had cancer done this? Caden stayed just inside the hospital room door, staring, knowing he should be feeling something but unsure of what. Mostly, right now, he just felt numb. He didn't know what to do with the vision before him.

His mother looked as though she had shrunk. Instead of looking larger than life, as she did in all his memories, she was a small, old woman, frail, propped up against pillows, lying on over-starched sheets. An IV dripped a clear liquid into the upper side of her hand. Her hair, usually dyed a fiery red, had at last lost the battle, and most of it was gray now, in need of a washing.

Caden swallowed hard. There was a selfish, fearful part of him that simply wanted to turn and tiptoe out of the room, to await Yvonne's arrival in the hallway. He imagined his sister's look of disappointment as she came down the hall to see him standing outside their mother's room like a coward and felt ashamed.

He took a few more steps, cautiously, like someone approaching a fearful wild animal. Finally, he stood at the edge of his mother's bed and looked down on her, watching the rise and fall of her chest as she slept.

Unbidden, a memory came to him.

He must have been five years old, not yet in school, because he remembered his mother had just read him a story—one of his favorites. He could still picture the Golden Book in his mind's eye and its title, *The Poky Little Puppy*. He snuggled against his mom, her flesh warm and soft, as she sang that old chestnut "You Are My Sunshine" to him, ending with:

You'll never know, dear, how much I love you.

Please don't take my sunshine away.

Caden closed his eyes, his lower lashes a little damp. When he opened them again, his mother stirred and opened her own eyes, green flecked with amber, to look up at him. His heart lifted as he saw what happiness suffused his mother's sallow features.

"Caden." Her voice came out tired, a whisper. It was so unlike her, a woman who was big in every way, including her voice. "I didn't know you were coming."

"I'm your surprise, Ma."

Caden bent down to embrace his mother. She felt frail in his arms, and he asked himself again: where had his mother gone?

"Well, it's a damn nice surprise. How long you in for?"

"No agenda. We'll see."

A look of pain crossed his mother's features, and he wondered what she was thinking—and perhaps not daring to voice. An open-ended stay, Caden thought, would be cause for concern in a mother who worried too much. He knew his mom well enough to know she would automatically think his visit and his indefinite plan indicated she was going to die.

Caden hoped that wasn't the case. "How are you feeling?"

His mother groped for the control to raise the bed. Her hands fluttered around her head, trying, he guessed, to make her flattened hair look somewhat presentable. She drew in a deep breath, and when she spoke again, her voice came out a little stronger. "Not too bad, not too good. I haven't been feeling real good for a while now. Tired. Sick. I didn't know why."

"Why didn't you tell me?"

She waved the question away. "Why? What are you gonna do about it all the way out there in Chicago? I didn't want to burden you. You're a grown man. You've got your own life."

Caden took his mother's hand and held it. "How my mom is feeling is *not* a burden. You should have let me know."

She didn't say anything for a few minutes, time enough for Caden to look out the window at the view. Below them the green/brown waters of the Ohio moved sluggishly along. On the other side of the river, the tree-covered hills of Pennsylvania rose up. "Did Yvonne tell you? I have cancer."

Caden squeezed her hand. "I know. She told me."

"Lung cancer. Doesn't that beat all? I have never taken one puff on a cigarette my whole life, and where did it get me? Your father smoked like a chimney all his life, and he didn't get cancer."

No, Caden wanted to say, because he died before it happened, most likely. And his smoke was yours, Ma; his smoke was yours. But he didn't want to voice any of that. His mother was smart enough and probably knew his dad's secondhand smoke might have played a large part in her predicament. But he knew her well enough to know she would never say anything bad about the man whom she had married and borne two children with. She certainly wouldn't blame him. It was easier for her, Caden supposed, to imagine her affliction as a mystery.

"I know. They treating you okay in here?"

"The good news is that I'm losing weight—finally! The bad news is the food sucks. I mean, really sucks. I don't know what they use for seasoning down there. Dust? Maybe you can sneak me in a sausage and peppers sandwich from D'Angelo's."

Caden chuckled. "I'll work on that."

"They're gonna cut me open tomorrow. Take out a part of one of my lungs. I'm scared."

His mother's face revealed little of the turmoil he knew must have been brewing beneath the surface, the fear he was positive she had to be feeling right now. He leaned over to hug her again, and she gripped him tightly.

In his ear, she whispered, "My sunshine."

Chapter Ten

It was a week before Kevin heard from Caden. A week of worry. A week of work. A week of school. Behind those last two distractions was always the thought—where is he? What's going on? Is he okay?

He had Caden's number and knew he could call, and it was perfectly reasonable for him to do so. After all, wouldn't it be nice of him to show his concern, to check in and see how Caden was doing? What news he had about his mother?

Yet something prevented him, and he wasn't quite sure what. He supposed the main thing was that they had only had two dates, and the first of those was really nothing more than a late-night hookup. Their real date had been aborted—and had turned out to be more about sex than anything else.

Oddly enough, and Kevin wondered if he was justified in thinking this way, he didn't know if he would be out of line in calling Caden. After all, this was such a personal thing, a family thing. They hadn't even gotten into talking about their families to each other yet, and he felt that maybe a call would be intrusive, inappropriate, from someone maybe Caden only saw as a trick.

He hoped Caden didn't see him that way, but it wasn't unrealistic to think so.

Things had been going so well too! Off to such a promising start! But all it took was something like this—a real world, grave intrusion—and it showed Kevin how fragile was the foundation upon which their relationship was built.

It was really nothing more than a house of cards. Still, he really cared for this guy and felt something for him that went beyond physical attraction. There was an emotional connection too, one that Kevin was certain could lead to something significant.

He had talked to Prunella, maybe too much, about his indecisiveness, his fear of simply picking up the phone.

She, with her common sense approach to life, chided him. "What? You think he's gonna be pissed at you for taking an interest? For showing some concern? Are you nuts?"

Maybe he *was* nuts, and maybe this paralysis of propriety was going to cost him the promise of a new relationship, but he simply couldn't help himself.

All of this ran through his mind as he huffed and puffed his way up the stairs after what had become his regular morning run. He didn't know what the future held or if he was screwing it up, but he did know that Caden would come home to a leaner, fitter Kevin, one worthy of a guy who looked like Caden.

So, in addition to eating healthy, he had taken up Caden's exercise of choice—running. He had ordered himself a pair of Asics from Zappos.com (the type of shoe he knew Caden preferred), spending a hundred bucks on a pair called the "Gel Foundation." After the shoes came, overnight, he had begun his running program—starting off with two miles between his apartment and the south end of Evanston.

Of course, he didn't *run* those two miles. The first day or two, he mostly walked them, running in sprints for two minutes, then walking briskly for five.

Even that much, at first, was hell, and made Kevin want to throw in the towel, come home, and order a pizza. His lungs burned. His legs ached. His back hurt. Even after two minutes, he sweated profusely and found it hard to catch his breath.

People did this for fun?

Caden had told him he ran every day, and that some days, he couldn't wait to get outside for his run, as though it was some kind of reward.

Kevin, sweaty and in sweats, approached his own front door, slid his key into the lock, and went inside. His breathing and heart rate were slowing to normal, non-gasping levels, and he had to admit to himself the running was getting easier every day. He had even built up, already, to running for three minutes and walking for three, and this morning, he realized as he was running, he had stopped thinking about the pain it was causing his body and had enjoyed, for a moment or two, the wide blue expanse of Lake Michigan as he ran along the boulders on Sheridan Road, across from Calvary Cemetery. Instead of wanting to clutch his burning chest and monitor his heart—was it beating *too* fast?—he admired the shifting colors of the leaves along the shoreline and felt the cool damp breeze wash over him, after sweeping across Lake Michigan's waters.

Inside, he took a quick shower and donned his robe to make breakfast—two poached eggs atop a bed of lightly wilted spinach with a little garlic. It was not bad. He almost didn't miss the toast and the home fries. Almost. He wasn't kidding himself, though, about missing the bacon.

He missed the bacon.

He ate and went into the little corner of his dining room where his desk and computer were set up. He'd check his email and then head into work. Today, he didn't have to be in until ten.

As soon as he opened his Gmail, he saw the subject line and his heart gave a little leap.

Caden DeSarro wants to be friends on Facebook.

He didn't get that many friend requests on the social network, and he knew absolutely no one else named Caden, so this had to be him. He clicked on the link that would take him to Facebook, entered his user name and password, and saw the friend request, complete with a thumbnail picture that threatened to make his heart beat right of his chest. It was Caden, scruffy, looking over one shoulder and smiling at the camera.

Smiling at him. It was almost as if their eyes connected.

Kevin pressed "confirm" before even one second had passed. He laughed out loud. Caden had gotten in touch!

He looked up at the icons across the top of the site and saw he had a message. He clicked on the icon and found that the message was from Caden.

"Hey, you. I am here in Pennsylvania and just thought I'd drop you a note when I realized I didn't have your email. A quick check of Facebook tracked you down for me. Just so we can keep in touch while I'm out here in the Keystone state, here's my personal email: cadenruns@gmail.com.

"I probably won't be back for another month or so. My mom had her surgery. (I'll fill you in on the details when we're face-to-face.)"

Kevin had to stop reading for a moment to breathe a sigh of relief. So Caden was thinking of another face-to-face meeting? That was good. Then he chastised himself for being selfish—Caden was in Pennsylvania for his mother, who he said was very sick.

Wipe that grin off your face, Kevin. He continued to read.

"Anyway, I worked it out with my job to work remotely for the rest of the month, and then we'll see. (It surprised me to see how little I actually need to go into the office.)

"I hope you're thinking about me. I sure am thinking about you. I hope you're saving a spot for me in your heart. I know it's unfair of me to ask you to wait, but we were off to such a damn good start...

"I'll shut up now before I make a complete ass of myself. Drop me a line or give me a call soon. Let me know—please—that you're thinking of me too."

Kevin leaned back in the desk chair, staring at the words on the screen. On his morning runs and his evening workouts at LA Fitness over on Clark Street, he had been certain that Caden, with all of his problems and the tenuousness of their connection, hadn't thought of him at all.

Yesterday, Kevin was almost ready to chalk up their promising beginning to a false start that had flared out quickly. Not because there wasn't anything there, but because life had intruded, as it often did, at the most inopportune time.

Kevin wanted to respond—immediately. He didn't care that such a response, whether it was written or over the phone, would cause him to be late for work. He needed to keep that line of communication open.

He grinned. Caden had been in touch. He had been thinking of him.

Now the question was whether he should write back to him at his email, on Facebook, or if he should just summon up the nerve, now that he knew for sure he meant something to the guy, and call him.

Kevin needed to hear his voice.

Without hesitating, without doing his usual song and dance of questioning himself about if now was the right time (What time was it in Pennsylvania, anyway? An hour earlier or an hour later?) or if he should interrupt Caden's family crisis, he snatched up his phone and hit the icon that would connect him to Caden.

Part of him—the shy part—hoped for voice mail. That way, he could leave a nice message, one expressing concern for Caden's mother and gratitude for his Facebook message and its sentiment.

Part of him thought he was a chickenshit for thinking this way as he listened to the distant ringing in his ear.

Another part was stunned when Caden's warm voice, not recorded, traveled through the phone lines and into Kevin's ear. Kevin had forgotten how velvety and deep Caden's voice was, bordering on raspy, masculine, and belonging in the bedroom. His dick awakened at Caden's "Hello" and lifted its head a bit, sniffing around.

Caden repeated himself, jarring Kevin into action.

"Hey, it's Kevin. I got your friend request and message."

"And?"

"Well, of course I accepted. I guess we're official, and now we're really significant others since we've 'friended' on Facebook."

Caden sighed. "There's no human bond that has more meaning—or depth."

Kevin laughed. "You said it. Anyway, I've been wanting to call, and your sweet message was just the shove I needed to get in touch."

"You needed a shove?"

"Well, yeah." Kevin wondered if he should have just written. Talking on the phone, even to the man he thought he was falling in love with, was always a chore. Kevin was a person who needed visual cues, body language, for full, unfettered communication. "I didn't want to intrude on your family stuff." Kevin paused, wondering if "family stuff" seemed insensitive when it was uttered in reference to one's mother's illness. He hoped not.

Kevin continued, "I mean, I didn't know if you'd be busy at the hospital." He sighed and finally asked, "How's your mom doing?"

Caden didn't say anything for a few seconds. "I don't know. She's pretty frail—lost a lot of weight and looks kind of gray, years and years older. It's almost like it's not even her, just some old woman pretending to be her, in that hospital bed." Caden paused. "They removed a good part of her left lung last week, and it's been touch and go."

Had Kevin heard Caden sniffle? Oh, how he simply wanted to reach through the phone and hold him!

Caden went on, "But Mom is a tough cookie. She'll fight this thing. They're going to start chemo soon, and they've already told us how rough that will be. I hate to see her going through this." Caden breathed in a quivering breath and said, "I wish I could go through it for her."

And this is why I love you. Kevin thought the words, yet still did not have the courage to say them. "You sound like a good son. I bet she's glad to have you there."

Caden didn't respond. After a while, he changed the subject from the pain of his mother's illness to Kevin. "So how have you been?"

"Oh, you know, just lots of work, going to my vet tech class, and studying."

"No late nights? No bars?"

"If you're asking me if I've seen anyone else, then no. Even if you're not, I've been leading a pretty dull existence—work and TV."

Caden chuckled. "That makes me happy. You save yourself for me, now, you hear?"

"Really?"

"Well, no, not really. I don't have any right to tell you what to do. We did, after all, only just meet." Caden sighed. "And I don't know how long I'm going to be back home here. Mom's recovery could take a while, and she needs me. Still, I hate the thought of me here and you there—with all the temptations the city has to offer."

Kevin thought it was sweet Caden was worried about losing him. In his own heart, he knew there wasn't much of a chance of that. Hell, the only reason he was glad they were having this separation was to give him time to lose weight to surprise Caden when he came home. He might not be as lean as Caden was, but he would certainly be a lot lighter than he was before Caden's abrupt departure to Summitville.

"Don't you worry about that, Caden. I'll be here when you get back—however long you need to be there. You just take care of your mom and support your family. I'm not going anywhere, and you've already spoiled me for other men."

"Hah! I doubt that, but it's nice of you to say so."

"I really mean it," Kevin said softly.

"I do too. I really look forward to getting back and picking up where we left off, seeing where it goes. I really like you, Kevin."

"Me too." Kevin glanced up at the clock. If he hurried, he would only be fifteen minutes late instead of half an hour. Yet there was so much he wanted to say—and not say. Just having Caden on the phone like this, hearing his breathing was enough.

But the real world, as was its habit, intruded.

"I gotta go," Kevin said. "Duty calls."

"Okay. We'll talk again soon. I'll be thinking about you."

"And I'll be thinking only of you," Kevin responded.

"Right. You probably have them lined up around the block."

Kevin shook his head. "Good God, man, how *do* you see me?"

"I'm not gonna answer that. Give you a big head. Now go on to work."

"Take care, Caden."

"Bye, Kevin."

They hung up, and Kevin wondered why he didn't mention the new fitness regimen or the changes he'd made to his diet.

He dropped his robe on the bed and went into the bathroom, stepped up on the scale.

He'd lost eight pounds.

Part Two

Chapter Eleven

The guy had been eyeing him when Kevin was running on the treadmill, taking the full measure of Kevin in, from head to toe. The starer had quit his exercise routine—conveniently—at about the same time Kevin did and had followed him into the LA Fitness locker room. He was a few lockers down, but Kevin would swear that every time he looked up, the guy was giving him the once-over.

Was there something wrong with Kevin's appearance? Was his hair sticking up? Was there spinach between his teeth? Skid marks in his Jockeys?

Kevin had turned his back as he peeled off his black sweats and Big Chicks T-shirt, and then wrapped a towel hurriedly around his waist.

The guy followed him into the shower, positioning himself in the one directly across from Kevin. Since the showers did not have curtains, the leerer could continue staring. He even smiled when he caught Kevin's eye.

What? Are you laughing at me now? Kevin turned under the spray of hot water, trying to ignore the stare he continued to feel, even though it was now directed at the back of his head, or perhaps a bit lower. Kevin chanced a quick glimpse over his shoulder and confirmed the man was not only looking at him, but also suggestively soaping his genitals, which seemed to be growing.

Kevin's face burned as he turned to the wall, grinning and feeling unnerved, all at once. *Surely he's not lusting after me. I mean, yeah, I've lost some weight and toned up some, but that guy's an Adonis.*

And it was true. The man across from him in the showers looked as though he had recently stepped from the pages of some fitness magazine, so toned, tanned, and ripped was his physique. To boot, he had a face that made him seem as though he was the love child of Johnny Depp and Gerard Butler—super manly and super sensitive. He was movie-star good-looking, model handsome, a hunk of masculinity, Kevin opined, far beyond his reach.

Did I forget to mention he was obscenely well hung? So, there is no way this creature that personifies male beauty and masculinity is staring at me, unless he sees something wrong, or worse, something funny.

Kevin shut the water off and wandered out to the area just outside the shower room, where one could place one's towel on a hook. He dried himself quickly, hands trembling and heart banging away, and not quite understanding why.

"Have a good workout?" The guy spoke from behind. Kevin turned and saw him simply standing there, naked, his balled-up towel clutched loosely in one hand at his thigh.

His penis hung halfway down to his knees.

And that body, my God…

"Uh, yeah," Kevin responded with eloquence, charm, and grace all rolled into one squeaky package.

The man moved forward, his penis moving lazily with his long stride, and held out his hand, "I'm Robert, but my friends call me Bobby."

Kevin swallowed, mouth suddenly dry, and grasped Bobby's outstretched hand. His grip was predictably strong, firm. "Kevin."

Bobby grinned at him, and Kevin couldn't help but notice how perfect his teeth were: uniform and blindingly white. One word flashed in neon in Kevin's brain: Chiclets.

Bobby gestured with a nod to the sauna opposite them. "Gonna get a little heat. Wanna join me?" An invitation twinkled in Bobby's gray eyes.

Oh, please! Really? Kevin felt shook up, more shook up than he had a right to, because he realized—suddenly and without a doubt, even to his dim, low self-esteem mind—that this guy wanted him. Yes, someone Kevin would have surmised was completely out of his league was coming on to him.

"Uh, no, I gotta run. I'm late for work." Without waiting for a response, Kevin hurried back to his locker to finish drying and to dress with shaking hands. His buttons would not line up right, and if he hadn't been wearing briefs, his zipper would have yanked skin right off his dick.

Outside, Kevin found his breath coming faster.

What in hell just happened back there? I am Kevin Allen Dodge. You do not attract men like the one back there. Sure, there's Caden, and Caden is hot, if I recall correctly, but he was the exception to the rule.

Flattered as he was by the flirtation and the rather heavy-handed cruise, Kevin couldn't suspend his own disbelief long enough to take in what had just occurred.

He caught a glimpse of himself in the glass of an empty storefront below LA Fitness and had a moment that reminded him of a movie he had loved as a little boy, one his mother would cluck her tongue at and roll her eyes whenever he insisted on watching it—*Gypsy* with Natalie Wood.

He should have known then he was gay!

Kevin was remembering the scene where Natalie's character was just about to go on stage to perform in her first burlesque. She wore a long satin gown, a fur stole, and elbow-length gloves. She looked at herself in the mirror, radiant and realizing something about herself for the very first time. "Mama," Kevin recalled her saying to her reflection, "Mama, I'm pretty."

As vain as it seemed, Kevin was having a similar aha moment right now, as he examined his own countenance in the window glass. The man looking back at him, an amused half smile pulling up his mouth at one corner, was virtually unrecognizable.

Six weeks. Six weeks had made all the difference. Granted, it was six weeks of running in the morning, building up until he could run three, then four, then five miles without stopping. It was six weeks of foregoing TV in the evenings and going instead to LA Fitness, where he lifted ever-increasing amounts of weight, building up his muscles, hardening and defining them. It had been six weeks of eating oatmeal with a little Splenda on it for breakfast, a salad with tuna and lemon juice for lunch, and something like a boneless, skinless chicken breast and steamed broccoli for dinner.

Although he had passed many a mirror during those weeks, he had always seen the old Kevin lurking there—the one with a bit of a paunch, a round face beneath the beard, a big ass. Almost magically, that Kevin had remained in the mirrors and any other reflective surface, even though his bathroom scale showed him he had lost ten, twenty, and finally thirty pounds.

It had taken a stranger's appreciation to change everything, to change the way he saw himself.

And now, as he looked in the glass, he couldn't believe it was himself staring back at him. Although he did *not* whisper "Mama, I'm pretty," he felt the sentiment deep within him just the same. It was not vanity, but a kind of joy, seeing that he had reached a goal. He hadn't quite internalized that he had actually attained this peak, this end of the road.

The Kevin looking back at him was trim. His face was no longer round, but strongly sculpted, his chin and jawline, even beneath his sandy beard, were angular. Dare he say patrician? In his black jeans, boots, hoodie, T-shirt, and leather jacket, he looked lean, no belly at all, shoulders broad, waist narrow and tapering down to thick, muscular thighs and calves.

He saw the Kevin Bobby had seen.

Kevin laughed. He turned around, checking out the high, taut ass that hours on the StairMaster and countless squats had sculpted.

Then he scolded himself. *Cut it out! You may have lost a few pounds and toned up, but don't get so full of yourself, mister. A box of Krispy Kremes and a week in front of the TV are all that separate the old Kevin and the new.*

He forced himself, at last, to walk away from the reflection he had seen with new eyes, reminding himself practically that he needed skim milk and grapefruit from Dominick's before heading home.

When Kevin came out of the grocery store, he all but ran face-first into Bobby, who was just emerging from the gym. Bobby looked ruddy and just as handsome clothed as he did naked. He wore a suede jacket, ripped jeans, and a pair of cowboy boots.

Bobby's gaze connected with Kevin's almost immediately, as if he had been looking for Kevin.

"Hey there, stranger," Bobby said. "I was hoping I'd run into you again. You hightailed it out of there so fast, I didn't have a chance to give you my number."

Kevin thought it was awfully presumptuous of the man to assume he even wanted his number, or that Kevin was even gay, for that matter. Was it that obvious? Kevin shook his head, grinning at Bobby, thinking it didn't matter. *This guy is so hot, he probably doesn't know what rejection feels like, and yeah, he could probably turn even a straight guy's head, so where's the risk in offering me his phone number?*

Kevin wasn't sure what to say, so he continued to grin stupidly. Caden was coming home tomorrow. His last email—complete with flight itinerary—had told him. But should Kevin blurt out that he couldn't take his number because he had a boyfriend?

Kevin wasn't even sure he *did* have a boyfriend. Sure, he and Caden had grown awfully close over the past six weeks, talking daily on the phone, writing countless texts and emails, and posting on one another's Facebook pages. And they had done a lot of sharing. Kevin liked to think he had been a great help, a virtual shoulder Caden could lay his traumatized head upon as he helped nurse his mother through her recovery and subsequent cancer treatment.

But now she was getting much better, back home, and Caden was bound for Chicago in less than twenty-four hours.

But to say to this guy he had a boyfriend just seemed stupid and premature. No mention of dates or even hookups had been uttered at this point. The polite thing would be to go ahead and exchange numbers. Kevin could explain his situation later.

So Kevin grinned and said, "Who said I wanted your number?"

Bobby grinned back, but Kevin could see the beginnings of scarlet flooding his cheeks, which served only to make the man even more handsome. "Well, of course you want my number. Everybody does. But only a few get it." He winked.

Kevin shook his head, both enthralled and put off a bit by Bobby's cockiness. What was he doing, anyway? Caden was coming home tomorrow, and Kevin had big surprises in store for him. He should just say something like "See you around" and be on his way. Yet, something— something like a drop-dead gorgeous man who was interested in him—held him back. He shifted his weight from one foot to the other, trying to think of a clever comeback.

"I see I've left you speechless. Got a cell or iPhone?"

"Huh?" *Gee, I'm glad you took the time to think of something clever to say.*

"A phone. I can give you my number and you can put it in your directory. I don't have a pen, and this way you can't make up any stories about how you lost the scrap of paper, matchbook cover, or receipt that I scrawled it on."

"Sounds like you've been the victim of such calamities before. And here I was thinking you were God's gift to homos, completely unfamiliar with the sting of rejection."

Bobby shook his head. "Ah...even the best of us strike out every few times at bat." He sighed and frowned. "So is this gonna be a strikeout?" Bobby stuck out his lower lip, like a child who was about to bawl.

Well, it's certainly not going to be a home run. But you're cute and nice in an obnoxious, full-of-yourself way—perhaps you'd make an amusing friend or a workout buddy. I could use some help getting abs like yours. No one said exchanging phone numbers meant the two of us would end up in bed. Yet, Kevin, damn him, had a flash of Bobby's naked body lying spread-eagled on his own bed, big dick pointing upward, practically screaming, "Jump on and take a ride, boy! Yeehaw!"

Now, that is no way to think. You have a much better specimen waiting to see you tomorrow.

In spite of his mental tango, Kevin pulled his iPhone out of his pocket. "Shoot."

"Love to." And Bobby recited his number. Kevin punched it in, thinking he could have only pretended to enter the numbers and walked away.

But he didn't.

And as he did, at last, walk away, Bobby called after him. "Hey you, aren't you gonna give me yours?"

Kevin turned around, a gust of wind catching him in the back of the head, and smiled. "I will when I call you."

Bobby called, "Really? Come *on!*"

Kevin relented, shouting out his phone digits as he walked away, thinking Bobby would never remember them, let alone call him, so where was the harm?

Kevin was pretty sure this Bobby probably gave his number out to lots of guys, and got numbers from tons of guys, all dying to get to know him better. This flirtation, temptation, whatever it was, would fade away, leaving Kevin with only a flattering memory, one that would buoy him up when he paused in front of the Swedish Bakery on Clark Street and eyed the calorie-laden delights always offered there.

Chapter Twelve

Everything was ready for Caden's return. Kevin did one final walkthrough of his one-bedroom, ensuring that everything was just the way he wanted it—welcoming, warm, a home.

He had cleaned the place from top to bottom. The hardwood floors gleamed, pillows were fluffed, magazines and books put away, bathroom and kitchen sparkling, as close to new as they could be in Kevin's vintage 1920s apartment. More importantly, he had stripped the bed, laying down a freshly laundered and brand new set of Ralph Lauren sheets that he had paid way too much for at the Macy's at Old Orchard Mall, but hell, this was a special occasion. He looked forward to getting those pristine sheets very soiled before the night was over.

So what if the come stains wouldn't come out? Kevin grinned.

On the counter, the makings for the dinner he had planned awaited him. It was going to be simple, healthy, and maybe just a bit more caloric than usual, but again—special occasion. Crimini mushrooms, cherry tomatoes, fresh garlic, fresh basil, and onions awaited Kevin's touch to transform themselves into a quick pasta sauce when all of the above were roasted into submission in a 450 degree oven, then pulverized in the blender Kevin had recently purchased. There was also escarole and artichoke hearts for a nice salad.

Cream-filled long johns, Kevin grinned, were all that was required for a filling and oh-so-satisfying dessert. He visualized Martha Stewart wiping some cream from the corners of her mouth and sighing, "And *that's* a good thing."

He glanced up at the clock and saw he had only an hour before Caden arrived. He was coming straight from Midway Airport to Kevin's place, taking the orange line to the red on the L. Kevin was honored, flattered, and thrilled that Caden didn't even want to stop at home first, as Kevin had asked if he wanted to do on the phone before Caden boarded his flight in Pittsburgh.

"No, I'm too eager to see you, man. It's been so long, and I just can't wait."

The words were burned indelibly into Kevin's brain. He would remember them forever. And he would make sure that tonight would be a homecoming Caden wouldn't forget, one that would build upon the relationship that was just beginning to blossom when Caden had been called away a month and a half ago.

Kevin now had just enough time to make sure every inch of his new, trim self was perfectly clean—inside and out.

One more hour, he thought, just one more hour. He headed toward his bathroom, dropping his clothes as he went.

Should I greet him at the door naked? Let him see the full measure of what he's getting?

Nah. Wrap that present. Half the fun of a gift is in tearing off the paper, so to speak. Kevin chuckled as he reached down to adjust the water for the shower to just below scalding.

*

Caden let his head rest against the glass of the subway car, bags heaped on the seat beside him. He was now on the underground part of his journey northward, and the dark tunnel outside, the gentle rocking motion of the train, and the relative calm of his silent car were almost enough to lull him to sleep.

He couldn't wait to see Kevin, to feel his all-encompassing warmth surround him as he took him in his arms. He pictured Kevin's stocky frame, his wheat-colored beard, his probing gaze and found himself filled with a combination of lust and, yes, tender warmth. All the time he was in Pennsylvania, nudging his mom back on the road to recovery—a road it looked like she would slip off more than once—he had thought a lot about Kevin and what he had left behind. He hoped the strength of their beginning was enough to hold the lusty man for the six weeks he had been gone.

Intellectually, he couldn't blame Kevin if he had been unable to wait. After all, he was a young guy—certainly horny—and he had his needs. It didn't even have to mean he wasn't always thinking of Caden. A quick encounter at the baths on Halsted or an online hookup would have been perfectly natural, logical even. A much-needed release. And Caden could surely understand that.

He could. He could. And his brain told him it was okay and did not have to be a threat to their burgeoning relationship.

But his heart—ah, that was another matter. Even if he imagined, for only a second, Kevin in another man's arms, the thought made him nauseous. It didn't matter if the other man was some anonymous hookup that Kevin would forget an hour after the deed was done, it still hurt. He couldn't abide it. Not emotionally. Emotion and intellect were two entirely different animals, and nowhere was this fact clearer than in the wilds of loving a person.

Caden shrugged, trying to position himself more comfortably. He did not want to arrive at Kevin's exhausted, but it had been a long day of travel. He told himself if Kevin had not been completely true to him in his absence, then he couldn't let it get to him.

What mattered was now.

And what came next.

He closed his eyes after the station at Grand and drifted into a fitful sleep.

*

There was the sound of a heartbeat and a succession of blurred images until he was with his mother again.

She had had the surgery, and the chemo had obviously begun, because her hair was falling out in clumps. Usually, she wore a bandana wrapped around her head to hide the loss, but now, in her bed here at home, she didn't bother. Her weight had plummeted, and she liked to joke, when she was feeling up to it, that she was now at the weight she had been on her wedding day. "One hundred and ten! Can you believe I was ever that thin? I was. Before you kids came along and wrecked my figure for good!"

But the weight loss did not look good on her. Her emaciated frame, coupled with her emerging scalp, made her look like someone frail, sickly.

Caden's heart lurched at the sight of his mother. He ached to make her feel better, and he knew the tender pain of helplessness when it came to protecting a loved one from suffering. There wasn't much he could do.

But he could make her eat. To get better, she needed her strength.

Now, he sat next to the bed with the bowl of chicken broth in his lap, the Ensure chocolate shake on the nightstand, trying to get her to take a sip of one or the other, or—miracle of miracles—both.

"Come on, Mom. You have to eat. You need your strength to get better, to fight those damn poisons they're using to cure you."

His mother's face was wan in the pale afternoon light that filtered into the room through partially open mini-blinds. Her lips were dry and cracked, and she ran her tongue around them every so often, to little avail. "I can't," she whispered. "The thought of food makes me want to throw up."

"Come on, Ma. Just try to get a little down, for me." Caden held the spoon out to his mother.

*

Caden awoke to the mechanical voice chiming that they were at Morse. Jarvis, Kevin's stop, was next. Caden forced himself to sit up, wiping the spit from his jaw and running a hand through his dark hair, which had grown out while he was in Pennsylvania. The dream images dispersed, replaced only by a sweet longing for his mother, the desire that she continue to progress in her recovery.

He would call her later—after he saw Kevin, after he kissed him, held him, and who knew what else?

The train could hardly move fast enough!

*

Kevin turned in front of the mirror, grinning. Caden would be so surprised! And he knew he'd be pleased. Kevin had gone from 220 pounds to 190 in the past six weeks, and he looked fit and lean in black Diesel jeans, topped with a formfitting cotton-spandex blend T-shirt, also in black. He had trimmed his beard way back to emphasize his more defined jawline, and had scrubbed himself so clean he expected to squeak when he moved.

The buzzer sounded from below, and Kevin hurried to answer it, but couldn't resist first making a quick run onto the balcony to peek down at Caden below. His heart just about stopped as he saw his dark-haired love, looking through the glass door of Kevin's vestibule, unaware he was being observed. A big duffel lay at his feet, and his backpack weighed him down. Still, he looked wonderful—tall, manly—his dark hair grown out enough to show Kevin that Caden's hair was curly.

What are you doing? Buzz him in! Buzz him in!

Kevin hurried to quiet the buzzer, which was just now sounding a second time. He stopped midway through the living room as he felt a draft at his back. He dashed back and shut the door to the balcony, then sprinted for the buzzer to press the button that would admit Caden.

His heart thudded in his chest, just this side of uncomfortable, as he heard the squeak and bang of the doors opening downstairs, and he sighed as he heard the thumps of Caden's footfall on the stairs.

Smiling, nearly breathless, he swung the door open.

*

Caden looked up as he heard the sound of Kevin's deadbolt turning. He rounded the landing and paused for a moment, waiting for the door to open.

When it did, Caden did a double take, one he later hoped wasn't immediately apparent to Kevin. At first, he thought someone else opened the door, that Kevin had invited a friend to join them.

But why would he do that? This was a reunion, a night to be alone.

But the person who was looking down at him now, all smiles, the pride telegraphing its way down the stairs to Caden, was Kevin.

A different Kevin.

A new Kevin.

A thin Kevin.

Caden smiled back, but his thoughts were in turmoil. *Where did my Kevin go? Where did the chubby, beefy, stocky man I fell in love with disappear to? This isn't him! It's just not him.* A part of Caden wanted to turn around, to hurry back down the stairs and just go home, to try to absorb that the person he had left when he had gone back to Pennsylvania was now an entirely different one.

And then Caden felt the heat of deep shame rise to his face. The impulse to flee was not one he was proud of, so he attempted a broader smile and continued his flight up to Kevin.

Before he could say a word, Kevin snatched him in the door and gave him only time to drop his bags before he pushed him up against the closed door and kissed him deeply. Kevin's body was pressed, inch for inch, up against Caden's own, and even this quickly, he could feel Kevin's erection pushing up against him. He could also feel the press of a different body, one that was harder, more angular, and not as soft and encompassing as the body he had left behind six weeks ago.

And Caden felt nothing.

This is moving too quickly, that's all. Caden wriggled away from Kevin, smiling but unable to meet his eyes. "Whoa, there, boy! Let's save a little of that for later, okay?" Caden squatted down to grope in his bag. He could feel Kevin's stare tingling at the back of his neck and could imagine the stunned expression probably on his face.

He moved clothes around in his duffel until he came upon a small tissue-wrapped parcel. He stood up and handed it to Kevin. "Here. I brought you a present."

Their eyes finally met, and Caden read hurt in Kevin's eyes. *No, I don't want to hurt you. This is so not how I expected things to go.* To compensate, Caden smiled warmly, but still felt like he was acting. He just couldn't get over the dramatic change in Kevin's physique. Why hadn't Kevin mentioned anything about losing weight in their many emails, texts, and phone calls during Caden's absence?

Caden was simply having a very hard time reconciling the two Kevins. He had come here expecting one man, and another had opened the door. How does one deal with something like this, anyway? Caden couldn't recall reading any dating advice on how to handle it when the person you fall in love with transforms himself into someone different when you're away for a while.

Kevin turned the present over in his hands, looking up at Caden. "You didn't have to get me anything. Believe me, buddy, just your being here is gift enough for me."

Did Caden detect a note of desperation in Kevin's tone? Had he picked up on Caden's discomfort? He hoped not.

Kevin unwrapped the gift. Inside was a beautiful red box with a bow. Kevin held the box out. "You brought me truffles."

"They're from Betsy Ann in Pittsburgh. They're wonderful." Caden stared down at the hardwood floor, which he noticed had been buffed to a brilliant shine. In fact, Kevin's apartment, like Kevin himself, looked almost new. An L train rumbled by outside, giving Caden a moment to consider how appropriate his gift of rich, delicious, and tempting chocolate truffles was to a guy who had just lost a lot of weight.

"Well, thank you. We can have these with our coffee after dinner." Kevin set the box on the dining room table behind him. "Speaking of which, I need to finish up in the kitchen. Do you want anything while I'm in there? I have beer, wine, soda. I can mix you up a cocktail if you'd like too."

"That's okay. I'll wait until we can sit down together. How about if I just get these bags out of the way and use your bathroom? It's been a long day, and I could use a little freshening up."

"Sure thing." Without another word, Kevin disappeared into the kitchen, leaving Caden standing alone to stare at the box of chocolates. Who was it who said "Life is like a box of chocolates?" What the hell did that mean, anyway? He remembered then. It was from *Forrest Gump*, the movie with Tom Hanks and Sally Field. He recalled the rest of the quote and how it explained precisely how life was like a box of chocolates.

You never know what you're gonna get.

Ain't it the truth? Caden thought as he turned to head into the bathroom.

*

In the kitchen, Kevin took a moment to stare out the window of his back door. Outside, the trees were bare against a rapidly dying twilight, their branches black silhouettes against the deep blue, almost purple, sky. He thought—rather melodramatically—that they looked like skeletal fingers, reaching toward the sky. Below, his neighbor, Kim, tossed a ball for Skip, her miniature schnauzer. Above stood the tracks of the L train, upon which a train was waiting to head into the Howard Street station, the northern terminus of the line. The train rumbled like a restless giant as it waited.

What was wrong? It was obvious something wasn't normal. Kevin saw it as soon as their eyes met in the hallway. He had been expecting Caden to be delighted, or at least pleased, with his new physique, yet if there had been any reaction at all it was—what? Kevin couldn't quite put his finger on it. Displeasure? Discomfort? Indifference?

And when he had kissed him, he quickly got the feeling Caden couldn't abide it, couldn't wait to be released from Kevin's embrace. Did he no longer feel the same? Had he met someone else in Pennsylvania? Maybe one of his mother's nurses? Or an old high-school fling?

Caden had seemed so eager to see him! In all of his communications with Kevin, there hadn't been one hint he was less than enthralled with their budding relationship, no indication his feelings were cooling. He remembered the text he had sent him as he boarded the train in from the airport.

"Can't wait to be in your arms again, to feel you all around me, surrounding me."

Yet, here, now, things were already stilted and awkward, as though they were strangers, set up on a first date where one of them—at least—didn't really seem to have his heart in it.

Don't overthink things, Kevin! He's been away for six weeks, and in that time, he's dealt with the very heavy issue of possibly losing his own mother, a real trauma and tragedy for just about anyone. Maybe you need to be patient and not expect everything to pick up right where you guys left off.

But he had wanted just that. He had expected it, dreamed of it, beat off to it. He had pictured the very moment their eyes met, there would be fireworks once more. And when they kissed? That would be magic, right? But it hadn't been. In fact, Kevin felt as though he was forcing himself on Caden.

Kevin couldn't imagine what the problem was. Perhaps it *was* just a bit of initial awkwardness, he hoped, as it had been a long time since they had last seen the other. *Sure, that was it.*

Still, it was a glum Kevin who turned to his pots and pans on the stove. He had brought everything to a certain point and then shut things down, hoping that when Caden saw him he would want to sweep him immediately into the bedroom. Kevin had imagined leaving a naked, sweating, and panting Caden on the damp sheets while he went into the kitchen to finish making their dinner.

He remembered thinking when they first met, "Life is short; eat dessert first." And that was kind of the concept he had in mind.

But it hadn't turned out that way.

Kevin took a quick peek in the oven to see how the roasting vegetables were coming along and listened for Caden's return.

*

In the bathroom, Caden scolded himself. *You need to pull yourself together and try to at least behave like you're happy to see him. I know it's tough to process the physical change, but you have to stop acting like there's something missing, something wrong. He's obviously gone to a lot of trouble to make a nice homecoming for you, and the least you could do is not act like a jerk.*

I know. I know.

I just need time to process the change.

Caden splashed water on his face and looked at himself in the mirror, the rivulets of cold water dripped down his cheeks, and his blood ran cold.

What if it's not just the change that has me so freaked out?

Caden gripped the sink as another realization washed over him.

What if it's more than that? What if—now that he's thin—Kevin is no longer attractive to me? What if the fire that burned so brightly has been snuffed out?

What if I've fallen out of love with him? Just like that!

Are you really so shallow?

I don't know if it's shallow or not. Who can explain why they're attracted to a certain type? I know lots of people probably find Kevin much more attractive now that he's lost some weight. Some people are attracted specifically to black men, and others aren't. Some like tall, lanky guys. Others prefer redheads. Is that a bad thing? Does it make a person racist because he prefers black men over white? Is sexual attraction supposed to have some sort of PC all-for-one and one-for-all universality?

It didn't work that way. For example, many of his friends thought the action film star—Caden hesitated to call him an actor—Vin Diesel was hot, but all Caden saw was some ridiculously overpumped muscle man that made him wonder about steroid use.

You like big butts. You like bellies. You want a man with a little meat on his bones. What's wrong with that?

"Honey," Kevin called from the kitchen, "do you want red or white wine with dinner?"

Caden would have to process the deeper questions later, maybe with his therapist. Right now, he needed to answer Kevin's query.

"Red," he said, quickly drying his face and coming out of the bathroom. "Red," he said again, smiling, in the entrance to the kitchen, now filled with the aromas of garlic, basil, onions, and tomatoes.

You be nice to this man, now.

Kevin is still Kevin.

*

Dinner, unlike the rest of the reunion so far, had turned out fabulously. Roasting the tomatoes, onions, and garlic before pureeing them into a sauce had brought out their sweetness and gave the sauce a depth of flavor that Kevin was proud of. The rich red gravy was a delicious accompaniment to the whole-wheat fusilli he had tossed it with.

Caden shifted a mouthful of pasta to one side of his mouth and said, "This is amazing."

"Thank you. And it's pretty healthy too." Kevin smiled, and the conversation stopped once more. Kevin wished he could attribute the frequent silences, made all the more defined by the clink of their cutlery against their plates, to being hungry, but he knew that wasn't the case. Or, maybe Caden *was* simply hungry.

But Kevin, somewhere along the way, had lost his appetite. He moved the food around on his plate, to make it appear he was enjoying the meal he had so lovingly prepared, damned now by a mysterious and almost palpable presence of unease in the dining room. Even Nina Simone's sultry voice could not help the mood.

Part of Kevin simply wanted the evening to be over—and that was a reaction he never would have predicted.

To break the silence, he asked, "So, with everything that was going on, were you able to have a nice Thanksgiving?" The holiday had just passed the week before, and Kevin had spent it alone, taking on a shift at the vet clinic to walk, water, and feed the dogs and cats boarded there. The whole time, he had tried to imagine himself next to Caden around a festive holiday table, set just for two.

"You know what?" Caden met Kevin's eyes for one of the first times that night. "It was really nice. Mom was out of the hospital and still weak, but able to join us all at the table. My sister went all out with the meal, I think because we knew that having our mother with us meant a lot more this year than ever before.

"I know it sounds kind of corny, but we always join hands before the meal and say our thanks. And then we all went around the table, as we always do, and said what we were thankful for." Caden paused for a moment, and Kevin could tell he was having trouble speaking. He wanted to reach out and cover Caden's hand with his own but instead took a sip of water.

When Caden looked back up at Kevin, his eyes were bright with unshed tears. "Every one of us—me, daughter, son-in-law, grandkids—were all thankful for the same thing: that Mom was there with us. She had to get up and leave the table for a minute. When she came back, her eyes were red and puffy, but she put on that tough demeanor I have come to love and scolded us all."

"What did she say?" Kevin asked.

"She said, 'You all ought to be ashamed of yourselves, making an old sick woman cry on a holiday. What's wrong with you?' She held up her wineglass and said, 'I'm giving thanks this year for booze.'"

"Your ma's not exactly sentimental, huh?"

"What gave you the first clue?"

And they both laughed. For just a moment, the tension in the room dissipated, and it felt good.

The tension came back almost immediately, when Kevin took the opportunity to ask the question that had been burning in the back of his mind since his gaze met Caden's out in the hallway. "So, you haven't said anything..."

"About?"

Kevin breathed out a sigh. "Come on, don't be coy." For the first time, Kevin felt himself growing a little angry. "Do I have to pull a comment out of you with a pair of pliers? Haven't you noticed I've lost some weight?"

Caden looked at him, and it was hard to register what was going on behind his gaze. Kevin was certain, though, it wasn't happiness, lust, or admiration. The food he had eaten churned in his stomach.

Caden said weakly, "Oh, I noticed. You look great." He became absorbed quickly in his food, breaking the connection they had made with their eyes.

The remainder of the meal was eaten in silence.

*

Caden was on the floor of the living room, going through Kevin's CDs. "Don't you have any dance music?"

From the couch, where he sipped his fourth glass of wine, Kevin asked, "What kind of dance? Surely you don't mean slow dance or swing?" He failed to keep the sarcasm out of his voice.

Caden turned and grinned at him, uncertain. He could feel the anger emanating off Kevin and wondered if he should leave. "No. I just mean something more upbeat." *Because we sure as hell need something to bring the level of this evening back up, give it a little life.*

"I think there's some Madonna in there. Some Black Eyed Peas." Kevin stood, crossed the room, and squatted beside Caden. "But I don't want that kind of music. I want Oscar Peterson, or hell, even some vintage Barry White." He took the CD jewel cases out of Caden's hand and set them on the floor. Then he grabbed Caden's face, forcing him to look him in the eye.

"I want to be close to you. I've hungered for you for weeks on end. I thought we'd have made love a couple of times by this point in the evening. I still want to. Don't you?"

And Caden realized he didn't know how to answer that question. Or if he did, he wasn't sure how to voice what was going on in his head without hurting Kevin. Why couldn't they just talk? Why was Caden so averse to conflict that he couldn't simply be honest with Kevin and tell him that he was weirded out by his new physique?

Because you saw the pride in his face when he opened that door, like he was giving you a gift. And Caden supposed Kevin was—he knew he had done the weight loss and the buildup of lean muscle all for him. It was obvious. *How can I hurt him by telling him the new look is what's making me uncomfortable? Unsure? How can I tell him that what drew me to him in the first place is now gone, and I don't know where that leaves us?*

So Caden said something stupid, something he didn't even know he was going to say until the words tumbled thoughtlessly out of his mouth. "Sure, I want to get with you, man."

"Get with me?"

"Right. But I was looking for some dance music because I feel like moving. I've been cooped up on a plane and a train. Wouldn't you like to go out and dance tonight?"

Kevin shook his head. "No. That's not what I was thinking."

Caden gnawed on his lower lip. "Maybe we could go out for a bit, have a few drinks, dance off a little of this lethargy from my travels. Then we can come back here and fool around, if you want."

"Fool around?"

"Yeah." Caden sorted through CDs, feeling like he could burst into tears. His heart, if it had a color at this moment, would be black. He realized that the only way he could make love to Kevin, at least tonight, with the confused feelings running through him, which made him by turns antsy and heartbroken, was to get himself good and drunk.

Kevin got up slowly and went back to the couch. "Listen, if you want to go out to the bars, feel free. I'm gonna clean up the kitchen." He stood and moved to exit the living room.

"Kevin. Come on. You can do that tomorrow."

When Caden saw the hurt on his face, he dropped the CDs to the floor and stared down at them.

"I'll do it now," Kevin said. "Maybe you should go."

"Go? Really?" Caden stood and faced Kevin across the room.

"Yeah. This night isn't going like I'd hoped, and maybe we can try a fresh start some other time." Kevin made no move to come closer to Caden, which Caden desperately wanted, but also felt frozen in his spot. "I don't know what's wrong, Caden, and until you want to tell me, I don't see the point." Kevin did move a couple of steps closer and said softly, "I just don't see the point."

Caden smiled, but it felt more like just grinding his teeth together. "We can have sex."

"Will you go?" Kevin's question was just shy of anguish.

Caden felt he had no choice but to comply. With shaking hands, he put his shoes on and then his coat and gathered up his bags. At the door, he paused with his hand on the knob. Kevin was turned away, staring out the dining room window, at what Caden wasn't sure, because only blackness pressed in. He wanted to say something, but the words caught in his throat, choking him.

Caden opened the door and started out. With juggling his bags, his coat pocket came open and caught on the doorknob, and Caden pulled, ripping the nylon of his jacket. He released himself from the doorknob, paused once more to grin sheepishly at Kevin, who still would not return his stare, and then left, closing the door softly behind him.

Chapter Thirteen

Dawn's gray light filtered into Kevin's bedroom like time-lapse photography. One second, he was lying on his back in near pitch darkness and then, quickly, the room began to lighten, at first making hulking shapes of the furniture around him and then, as the light continued to brighten, defining the shapes.

Kevin had lain awake most of the night, trying to figure out what had gone wrong. He had tossed and turned, trying to find that elusive position that would allow him not only rest but, more importantly, an escape from the anguish he felt.

He went over possible reasons for Caden's distance and lack of enthusiasm at seeing him. All he could come up with was either he had met someone else back home or the sight of Kevin was simply different from what Caden had expected. Sure, Kevin looked a lot better than he had before Caden left, but maybe Caden had nursed an idea in his head, an image while he was gone that was not really Kevin. And maybe being together made him realize that his idea of Kevin and the reality of him did not mesh.

Who knew? Caden himself wasn't talking; that much was for sure.

With a pain in his gut, Kevin realized that they had built very little before Caden's mom got sick—they had had, after all, only a couple of dates. How well did they really know each other?

Yet he answered himself back with the fact that, even while he was gone, Caden had been in touch almost every day. They had shared a lot in their short and long communications, getting to know one another. Sometimes you don't have to be physically with a person to get to know him.

This led him back once again to why Caden was so distant. So strange. And it was thinking like this that had kept him awake most of the night.

Now, his back hurt from lying in bed, and even though the digital alarm clock on his nightstand told him it was only a little after six on a Sunday morning, he rose from bed, feeling his eyes burn and a bone-deep fatigue that made his movements slow. "What a great way to start the day—feeling exhausted and depressed," he said to himself.

He wandered into the kitchen, thinking caffeine might help his mood, give his clouded brain a little more clarity so he could decide what he should do about Caden. He was certainly not ready to write him off as a lost cause, but he also couldn't take much more of the tension and lack of feeling he had experienced last night.

Kevin filled the Mr. Coffee reservoir with water, ground some beans, located a filter, and started the coffee maker to brewing. He looked out the back window, and the weather matched his mood. Gray, low-hanging clouds pressed in, and he could see that those same clouds were spitting out a mix of freezing rain and the season's first snow.

He thought of how weather like this, if last night had gone as he hoped, would have been cozy, with him and Caden in bed together, watching the flakes come down, feeling safe and warm in each other's arms. For a moment, Kevin allowed himself to imagine that alternate reality, the two of them, sleepy, turning to each other with morning erections. Their mouths finding each other in the fuzzy dawn light—making love.

He forced the imagery out of his mind; it was only making him feel worse. At least the coffee, now almost done, smelled good.

Kevin got out a mug, put in a teaspoon of Splenda, and filled it. He went into the living room to sit on the couch and consider how he should spend his Sunday and if, most importantly, he should call Caden, or wait for Caden to contact him.

After all, it was Caden who had behaved like an ass.

*

Three hours later, Kevin was feeling marginally better, at least physically. He had eaten a bowl of oatmeal and gone for a run along the lakefront all the way up and into Evanston, turning around just south of the Northwestern University campus. During his run, he forced himself to concentrate on his breathing, the sight of the roiling slate-blue, white-capped water of Lake Michigan, and pushing himself beyond his endurance.

He would not brood about Caden.

When he got home, he took a long, hot shower and made himself more coffee. He had just sat at his computer to look up movie show times on Google when his cell rang.

His heart gave a little flutter, hoping the caller was Caden.

But it wasn't. The caller ID simply said "Bobby," and for a moment, it didn't even register who Bobby was. Quickly, though, Kevin's brain clicked into place, and he recalled the drop-dead handsome guy he had met at LA Fitness.

He debated whether he should pick up the phone or not. On the one hand, he was in no mood to be flirted with, not with Caden's distance and awkwardness still tasting sour in his mouth. But on the other hand, a deeper level of his subconscious told him that the attentions of a gorgeous man could go a long way toward validating his desirability, something he just might need after last night's fiasco of a reunion.

So he picked up the phone. "I really didn't think you'd call."

"And good morning to you too. How am I? Oh, fine, just fine. Weird weather we're having, right?" Bobby chuckled, and Kevin had to admit he liked the deep-throated growl of his voice. "Are you always so direct? Why didn't you think I'd call?"

Kevin paced around his living room, glancing outside, noticing the wind had picked up. The naked branches of a maple tree danced in it. "Oh, I know your type. Good-looking. Always on the make. Guys like you usually don't go for guys like me, so I just figured…"

Bobby said, "I don't know what you're talking about."

And Kevin realized he was speaking as his older, chubbier self. He might have lost weight, but his confidence had not caught up to the pounds he shed. He saw Bobby in his mind's eye and still could not resist thinking that the guy was out of his league. It would take Kevin a long time to boost his self-esteem. "Slick Rick. That's what I'd call you if your name wasn't Bobby." Why was he being this way? Maybe he shouldn't have picked up the phone at all.

"O-*kay*," Bobby said, an edge of nervousness in his voice, nervousness Kevin was sure he inspired. "I was just calling to see what you were up to today."

Again, Kevin felt the urge to tell him that he had a boyfriend, and again, the same arguments came back at him. One, he wasn't really sure he did have a boyfriend. And two, the assumptions such a statement would make were not only inappropriate but ran the risk of making Kevin seem like a conceited ass. So, he simply told the truth: "I was just about to sit at the computer and check movie times. Thought I might see a matinee and then head over to Argyle for some Vietnamese for lunch. I know a place that makes a mean green papaya salad."

"That sounds like the perfect way to spend this shitty day." Bobby laughed. "I know it's forward, but would you mind some company?"

"How do you know I don't already have company?"

"Well, I don't. But hey, my motto is nothing ventured, nothing gained. So you already have plans with someone? Who's the lucky guy?"

There was a plaintive note to Bobby's voice, and Kevin was surprised, because in that note, he could hear loneliness. *A guy that looks like Bobby is lonely? You must be out of your mind.* Guys like Bobby were never alone, or if they were, they never should be. Kevin couldn't imagine a man as handsome as Bobby without a long line of admirers snaking around behind him, desperate to curry his favor.

Kevin sighed. "No. I was thinking of going by myself. I kind of had a bad night last night and thought I'd escape from it with a mindless movie and some good food."

"Look, I really am not trying to horn in on your day, even though it sounds like I am, but if you'd like some company, I wouldn't mind getting together. And if not, I understand. Maybe we could do coffee or a drink later this week. That's what I was calling to ask you, anyway."

Ah, the plot thickens. Does he really want to ask me out on a date? Or is he just being friendly? Sometimes, between gay men, the distinction was often hard to make, which is why Kevin supposed they often went straight for the crotch. It was simpler that way.

Kevin wondered, then, what he should do. Things with Caden were still so unresolved. But after his behavior last night, Kevin did need an escape, a little time to just put what happened behind him. He had originally thought that time was going to be spent alone, which was fine with him. But now he had a new consideration—spending it with a gorgeous man.

Why are you even asking? Go for it! Jesus! Just because you get together with him for lunch and a movie doesn't mean you're getting involved sexually, romantically, or for that matter, that you even have a future as buddies. So Kevin said, "Yeah. Why don't you come along?"

Kevin was surprised at the sound of relief and happiness in Bobby's voice when he said, "Great! I'd love that. Now, what were you thinking of seeing?"

*

An hour later, Kevin looked out his window to see Bobby on the sidewalk below, waiting for him, just as they had planned. There was a giddy moment when he couldn't help but think, "That's for me. That man, that hunk, that hottie, is waiting for me."

He grabbed his jacket and headed outside. "Here goes nothing," he whispered to himself as he locked his door. He realized his spirits had lifted quite a bit since last night, a feat he wouldn't have thought possible when he woke this morning.

He had just started down the stairs when his phone rang. He extracted it from his pocket, and with a certainty about how the universe worked, Kevin immediately thought Caden would have chosen this moment to call and talk.

He was right.

Kevin sat down on the stairs and answered the phone, even though a part of him told him to let it go to voice mail. "Hey," he said softly into the phone.

"I'm sorry about last night."

Kevin didn't say anything for a moment—partly because he wasn't sure what to say and partly because he didn't know if he was quite ready to forgive. Caden had built up his expectations, making him think that the two of them would have a loving reunion, one filled with happiness, reconnection, and yes—damn it—lust. And then he acted like a different person, one Kevin wasn't even sure he wanted to know.

"I'm glad," Kevin said.

"I'd like to talk to you about things. Could I come over?"

Kevin stood and walked down the stairs so he could look out the window on the landing. Bobby still paced outside, but Kevin's gaze must have penetrated his thoughts because he looked up and met Kevin's stare. Kevin held up a finger, indicating he'd be a second. Bobby nodded.

Kevin swallowed, his throat suddenly dry. He didn't really want to say the words, but what else could he do? "Listen, Caden, I'm sorry, but I have plans this afternoon. Can we make it later?" Kevin really wanted to drop everything to see if he and Caden could make sense of the ruins of their evening. But that wouldn't be fair to Bobby and in a way, Kevin thought, to himself.

"Oh?" Caden sounded as though he expected Kevin to reveal more. And that, for reasons Kevin didn't really want to consider at the moment, was something Kevin wasn't willing to do.

"Yeah," Kevin said. "So can we meet up later?" He was about to say for dinner but didn't think Caden deserved another shot at dinner or even, for that matter, another shot at being alone with him. "How about I meet you at Big Chicks tonight around seven?"

"I thought we could be alone."

"And I think it would be better this way. We can still talk." Kevin heard Caden begin to say something else, but he cut him off. "Listen, I gotta run. I have someone waiting for me." And Kevin hung up, feeling a paradoxical burn of shame and one of triumph, all mixed up together in one big sloppy package.

He tucked his phone in his pocket and hurried down the stairs to meet Bobby.

Chapter Fourteen

Big Chicks was crowded this early Sunday night. It wasn't surprising. The club was a popular neighborhood gathering spot because of its easygoing atmosphere, friendly bartenders, vintage bar, and the scores of amazing paintings and photographs (from the likes of none other than Diane Arbus and Lee Godie) lining its walls. Big Chicks was more of a relaxed gathering space, as opposed to a pickup spot, although Kevin supposed that happened there with regularity too. But if you were looking for a meat market in Chicago, you generally headed south to Halsted or north to Andersonville.

Now, Kevin sat alone at the bar, his jacket laid over the stool next to him to reserve a space for Caden when he showed up. Kevin had gotten there early because he wanted some time before meeting up with Caden, with whom he feared there could be a confrontation, or at least an unpleasant scene. After last night, Kevin would not have been surprised at all if Caden broke up with him, even though they weren't far enough along in their fledgling relationship to even call it that. It was more like a premature ejaculation—and just as bad.

He had ordered a white wine, which made him stand out among all the beer and martini drinkers who seemed in the majority, but he thought that was the drink that would have the fewest calories.

He looked around the bar, listening to the ice clinking in glasses, the bass thump of an old Moby song playing over the bar's speakers, and the additional music of conversation. It was a mixed crowd of men and women, gay and straight. There was even one person, dressed all in black with heavy eyeliner, nursing a Cosmo in the corner, whose gender was indeterminate.

Kevin had gotten several appreciative stares and even some come-hither looks. The bartender—a gorgeous little hunk who could have been no more than five five, but beefed up with lots of tattoos, muscles, and a shaved head—had been especially attentive.

Kevin was flattered by the attention and trying to get used to it. Since he had been eating right and exercising hard, he had stayed out of the bars. For one, he didn't want all the empty calories that came with alcohol. And for another, he was saving himself for Caden's return, a move he now questioned.

Had he been a romantic fool?

He took a sip of his wine and recalled the afternoon he had spent with Bobby. They had headed south first on the L, getting off at Argyle, which was right around the corner from where he was now, and gone to Hai Yen, Kevin's favorite Vietnamese restaurant, which was saying a lot because the uptown neighborhood overflowed with excellent Vietnamese food. Bobby was new to the place, and it was Kevin's pleasure to introduce him to things like *goi cuon* (fresh spring rolls with shrimp and bursting with herbs and vegetables), *chao tom* (ground shrimp on a skewer of sugar cane), *goi du du* (green papaya salad), and lemongrass pork bun (vermicelli noodles). Concentrating on the food, explaining it, and savoring it rescued Kevin from Bobby's leers and suggestive comments. (For example, he actually had the balls to say, albeit with a wink and a self-mocking grin, "If I told you you had a beautiful body, would you hold it against me?") By talking about food, Kevin could shut down the conversation when it moved in the direction Bobby obviously wanted it to head.

After a while, Bobby gave up, seeing he was getting nowhere with Kevin, although Kevin was certain he wasn't through with him yet. The sexual attraction—and Kevin admitted, on a very basic level, the feeling was quite mutual—was for the time being set aside. He made it clear to Bobby, without mentioning Caden, that he wasn't really looking for anyone at the moment, not even for a hookup, without coming right out and saying so in so many words. He did it by steering the conversation back to the food—again and again. Like a puppy, Bobby seemed to learn through repetition.

After lunch, they had headed down to the Music Box on Southport and laughed through a showing of *Best in Show*. The theater, a mainstay of independent cinema and revivals, was having a Christopher Guest festival.

When they parted, Kevin felt he had been successful in keeping his fears and anxiety about Caden at bay. It also didn't hurt that the heavily gay audience stared appreciatively at him and Bobby. They must have thought they were a hot couple, and Kevin was pleased to imagine they did.

At the Southport L station, they had said their good-byes and kissed—but it was a chaste kiss, even though Kevin had to work hard to keep his lips sealed shut against Bobby's flickering tongue.

The man never gave up!

Bobby had asked if he could see Kevin again, and before hurrying off to catch the train he could hear rumbling into the station, Kevin had coyly called over his shoulder, "We'll see."

Now, Kevin eyed the door, thinking Caden could arrive at any moment. The day had kept this meeting far from his thoughts, but now they returned to him with the force of a sledgehammer to the forehead.

Would this meeting go well? Or would Kevin ride home alone, thinking he had been so close to meeting someone he considered *the one* and yet lost him just the same?

And no, it wasn't any consolation that Bobby was, perhaps, waiting in the wings—Bobby and, apparently, scores of other guys, right here tonight.

If things weren't put right with Caden this evening, or at least moved in that direction, Kevin wasn't sure how much he'd want to do with any man in the near future. It would simply hurt too much, be too much of a reminder of what he had lost.

Now, don't think that way! Try to at least be optimistic!

But it was hard, and Kevin's nerves got the best of him. He felt butterfly wings flapping against the inside of his gut as it suddenly became real how tonight he could lose the man he had put all his hopes and dreams on.

He needed a drink.

"Hey, Luke," he called out to the bartender, who had told him his name when he sat down half an hour ago. "How about something with a little octane in it? This wine is for sissies." He shoved the wineglass away.

Luke came back with a big smile and his smoldering brown eyes beaming. "What do you think you want, Kevin?"

"How about a Jack and Coke?" *Calories be damned!*

Just as Luke was about to turn away, a voice from behind, a very familiar voice, said, "Make that two."

Kevin swiveled on his stool and turned to see Caden standing behind him, smiling. Kevin's breath was nearly taken away. Caden looked good enough to attack right there in front of Luke and everyone in the bar. What was it about this man that got to him so much? Yes, he was good looking and had a nice physique, but there was something about him that set off alarms all through Kevin's body. Kevin could not remember when another man had affected him so.

Sure, Bobby was a hunk and a half. But there was something almost plastic, something very Abercrombie about his looks, as though he worked too hard at them and believed too fiercely that he was God's gift to gaydom. His vanity and cockiness were a double-edged sword, attracting and repelling all at once.

But Caden... Kevin didn't say anything for several long moments as their eyes met. In Caden's, he could see, instantly, everything that had transpired between them before Caden was called away to care for his mother. Yes, the sex, but there was also that rapturous closeness and comfort they had shared, as if they were two parts of the same whole.

What was the name of that Duke Ellington tune Kevin loved? "I Got it Bad (and That Ain't Good)." Gathering up his jacket off the stool next to him, Kevin grinned at the memory as Luke hurried away to fetch drinks. "Sit down, sit down. I'm so glad you're here." Kevin had wanted to play it cool, but it was hard to keep the relief and warmth out of his voice. He just wanted to touch Caden, to kiss him, to tell him, "Let's get the hell out of here. Whose stupid idea was it to come here, anyway?"

But he *did* have enough strength, courtesy of the tense evening prior, to rein in those impulses. Nonetheless, he couldn't resist saying, "You look great."

"Thanks," Caden said, sitting. "So do you."

And the tension slammed back into Kevin's heart, because he felt as though Caden was just mouthing the words, returning the compliment because it was the polite thing to do.

For a while, the two men sat, side by side, sipping their cocktails and not saying anything. Finally, Kevin could stand it no longer. He drew in a deep breath and summoned the courage to bring things right to the point. "So are you going to talk to me about what's bothering you?" Kevin felt a small surge of anger veer in out of nowhere as he remembered how Caden had treated him last night and wanted to say more, something along the lines of "Or are we going to sit here and let this anxiety, stiffness, awkwardness, whatever it is, seep through us like acid and pretend everything's okay?" Again, Kevin was grateful he had the fortitude to resist being bitchy. He took a swig of whiskey and Coke and thought if he had many more of these, his inhibitions could loosen and he very well could say something he might later regret. *Pace yourself.*

Caden's gaze moved around the bar, and Kevin could tell he was nervous. Kevin put his hand over Caden's. "Look, whatever it is, I can take it. I'm a big boy."

Caden looked him up and down. "Not as big as you used to be." There was something wistful in his voice when he spoke.

"No. And thank God for that." Kevin realized, suddenly, what might be eating at Caden.

And he didn't like it.

Caden sipped and shook his head. "Beauty is in the eye of the beholder, Kevin."

"What?" Annoyed and unable to stop himself, he asked, "Are we going to sit here and talk in platitudes? Or can you tell me what it is?" Kevin had an inkling, though—he already knew.

"I'm sorry. I don't mean to be obtuse."

Suddenly, the music in the bar seemed too loud, the conversation and laughter around them grating. Kevin had imagined they would be in their own little bubble right here in the crowd, but that wasn't the case. "Would it be easier to talk if we went outside?"

"Back to your place?" Caden asked.

"I don't know. Could we just take a walk?"

Caden nodded and quickly drained his drink. Kevin did the same, and, wordlessly, both struggled into their jackets and went outside. Kevin left a twenty on the bar for Luke.

Outside, the almost total darkness was winter's way of reminding them she was almost ready to settle in for her annual visit. The sky above them was shades of navy, lavender, and gray, and Sheridan Road was relatively quiet.

"Should we walk over to the lakefront?" Caden wondered.

"With the wind whipping off the lake right now? We'll freeze our asses off, especially with you in only that hoodie for protection. Let's just walk up Broadway."

They headed west, over to Broadway, and started walking north, still not saying much, not getting to the heart of whatever awaited Kevin. He noticed, fairly soon, that Caden was shivering. After a block or two, they came upon a brightly lit café called Nerves, and Kevin saw it was empty. He also thought the name was perfect for their situation.

"Why don't we go in and get a coffee? Warm up? It looks pretty peaceful in there." Without waiting for a response, Kevin went inside. Caden followed.

After they found a table in the corner and Caden had his latte and Kevin his "regular old drip coffee—black," they got back to the conversation that had begun in Big Chicks.

"So you were saying 'Beauty is in the eye of the beholder.' You want to tell me what that was supposed to mean?"

Caden leaned forward, and Kevin could see the concentration on his face, looking as though he was preparing to say something big. *Brace yourself.*

"I only meant that I liked the way you looked."

"Thanks." Kevin played dumb. Or maybe he just wanted to be clueless.

"No. What I meant was..." Caden's voice trailed off, and he sucked in a deep breath. "What I meant was, I liked how you looked *before* I went back home."

Kevin cocked his head. Even though, somewhere in the back of his mind, he thought this was coming, he still didn't quite believe it as the words issued forth from Caden's mouth. "Seriously? You liked me better fat?" Kevin thought of the long hours of running he had put in, depriving himself of sweets, torturing himself with weights and aerobic machines—what was it all for? A voice answered him. *You. Yourself—you can't do what you did for anyone but you. Not really, even though Caden was a motivation.*

"Not fat, Kevin. You weren't fat. You were beefy."

Kevin waved him away. "That's just another word for fat."

"No, it isn't." Caden traced an abstract pattern in the scarred surface of the wood of their table. He met Kevin's eyes. "I have always liked heavier men, stocky guys, big-boned boys, football-player builds, whatever you want to call them, but I like, as some song goes, a man with a little meat on his bones." He smiled, but he looked nervous, as though he had just revealed that he liked to masturbate while riding on the L at rush hour and eating cotton candy. Caden grabbed Kevin's hand and squeezed it within his own. "It's what drew me to you."

Kevin thought of all the online sites, the Craigslist postings that used to make him feel inadequate, the ones that said "No fats."

"So you liked me better heavy? With a gut?" Kevin smiled, but he felt no happiness. *And finally—for the first time—when I'm just beginning to actually see a six-pack.*

Caden bit his lip and nodded.

Kevin glanced over at the other side of the café, where there was a glass case filled with croissants and pastries. "You want I should give a half dozen of those sweets a whirl? Snarf 'em down?"

Caden couldn't meet Kevin's eyes. "No," he said softly, voice barely above a whisper.

"What then? Where does this leave us?"

Caden stared down at the table, as if an answer was written there. "I don't know."

"I mean, because what I'm getting out of this is that you're no longer attracted to me." Kevin wanted to sound strong, but it was hard keeping the hurt out of his voice. He had spent many long hours pushing himself, all the while imagining Caden's delight when he at last laid eyes on him. He had imagined them running together, something new they could share and have in common.

Thinking of Caden by his side at some point in the future was what kept him going on his runs, especially in the beginning, when Kevin wasn't sure which would give out first—his legs or his lungs. He asked, in a voice that betrayed his uncertainty about whether he really wanted to know, "Are you still attracted to me? You're not, are you?"

The words hung in the air for a moment, their import, their ability to change the course of the two young men's lives unquestionable and grave.

Caden shook his head. "That's not true. I still care very deeply for you."

"You *care* for me? That sounds like something you say to someone you're giving the brush-off to, or someone who has just said he loves you and you don't return the feelings. You *care* for me? Please!"

"Yes. I care for you. Kevin, you don't understand. I was away for six weeks, and in all that time, I had no idea you were working out, dieting, however you lost the weight. I don't know why you chose not to tell me—"

Kevin cut in. "I wanted to surprise you," he said, barely audible. "Guess you were surprised, just not in the way I was expecting."

Caden nodded. "Anyway, the point I'm trying to make is I'm a little confused right now. I left one person, and I've come back to a different one."

"That's bullshit. I. Am. Still. Me. And don't you forget it."

"I know, but try to understand. I had an image in my head the whole time I was gone, and maybe I'm just having a little trouble reconciling the old image and the new one. Is that so hard to comprehend?"

Kevin didn't answer immediately, although there was plenty going through his head. *Yeah. Yes, it is hard to comprehend. I mean, most guys would think I look a hell of a lot better than I did when I was thirty or so pounds overweight. Most guys would congratulate me on working so hard. But that's not what I want from you, Caden. I don't want your congratulations, your praise. I want you to look at me and want me.*

I just want you to want me. I felt that once, and I don't feel it anymore.

"Kevin? You gonna say something?"

"I don't know what to say."

They both stared into their coffee for a long time, neither uttering a word. People came into the café, laughing, talking. As the evening deepened outside, Nerves got more populated until finally Kevin said, "I'm gonna go home now."

He stood, feeling he had nothing to lose. "You wanna come with me?"

"Gee, when you put it so romantically, how can I resist?" Caden rolled his eyes. "Sit down."

Kevin slumped into his chair once more.

"Can you give me a few days just to process that you're different? Maybe I'll talk to Camille...."

"Camille?"

"My therapist. I thought I told you about her."

Kevin shook his head.

"Anyway. Just a few days, Kevin. I'm sure it's all gonna be okay."

Kevin hung his head. "This is so not the scenario I imagined when I heard you were coming back."

Caden grinned. "There's a lot neither of us imagined."

Kevin shrugged. "Fair enough." He stood again. "Listen, I'm not big on expressing my feelings. Maybe that's why I work with animals. So just know this takes a lot for me to say, but..." Kevin paused, struggling to zip his fleece jacket and having trouble getting the pieces to connect. Finally, he gave up, leaving the jacket to hang open. "But I'm hurt. I'm disappointed." He paused again, drawing in a breath that he knew was quivery. "Maybe you didn't expect me to be thinner—and I foolishly thought you'd be happy about that—but I didn't expect you to be like this."

He turned and walked out into the night. He didn't turn around, but he kept an ear cocked for the sound of the plate glass door of the coffee shop opening, for Caden's plaintive "Come back, Kevin!"

But he never heard either.

He finally got the jacket zipped and started north on Broadway. He would walk the couple of miles up to his place on Fargo. Hell, he'd pass a Popeye's on his way home. Maybe he should just go in and order himself up some spicy chicken, biscuits with butter, and some dirty rice. Wash it all down with a tanker-sized order of Coca Cola. *And don't be bringing me any of that nasty diet stuff, either.*

His mouth actually started to water as the orange and white sign for the restaurant came into view in the distance. And he really started to think he might as well. What did it matter, anyway? The man he loved liked 'em fat, so starting at Popeye's would be a good choice, right? Caden would love that.

Farther up on Broadway where the street turned into Sheridan Road near Loyola University, there were any number of convenience stores before he got home. Sure.

He could follow up his Popeye's Pig Out with a stop at one of them for dessert. Wouldn't a box of those chocolate Entenmann's doughnuts be delicious with a tall glass of whole milk for dunking? And he could grab a couple tubs of Ben and Jerry's for good measure while he was there. The happy couple had been banned from his freezer for the past six weeks.

"Welcome home, boys!" Kevin blurted out, laughing.

A homeless woman, pushing a shopping cart, turned to stare at him.

Great. Now you've got homeless people staring at you. Kevin had reached Popeye's. It was across the street from him, beckoning with its promise of salty, greasy delights, a siren's seduction with its bright lights and promise of warmth. All that orange just made him hungrier.

Are you really thinking of doing this? Seriously? Kevin was no longer walking north. He was frozen in place, facing Popeye's and thinking how easy it would be to simply go inside and order himself a meal. It was as though his taste buds flashed back to the memory of fried chicken, the doughy goodness of biscuits, the sweet creaminess of melting butter as it spread its luscious self across the surface of the bread...

Why not? It would be much easier, Kevin knew, to gain back those thirty pounds than it had been to lose them. Within that few days Caden wanted to think, Kevin bet he could pile on ten, maybe even twenty pounds easy.

And the upshot was he could revel in all those foods he had denied himself—Snickers bars, Doritos, apple turnovers from the grocery store, a big bowl of spaghetti and meatballs with a side of garlic bread (Hold that salad, mister!), chocolate shakes, Cap'n Crunch cereal. There was a whole world of junk food gastronomic delights he had forbidden himself out there waiting, just waiting to be ravished.

The best part of it all was, he knew Caden would love him, want him, once again, if he only went back to his thirty-six-waist jeans.

So what's stopping you? Cross the street. Enjoy.

Kevin took the few steps that would take him to the corner of Broadway and Devon, where he could cross at the light and then head back south on the other side of the street to Popeye's.

Just outside the fast-food restaurant entrance, he stopped. He remembered when he used to binge eat and why. It was very simple, really. He did it to console himself. And he knew that's what he was doing right now.

If he truly believed consolation awaited him at the breast of some deep-fried chicken, then so be it. He should eat that bird. But the truth was, Kevin had done more than his share of eating for consolation, and he knew it only brought emptiness afterward.

Guilt.

Heartburn.

Pounds.

He wasn't really sure he wanted any of those things.

When the light turned to green, he drew in a deep breath and began to run. He would run all the way home.

Chapter Fifteen

Caden sat watching the door of the café for several minutes after Kevin exited through it. He half expected to see Kevin return again, his face contrite, wanting to talk some more. Isn't that what all the love advice people said you should do? Talk? "There's no problem too big," his mother had once told him, "that a good talking through, really talking, can't solve."

Caden felt a pang at the thought of his mother, wondering how she was doing, if it was too late to call her. He had told her about Kevin, and she had smiled when he revealed that he was a "little broad in the beam."

"Then he won't mind when I give him seconds of my rigatoni and meatballs." Actually, Caden's mother seemed delighted he had found a man with some meat on his bones. "Maybe he'll rub off on you. God knows you're too skinny." His mother was forever telling him he was too skinny, even though all the websites and health magazines told him his weight was ideal for his height. Even his regular doctor said so.

But Caden slouched down on his seat, unsure how sage the wisdom his mother had dispensed about communication really was. After all, how much talking would it take for Kevin to look the same to Caden once more? Caden couldn't help it if he liked Kevin on the beefier side, if that was the kind of look that rocked his world. Sexual attraction wasn't based on logic, and it sure as hell wasn't always rational. So how would talking give him that odd, indefinable, and delightful feeling in the pit of his stomach he'd felt when he had first laid eyes on Kevin almost a couple of months ago?

Would talking through it make him magically grow a hard-on at the thought of the "new" Kevin, naked?

Caden didn't know. *You're not even giving yourself the chance to find out. All you've done to the poor guy is dash his excitement and probably make him feel all his hard work was for naught.* And Caden was sure it had been hard work—one didn't just shed that many pounds in such a short period without a lot of sacrifice.

Wouldn't it be worth it just to kiss him, to maybe even get into bed with him and see how it feels? Caden felt oddly repelled at the idea, as though entertaining it was cheating on the "old" Kevin, as ridiculous as that sounded. The simple truth, plain and unvarnished, was that he no longer wanted to do either of those things.

The heart knows what it wants.

So does the libido.

And if Kevin had looked the way he did right now when he first saw him at Sidetrack, Caden knew he probably would have never given him a second look. He wouldn't have been his type.

Was Caden really that superficial? Usually, he thought of Bobby as superficial, only going after guys who fell into his hallowed category of "fucking gorgeous," but really, was he any different from Bobby? Caden had to be quirky and different and be superficial because he wasn't interested in a guy who was *not* overweight, when most of the gay men he knew were superficial in exactly the opposite way.

But really—was it any different? Didn't it all just boil down to basing everything on the outside, the shell?

Caden's cell rang, and he glanced down at the display. Bobby. Speaking of shells. It was as though his friend knew Caden was thinking about him. He had been meaning to call Bobby since he returned to Chicago, but all the business, drama, whatever one wanted to call it, with Kevin, had prevented it.

"Hey!" he answered, trying to sound cheerier than he felt, which wasn't hard—you can only go up from the bottom of a pit.

"Caden! What's up, man? Are you back in town, then?"

"Yeah, yeah. I got home yesterday."

"You did? Why haven't you been in touch?" Bobby sounded hurt, but Caden knew he'd get over it.

"Long story." Caden hesitated for a minute, trying to decide if he wanted to share what he'd been going through with this person he called his best friend. In the end, he knew there was no one better suited for it, simply because Bobby was there. His therapist, Camille, was not. He probably wouldn't be able to get in to see her for a few days at least. And while Bobby would probably be hard-pressed to understand why Caden no longer lusted after a man who'd developed a killer bod just for Caden, at least he'd be someone who'd listen. Caden asked, "What are you doing right now?"

"Now? I'm on Manhunt, cruising for dick. You expected maybe I was baking cookies? Cleaning the grout in my bathroom with an old toothbrush?" Bobby laughed. "Nothing's changed here, bud."

"How are the prospects looking?"

"Pretty dead. Everybody online right now is either old or fat—or I've had them before." Bobby laughed.

"Well, I guess that's good to hear, because I was hoping you'd want to meet me for a drink."

"Big Chicks?" Bobby asked. "They have a good Sunday crowd."

Caden thought it was amusing that Bobby would pick the one bar, out of the dozens he could have chosen, where he'd just been with Kevin. But he didn't feel like suggesting another place, and besides, it was within walking distance. "Meet you there in fifteen?"

"Make it an hour. I need time to shower, shave, and make sure I am looking particularly alluring tonight."

"Why's that?"

"Duh! The reason's the same every time I go out in public, sweetheart—one never knows when one might meet a man."

"Right. See you in a bit." Caden disconnected.

Bobby didn't need an hour to look gorgeous. He didn't need ten minutes. In an old flannel bathrobe, rolling out of bed with a hangover, Bobby still looked better than most men on the planet. Bobby was always the perfect ideal of male beauty.

And that, Caden thought, is why we're just friends and not lovers. He had never even been tempted by Bobby's good looks. It would have been too strange and, after they had become friends, almost like incest. Perfection had never played a part in Caden's attractions.

*

Big Chicks had gotten even more crowded since Caden had left with Kevin. He had to press through a crowd of bodies to find space along one wall at the back by the pool table and underneath a painting of a big-busted nude woman. At least here, there was a little bench on which he could sit.

Caden allowed himself a couple of beers before Bobby showed up. He wanted his tongue loosened for talking. He was ready to pour his heart out and only hoped his friend could ease his preoccupation away from hunting for cock long enough to listen.

"Maybe, my dear, it's time to get yourself a new best friend," a voice said in the back of his mind, one that sounded suspiciously like his mother.

Ah, Bobby was okay, Caden thought, once you got past the superficiality and the vanity. At least he was always there for him. Who else could he say that about?

There he was. Caden leaned back against the wall and sipped his beer, watching Bobby's progress through the crowd. Tonight, he wore a pair of faded jeans, ripped at the knee, with cowboy boots and a rust suede shirt, the top three buttons undone to show off his tanned, hairless, and defined chest. His hair was gelled and tousled in such a way that Caden was sure he had taken a long time to get it to look that careless. His face, under a sheen of perfectly applied bronzer, looked as though it belonged on a runway in Paris or a red carpet in Hollywood. Caden smiled, savoring this moment, sure Bobby was not aware he was watching. It was interesting to see the conversations go quiet, and observe the eyes following Bobby, checking out his ass as he passed. Then, the boys would turn to one another once more, giggling in a way that was way too reminiscent of schoolgirls, casting long and longing glances toward Bobby's departing figure.

Finally, Bobby stood in front of him. He pulled Caden up, gathering him in his arms. Caden smelled Terre d'Hermes cologne and felt the steel of Bobby's rock-hard body pressed against his own. As Bobby squeezed him, burying his face in Caden's neck, Caden had the absurd urge to call out over his shoulder, "Eat your hearts out, girls!"

But he didn't.

They settled onto the bench, next to one another, Caden with his beer and Bobby with his bottled water.

"Not drinking tonight?" Caden asked, gesturing toward the water.

"Nah. School night, plus, alcohol can sometimes make my face look bloated."

Caden grinned. "It's all about the face."

"You got that right." Bobby took a swig of water and arranged that same face into a serious, concerned mien. "So, how was Pennsylvania? How's your mom?"

And, at least for the next twenty minutes or so, Bobby listened, really listened, as Caden told him all about his trip back home. About visits to the ICU; about his mother looking like a stranger to him, as if someone had spirited her away and replaced her with a frail old woman; getting her through the sickness that came with chemotherapy; trying to keep her spirits up; trying to ensure she had a will to fight, a will to eat, a will to live.

Bobby shook his head. "Sounds rough." His gaze roamed the crowd, and Caden noticed it lighting on the very handsome face of a buzz cut blond with three-day stubble who looked like the porn-movie version of a Marine. The blond winked at Bobby, but Caden couldn't tell if Bobby winked back.

It was better that he didn't know.

"Yeah, it was. It was rough, but it was good too. I'm so glad I took all that time to go back and be with her. It brought us closer—and I like to think I helped."

"I'm sure you did."

They chatted for a while longer about Pennsylvania, each other's jobs, the plot of the latest episodes of *Glee* and *Modern Family*.

Caden went and got another beer, hoping someone wouldn't approach Bobby while he was gone. He was finally ready to talk about Kevin, and he and Bobby had been doing very nicely in their own exclusive bubble back by the pool table. But Caden knew that leaving Bobby alone, even for a minute, was an open invitation to the predatory wolves lurking in any bar.

Fortunately, when he got back, Bobby was still alone, although it was obvious the swarthy looking gentleman holding up the opposite wall had eyes only for Bobby. Caden met the man's dark-eyed stare. *Get away, bitch. He's mine, at least for a little while longer.*

Caden scooted close to Bobby. "So I wanted to talk to you about a guy."

Bobby's eyebrows went up. Here, at last, was his favorite topic. "Someone you met back in the Keystone State?"

"No. He's here."

Bobby placed a hand on his heart. "Horrors! And you haven't told your BFF? What have you been keeping from me?"

Caden smiled. "No big deal. I met him before I left to go home." Caden summarized his brief relationship with Kevin, sparing Bobby no details about their couple of dates and about the hot sex. "But it wasn't just the sex—"

Bobby cut him off. "Honey, it's always the sex."

"Get your mind out of the gutter. I really was falling for this guy. I mean, like I could see myself spending serious time with him, like maybe forever, if things kept going as planned."

"So, this guy, you think he was 'the one'?"

Both grew silent as they contemplated the holy grail of gay romantic love.

"Maybe." Caden's mind went to a homespun image of Kevin in his kitchen, making him breakfast. He would never admit this to Bobby, but that memory was just as nice as the lusty, hot ones in bed. "Maybe—he had everything I wanted."

Bobby picked up on Caden's use of the past tense. "Had?"

"Ah...that's the problem. He changed while I was away."

"Did he get into drugs?"

"No! No, nothing like that." Caden wasn't sure how to put what he wanted to say next, so he just blurted it out. "He got thin."

"Too thin?" Bobby asked. "Because that's a sign someone's gotten involved with that bitch, Tina. I've seen it happen too many times." With his mention of Tina, Bobby referred to crystal meth, the abuse of which was running rampant in the gay community.

"No! No, really. He looks good. But, before I left, he had—how shall I say it?—a little meat on his bones. His was a stocky football player build, as they like to say online."

"He was fat." Bobby took a swig of water.

"Not fat. Beefy." Caden laughed, feeling like Bobby wasn't buying his euphemism; except they weren't euphemisms, they were the truth. Kevin had been ideal. His added weight had just made him manlier and more solid.

"Whatever." Bobby rolled his eyes. "So he lost weight? And now what, he's skinny?"

Caden shook his head. "Actually, you'd probably think he had a really nice body. He's been running and working out hard at the gym—and he has the muscles and definition to show for it."

"And you're complaining? Are you insane?"

Caden sighed. He figured it would go this way.

"Where does this guy work out? Maybe I've seen him."

Caden said, "Kevin works out at LA Fitness, the one on Clark up in Rogers Park." Caden grinned. "You know, the one you go to sometimes because you've already had all the hot guys at the one in Century City."

"Bitch." Bobby playfully slugged Caden's shoulder. "So has he changed in other ways? Is he still this nice, warm, giving guy you talked about?"

"Yes, of course."

"I'm not seeing the problem here."

"It's just that I went away, leaving behind this gorgeous three B."

"Three B?"

"Beefy, bearded, blond. And I come back to a 2B."

"With a perfect body?"

"Pretty much so." Laid out like this, Caden couldn't help but think how ridiculous it all sounded. Here, half the guys in the city were probably searching for a man as perfect as Kevin, who was not only handsome, but fit, masculine, and nurturing to boot, and Caden couldn't get with the program. He shrugged. "I like big guys. What can I say?" He scanned the crowd. "Like that one." Caden gestured quickly at a redhead in the corner. He was your typical bear—thick beard, flannel shirt, rotund gut, and hair sprouting out of the collar of his shirt.

Caden knew all Bobby saw was a fat guy.

But Caden saw dreamy.

Still, he was not ready to simply move on to the next man who happened to be a few pounds overweight.

Kevin still offered so much. Why did he have to go and change?

"And you said this guy's name was Kevin?"

"Yeah."

"Tell me again what he looks like." Caden picked up on an interest flickering in his friend's eyes.

Caden described Kevin right down to how even his sandy beard was now trimmed closer to his face. Then he stopped, eyeing his friend. "Wait a minute. You're not gonna tell me you know him? You are *so* not gonna tell me you've had him?"

It had happened before. Bobby got around. But the old Kevin would not have piqued Bobby's interest. The old Kevin was too heavy, which was another point in his favor.

So that would mean...

No.

Caden was relieved to see Bobby shaking his head. "No worries, little brother. I don't know the guy." Bobby sipped his water and looked away.

"Are you sure?" Caden hadn't missed the fact that Bobby had seemed a bit too interested in the particulars about how Kevin looked, even asking where he lived and what his last name was.

Bobby held up his hands in defense. "Don't go getting all paranoid on me! I've got more guys than I can handle. I don't need yours too."

"Okay. So what do you think I should do?"

Bobby still seemed preoccupied. Maybe he had spied a likely prospect in the crowd. Sometimes Caden wondered how many STIs Bobby acquired, you know, in a typical week.

"About what?"

"About the guy!"

"How should I know? I honestly don't know what the problem is. Here you have this gorgeous, built guy, who's not only sexy, but kind and warm, too, and you seem like you're not interested in him. But Fat Albert over there, hugging the wall, is just your cup of tea." Bobby shrugged. "I guess my advice would be, if you're no longer attracted to Mr. Kevin, you should move on. Because, honey, once the sexual spark is gone, there ain't nothin' left." Bobby polished off his water, crushed the plastic bottle, and set it on the bench next to him. "If you like fat, go after fat. I don't get it, but maybe the man of your dreams is twitchin' down at a Weight Watchers meeting." Bobby grinned and poked Caden. "That's it! You should start hanging out at gay Weight Watchers. I bet there's a group in Chicago!" Bobby pulled out his phone and started looking for the information.

"Stop it." All Bobby was doing, with his utter disregard for Caden's feelings and his refusal to take his problem seriously, was making him want to see Kevin even more. He knew Kevin well enough to know he was the kind of man who would be a sympathetic listener.

Suddenly, Caden was very tired. Maybe, he thought, his fatigue was bringing on all this indecision and uncertainty. Perhaps, if he went home now and got a good night's sleep, he would feel differently about Kevin in the morning. He told Bobby as much and added, "Maybe I could call him and see if he's up for meeting for lunch."

Bobby shook his head. "No. Don't call him yet. Give yourself some more time to think." For once, Bobby's handsome face went serious and sincere. "You need time to sort out your feelings. Don't rush yourself. If things were as good as you say with this guy, he'll still be there if you call in a few days, or even a week. But you need to decide if he's what you really want. Sometimes, it's good to simply listen to your heart."

"Look who's dispensing advice about listening with one's heart: the guy who thinks with the little head down south."

"And proud of it." Bobby grinned and looked over at Caden. "So you gonna go get some rest? A little sleep?"

"Are you trying to get rid of me?" Caden scanned the crowd. "Want me out of the way so you can hook up?"

"Brother, you know me too well." Bobby winked and smiled at his friend. "Beat it."

The evening had run its course, Caden conceded. As Miss Scarlet once opined, tomorrow *was* another day. Caden slipped his jacket on, kissed Bobby, and said he'd call him later in the week.

"Sure thing," Bobby said, but it seemed as though he wasn't even listening.

Caden headed out of the bar, thinking how his friend had a one-track mind.

Chapter Sixteen

Bobby *did* want to hook up, but there was no one in Big Chicks he was even remotely interested in. No, the man he was interested in was, at this very moment, Bobby hoped, home alone and a few miles north of Big Chicks.

The fact that Kevin had once sort of belonged to Caden only made him more attractive to Bobby, more of a prize.

What was it Pat Benatar had once sung? Love is a battlefield? Well, to the victor go the spoils... And no, he did not think he was betraying his friend. His friend, for Pete's sake, wasn't even sure he was interested in hot, sexy Kevin.

Bobby was interested, and if Caden didn't want him, suddenly Bobby did—all the more. He tossed his water bottle in a recycling bin and stepped outside the bar to make the call.

The night had turned nippy, and Bobby shot his collar up to protect himself from the wind. He turned away from the smokers gathered outside the front entrance, hoping their exhalations were not tainting his scent. After all, Terre d'Hermes did not come cheap.

He listened to the distant ringing and pictured Kevin alone, wearing a pair of boxers and a tank, his feet up on his coffee table, drinking a beer. He imagined the tank top exposing a nipple and his cock lazily peeking out the bottom of the loose boxer shorts. Bobby remembered first seeing Kevin in the locker room and remembered just how fine the man was—toned, in shape, and best of all, totally unaware of how good-looking he was. A man who was hot and didn't know it just made him all the hotter.

"Come on, pick up." Bobby shivered and hitched his shoulders up against the cold wind blowing in out of the north. Perhaps Mr. Kevin could keep him warm tonight, keep his fires stoked, so to speak.

*

Kevin lay in his room, wishing sleep would come. As always, sleep was elusive when he most wanted it, as if slumber, personified, was some capricious mistress who took pleasure in always being just out of reach.

He turned over on his left side and folded his down pillow in half, thinking maybe that was the magic combination that would bring sleep, but all he did was stare at the darkness pressing into the glass of his bedroom window and listen to the rumble of an L train going by outside.

It was no wonder he couldn't sleep. Things were still so unresolved with Caden. Part of him just wanted to call the guy and give him an ultimatum. "No," he would say, "you cannot have a few days to sort things out, or whatever you want to call it. You either want me or you don't. Which one is it going to be? Want me—as I am now? Or not? Pick one, and let's move on."

Kevin smiled in the darkness, wishing he had the capacity, and perhaps the lack of heart, that would allow him to be so direct. But the truth was, he couldn't stand taking the risk that Caden would simply walk away. He didn't think he could bear that. It tore him up inside to think Caden no longer found him attractive when, suddenly, so many other men did.

Paging irony, party of one.

He would give him some time, but Kevin would not stand by forever. He thought too much of himself to allow himself to wait around for a call that might never come. It would hurt a lot, and the disappointment of letting go of what might have been would claw at his heart, but he was strong enough to know he would be okay, that there were other men out there who would find him worthy, who would want him.

Still, he wished Caden would call…

As if in response to the turmoil in his head, his phone rang on the nightstand next to him. Kevin really didn't think Caden would be calling him so soon, but was still disappointed when he glanced at the display and did not see his name there.

What he saw instead was the name Bobby.

Kevin blew out a sigh and slumped back on his pillow, holding the phone above him and staring up at it as it rang. It was getting close to ten, and he needed to be up early to go into work to check in the folks who were bringing in their pets before work for surgery.

Did he really want to answer?

What the hell? He pressed Accept.

"Hey, Bobby. What's up?"

Bobby snickered. "Wouldn't you like to know?"

Kevin rolled his eyes, wishing he had just let the phone go to voice mail. Now he was stuck.

There was a moment of silence while Bobby obviously awaited a comeback for what he must have thought was a witty line. He could wait a long time.

Finally, Bobby must have given up. "So what are you up to, handsome?"

Kevin smiled. Being called handsome by a man who looked like a god was flattering, no matter how inane that god might be. "Actually, I was in bed. I've got an early start tomorrow, and then a class after work. So, not only is it going to be an early day, it'll be a long one."

"I like long ones," Bobby said wistfully.

Kevin shook his head. He was tired, maybe not sleepy, but tired, and definitely not in the mood for juvenile innuendos. "Anyway, I was just lying here, about to drift off, when the phone rang."

"So you weren't asleep?"

"Nah. Got a lot on my mind."

"Man trouble?" Bobby asked.

Kevin chuckled. "You're pretty perceptive. How did you know?"

Bobby said, "It's always man trouble. Want to talk about it?"

"I so do *not* want to talk about it. Right now, I just want to quit brooding and go to sleep. But it seems the harder I try, the more out of reach that possibility seems."

"If I was this guy you're brooding about, well, I'll tell you one thing—you would not be alone in that bed, and you would be having no trouble sleeping. You'd be too worn out."

"Big talk."

"You think I'm kidding?" Bobby's voice grew low and seductive. "Why don't you let me prove it to you? Around the corner from where I am is a nice little liquor store with a pretty good selection of wines. I could pick up a nice bottle of, say, a California Syrah, and be over to your place in, oh, ten or fifteen minutes."

For a moment, it did cross Kevin's mind that some company, especially hot company with a bottle of decent wine in tow, would be a nice alternative to lying there tossing and turning, chasing sleep. But no, at this late hour on a Sunday night, with the hints Bobby was throwing around, Kevin could not blame the guy for assuming this was a booty call if Kevin allowed him to come over.

Still, a vicious little part of him Kevin was loath to acknowledge that it would be just what Caden deserved— to have Bobby over, to have a hot time with him. He could rub Caden's nose in it, show him what he was missing.

But Kevin wasn't like that.

He comforted himself with the fact that a thought crossing one's mind was not the same as an action. And he also knew, deep in his heart, there was only one man he wanted in his bed tonight—and he was *not* on the other end of the line.

"Oh, Bobby, Bobby, Bobby—you do tempt me. But I'm settled in for the night and, as I said, have an early day tomorrow."

"I thought you just said you couldn't sleep."

"Yeah. I'm counting sheep, but they're keeping me awake by singing and dancing instead of jumping over that damn fence post."

"So? Let me bring you some wine. We'll just talk. No pressure."

Kevin chuckled. "You almost sound sincere."

"I am. I am!"

"Said the spider to the fly." Kevin shifted in bed, drawing the comforter up to his chin and actually relaxing a bit. "I've been around long enough to know how calls like this one usually end up—and I'm kind of involved right now."

Bobby didn't say anything for a minute. Then he asked, "If you're so involved, where's he at tonight?"

Kevin didn't really think he owed the guy an answer. After all, it was none of his business. But suddenly, a sympathetic ear—even if it was an ear he knew had a shitload of vested interest—sounded good right about now. He knew he'd see Prunella at work tomorrow and he could share his woes with her, but as much as she might talk like one, act like one, even sometimes smell like one, she was not a gay man. Plus, she had been happily married for so long, Kevin figured she would have little real notion of what it was like to be dating someone new, to be infatuated, to think things were going so well—until they weren't.

"That's a good question, Bobby."

"Why don't you let me come over, and we'll talk about it?"

"You are relentless!" Kevin laughed. "That is not going to happen. I am not admitting gentlemen callers this evening. Period."

"Not even handsome ones? Ones that have eyes only for you?"

"Now I'm starting to gag." Kevin sat up more in bed, fluffing the pillows against the headboard and thinking, *Let's just see if this guy is capable of being not just a lover, but a friend.* "So, do you have a few minutes to talk? Just talk? As in, on the phone?"

"Sure."

Kevin felt as though someone had lifted a weight off his chest as he told Bobby all about Caden. He led him through their initial meeting, their few, yet wonderful times together, their heartfelt phone calls and messages while they were apart, and right up until Caden had confessed, tonight, that he didn't know if he felt the same about Kevin. Kevin had to admit Bobby was a good listener, never butting in, but letting him pour his heart out with only sympathetic assurances to go on.

Finally, Kevin asked, "So what do you think?"

"You want the truth?" Bobby chuckled and quoted a line Jack Nicholson had once uttered, in *A Few Good Men*: "You can't handle the truth."

"I think I can. What? What do you think?"

He listened as Bobby drew in a breath. "Okay. Being totally honest here. This Caden guy sounds like a jerk, a superficial jerk who seems to think that what counts is what's on the outside of a person."

"But—" Kevin's first instinct was to rush to Caden's defense.

"Now, hear me out. You said you wanted the truth, wanted to hear what I thought. Let me finish here, okay?"

"Yeah, you're right."

"So this Caden—a person might think he didn't care about what's on the outside because he was attracted to you when you were a lot heavier and out of shape. That seems like a fellow who really does take the measure of a man by what's on the inside. But then he goes away, you lose weight—to please him, I might add—and he comes back and says he isn't sure how he feels anymore.

"To me, that just says the guy is superficial, all about appearances. Yeah, he liked you heavier, but that just means he's a chubby chaser. You know what that is?"

Kevin felt heat rise to his face. He knew all too well the term and how it applied to those in the gay community. "Yes, I know," he said softly.

"Caden is a chubby chaser, and when you no longer fit his ideal...well, he's no longer sure he wants you anymore." Bobby paused for a second. "Now you tell me how that makes him any different than the guy who will only go out with great-looking men, or men who drive expensive cars, or Hispanic men, or black men, or Asian men. It's all about the surface—and never looking past it."

Maybe this Bobby character wasn't as shallow as he first came across, Kevin thought. He lay back in bed, thinking how what he was saying made a lot of sense. It wasn't happy sense; there was no joy or relief in the words he spoke.

But there was truth.

And that truth, right now, was making Kevin feel sick to his stomach. He didn't want what Bobby was saying to be true, no matter how rational and credible it sounded.

"You're not saying anything. Did I go too far?"

"I don't know. I just don't know." Kevin sighed. "Would you be offended if I just said goodbye right now?"

"Are you okay?" Bobby asked, concern radiating in his voice.

"Yeah, sure, I'm fine. You've just given me a lot to think about."

"I hope I wasn't too frank. I was only trying to help. I realize we don't know each other that well, but I like you. I care. I don't want to see you hurting, especially at the hands of some insensitive guy, who, in my opinion, doesn't deserve you if he can't see the prize that's right in front of his face."

"Well, I don't know about that. Caden just said he needed some time. Maybe it'll all turn out okay." Why did these words feel empty, like lies, coming out of Kevin's mouth?

"I hope so. I really do." Bobby paused again, and it was almost as though Kevin could hear him thinking through the phone. "Listen. Do you want to get together sometime this week and talk some more? It sounds like you have a lot on your mind, and maybe I can help. No pressure and—believe me—no strings. We can even meet up at a coffee shop, somewhere public."

"That would be nice. Thank you, Bobby." Kevin got out of bed. He'd use the bathroom and make himself a cup of Sleepy Time tea. Then he'd try again. If nothing more, he would rest.

"I'll call you tomorrow, and we can set something up."

"Sounds good."

"And Kevin? We're just friends, okay?"

"Okay. Thank you."

"But you can't blame me for hoping that might change one day."

Kevin chuckled. "Good night, Bobby. Talk soon."

"You bet."

*

Bobby paused for a moment after hanging up. Christ, it was freezing out here. He hurried to get back inside Big Chicks. He may have struck out with Kevin for tonight, but he still needed dick. And he was certain there was at least one lucky guy inside who would be ready, willing, and able to board the Bobby Express. He grinned. Maybe even two—couples could sometimes be fun.

He pulled open the door and put on his best and most alluring smile.

He would *not* go home alone tonight. Let Caden and Kevin stew in their isolated, lonely beds.

Chapter Seventeen

The Bored Room was not Starbucks. Located on Sheridan Road in Rogers Park, it was an old school café, with mismatched chairs, scuffed tables, an old checkered tile floor, a glass case with a few pastries in it, and a gorgeous, busty Greek female cashier/server behind the counter. When Kevin had ordered, she had told him her name was Venus. "You just call Veenie if you need anything else," she had told him with a wink. The term for Venus was most decidedly *not* barista. The place predated the trendy coffee venues by years.

Kevin liked the Bored Room for precisely those reasons. It was not pretentious, and now, as he waited for Bobby to show up on this Monday evening, he wondered if he was doing the right thing. All day long, he obsessively checked his phone for a voice mail, text, or even an email from Caden. Each time, he would put the phone down in disappointment. Hell, he'd had more contact with the guy when he was in Pennsylvania.

In spite of everything, he missed Caden. It felt as though life had ground to a halt while he waited for some sign from him that would indicate which way their relationship would go. In his lowest moments, Kevin even thought he would be relieved if Caden simply called the whole thing off. At least then he could move on, be released from the prison of this limbo of hanging on and waiting for the man he loved to come to his senses and decide he loved Kevin.

Or not.

Kevin had a cup of black coffee in front of him and stared down into the steaming black liquid, thinking again of the lovely cherry Danish he had spied in the glass case at the front of the café. There was a part of him that told him to go ahead and have it, relish its tart sweetness, its sugary glaze of white drizzle on top, and its flaky dough. Why not? It would only help him pack pounds onto his newly thin frame, a frame that seemed to give poor Caden no thrill at all.

Poor Caden, my ass.

Kevin thought enough of himself to not eat the pastry, to stick with his black coffee with one Splenda.

He looked up at the traffic, almost always heavy except in the wee hours of the morning, coursing north and south on Sheridan Road, a river of headlights. Everyone in the world seemed to have somewhere to go tonight.

In spite of himself, he took out his phone and checked it one more time for a message or evidence of a call from Caden.

But there was nothing. He set the phone down on the table and resumed staring out the big windows at the night. A group of what he presumed were Loyola students hurried by, all talking at once and laughing. *I must be getting old, because right now I envy them their youth and the carefree way they seem to be going about their Monday night.*

As he was looking outside, he saw the most gorgeous man hurry by. The guy was so hot, it nearly took Kevin's breath away.

"Look at that one," Venus remarked from behind the cash register. "I wouldn't kick that one out of bed for eating crackers. Or anything else!" She laughed. "And I don't even like men."

The guy outside had broad shoulders encased in a black leather biker jacket, faded jeans, and a pair of combat boots. He was a delicious morsel of maleness.

It took him a second to actually absorb the fact that this was Bobby—and he was on his way to see him.

Kevin sat up straighter, painting a smile on his face as Bobby entered the café and looked around, presumably searching for Kevin. He noticed how the other patrons stopped talking and stared—male and female alike—at Bobby when he came in. Kevin couldn't blame them. It was as though a Mr. Brad Pitt or a Mr. George Clooney had decided to drop by for a latte on his way to some premiere. The way Bobby carried himself, his smile, the confidence he exuded all possessed a kind of star wattage.

Kevin shook his head. *This guy is interested in me? In what world can this happen?*

Their eyes met, and Bobby smiled, pointing to the counter to indicate he was going to grab a coffee before joining him.

"So, how's Kevin tonight?" Bobby said, sitting down with his coffee.

"Tired."

"I'll bet. Did you get any sleep last night?"

"Not much. And it was a long day. How was yours?"

Bobby told him about his day at the office and his workout at LA Fitness. Kevin thought he must put in countless hours to maintain a body like that. They chatted about nothing much for the first fifteen minutes or so, and then Bobby said, "So, I hope I didn't come on too strong last night. I just wanted to give you my honest impression."

"No, no. I'm glad you felt comfortable enough with me to tell me the truth. I've thought a lot about it, and I'm kind of thinking right now, if things don't go my way with Caden, I dodged a bullet."

"Yeah?"

"Well, as much as I think I was falling for the guy, if he can't see what a catch I am—" Kevin grinned to show he was kidding, sort of, and not being vain. "Then maybe I haven't really lost anything if he moves on, simply because I look a little different."

Bobby leaned back in his chair, tipping it back on two legs and spreading his denim-clad legs wide apart. "That sounds very healthy, Kevin."

Kevin, albeit still in the throes of infatuation for Caden, had trouble drawing his gaze away from the widespread thighs, their thickness and the tempting bulge, fetchingly faded, nestled where they came together. It was enough to stop a person's heart. He made a point of dragging his gaze back up to Bobby's gray eyes, which were equally fetching, yet in a different way. "That doesn't mean, though, I won't be sad."

"And I will be here to comfort you." Bobby smiled, his even white teeth lighting up his face. Bobby touched his hand for a moment, long enough to transfer a jolt of heat from his flesh into Kevin's.

Kevin thought Bobby's comfort might not be such a bad consolation prize if he lost Caden. But he *so* did not want to lose Caden. Before Caden had gone back to Pennsylvania, it really seemed like something special was starting to bloom between the two of them, something rare enough that it wasn't easy to simply shrug and walk away from it.

"Thanks. I think I have an idea of what that comfort might involve," Kevin said, grinning, teasing.

Bobby held up his hands in a gesture of blamelessness. "What can I say? Guilty as charged, buddy! I'm a passionate guy—I'm not going to lie. I would so like to comfort you. And if we happened to be naked during that comforting...well, all the better." He winked.

Kevin stared down into his coffee, feeling heat rush to his cheeks, embarrassed, intrigued, and repelled all at once. He sighed. "Let's not go there."

"Too soon?"

"Way too soon. Premature, actually."

Bobby grinned, nodding. "I can wait."

*

Caden got off the bus, having no idea what he would say to Kevin. He didn't know why he had opted for the bus tonight. Usually he was pretty faithful to the L, but the Sheridan Road bus would take him straight from his neighborhood to Kevin's, and when he got off, the few blocks' walk west would give him time to think. Maybe in the chill and darkness of night he would find the right words, would understand something key about himself that would allow him to cross this bridge he found himself standing at the other side of.

He strode north on Sheridan Road, the thoroughfare bustling as usual with traffic and pedestrians. On one corner, a *Streetwise* vendor hawked his newspapers to passersby, and Caden stopped to give the guy a dollar. He waved the paper away and told him that he hoped the money would help the guy find a place to sleep tonight. He started to walk away, then turned around and gave the man another dollar.

He passed the lighted windows of a little coffee shop called the Bored Room, thinking how warm and inviting it looked inside. The night air's chill crept into Caden's bones, and he thought of how close this place was to Kevin's apartment, how maybe the two of them might have ventured over here one night to share coffee and conversation.

He almost didn't see them.

His reaction was very much like the kind of double take one would see on a sitcom or in the movies, where the person spies something so outrageous it doesn't register for a second. Then the witness would stop in his or her tracks, eyes wide and mouth open, and back up. That's exactly what Caden did, reversing in his tracks to look again. He told himself he could not possibly have seen Kevin with his best friend, their heads bent close together, as if conspiring.

But it *was* them, and the sight of the pair was almost surreal, as if he had stepped into another world. He didn't even know the two of them knew each other, so the shock of seeing them together on some sort of coffee date made Caden question his grip on reality. He stepped back from the windows a bit, secreting himself in the shadows and watching as Kevin talked to Bobby, as the two of them laughed together, looking like two friends or—worse—two gay guys out on a casual date.

Caden wasn't sure what he should do. He moved back farther, hiding in a bus stop shelter. Obviously, his plan to drop in on Kevin was now out, since Kevin was clearly not home, and occupied with another man.

Another man who happened to be his best friend.

What was going on, anyway? How had these two met? What were they talking about? He watched, and his stomach turned as he saw Bobby place a hand over Kevin's, staring into his eyes with a soulful expression Caden had seen dozens of times in bars and gay meeting places all across the city. He recognized it as Bobby on the make.

Wow. Kevin certainly didn't wait long to find a replacement for me. How ironic, in a city of millions, and hundreds of thousands of gay men, Kevin had managed to latch onto Caden's own best friend.

It was weird. Were they aware of the connection? Were they talking about him? How—he wondered again—had they met in the first place?

Caden recalled telling Bobby all about Kevin, describing him, giving his name and even mentioning where he lived. While it was possible Kevin might not realize Bobby's connection to Caden, it was almost impossible for him to believe Bobby wasn't aware of who Kevin was and what he meant to Caden. Caden had talked to Bobby at length about it only last night at Big Chicks.

And the whole time they had talked, Bobby had never given any indication he knew Kevin personally.

His best friend was a horndog, that was for sure, and Bobby often jokingly said he'd had more dicks than a convention of Richards, but he wouldn't go after the one man Caden had said he thought he was falling in love with, the man he was so conflicted over.

Would he?

Caden crossed the street, feeling painfully aware of his own body, sure Kevin would look up and see him outside. He hurriedly walked south on Sheridan, searching for the next bus stop to take him home, a bus stop that would not be in view from the windows of the Bored Room.

He waited at the little shelter, stomach churning and hands shaking. Maybe, he told himself, they had met only recently and by coincidence. That had to be it, and Bobby just hadn't had time to mention it to him.

He pulled out his phone and sat on the bench at the bus stop. He texted Bobby: "*What are you doing tonight? Thought we might meet up at Roscoe's for a drink.*" He pressed Send, knowing he was being duplicitous, but also thinking he was only giving his friend a chance to come clean. Surely, if there was nothing going on between Kevin and Bobby, Bobby would be honest when he texted him back.

He listened for the sound of a returned text. He gripped the phone too tightly in his sweaty palm and was about to give up as he saw the bus headed down the road. Maybe Bobby hadn't gotten his text yet. Caden stood to board the bus. He got on and headed to the back for a seat, staring down at the phone's screen the whole time.

Finally, a response from Bobby came through, just as Caden sat.

"*Sorry, bud. Hot date tonight. Not sure when I'll be home. But would love to see you soon. Call or text me in the morning and we'll make a plan.*"

Caden felt like he was going to throw up.

He pressed his forehead against the glass, reveling in the coolness of it against his burning face. His stomach continued to churn.

What was going on?

Should he text back? Should he say something along the lines of knowing exactly who this hot date was with and how could Bobby betray him like this? He always remembered Bobby's refrain whenever he abandoned him at a bar for yet another pickup—sorry, man, it's the law of the jungle.

Caden couldn't bring himself to do anything at the moment. He was too numb. He was also afraid he might get yet another lie from the stranger he thought was his friend.

Caden stared down at his knees as the bus lurched forward, thinking somehow this all had to be a big misunderstanding. The whole last twenty minutes of his life suddenly seemed completely unreal and dreamlike.

*

"I should get going, Bobby. I'm beat."

"You sure you don't want me to come home with you? I give an awesome backrub. It'll relax you." Bobby smiled a smile that, under other circumstances and at a different stage of his life, might have made Kevin melt. "No strings attached. Really."

Kevin shook his head. "You know I wouldn't trust you as far as I can throw a grand piano."

Bobby laughed. "You're a wise man, Kevin. A wise man. You really want to just go home by yourself?"

"Yeah. Caden might call. Or maybe I'll just say to hell with it and call him. Whether he needs time or not, *I* need to talk."

"Okay. If you need someone *else* to talk to later on, just give me a buzz."

Kevin stood. "You gonna go now?"

"I think I'll finish up my coffee."

"Well, maybe we'll talk tomorrow."

"I'm here for you, bud."

"Thanks, Bobby. I appreciate that."

Kevin took his leave and wandered out into the night. The walk home was only a few blocks, and the cold, brisk air would do him good. All the coffee he had consumed had left his nerves feeling electrified. He almost felt shaky, overstimulated.

He would call Caden when he got home.

*

Bobby didn't say anything as he watched Kevin leave. He knew he should call out to him, tell him he had left his phone on the table. It would be what a friend would do. But for some reason, having the phone gave him a sense of power, so he stayed quiet, watching as Kevin walked away.

He sipped his coffee, waiting and fully expecting Kevin to return for his phone, ruefully shaking his head at his forgetfulness.

But after twenty minutes, he realized Kevin wasn't coming back. He pocketed the phone and left the café.

*

Kevin didn't notice his phone missing until much later that night. In spite of his good intentions to call Caden, he wasn't ready to face making the call once he got back inside his apartment. Still feeling jittery, he slipped into sweats and a fleece and took a long run, all the way up to the Northwestern campus and back.

After his shower, he sat down to call Caden, hoping it wasn't too late. He missed the guy so much; he simply needed to hear his voice.

But his phone wasn't in the pocket of his jacket where he thought he had left it. He looked on the dining room table, where he often dropped it when he got home. Not there. He checked his nightstand, his coffee table, the back of the toilet, and the kitchen counter, to no avail.

Then he stopped—and remembered taking the phone out just before Bobby had arrived at the café. He had admonished himself at the time for obsessively checking for messages from Caden and had set the phone down on the table. That was when he had spied Bobby coming up the walk outside.

Kevin didn't have a landline or he would have called the Bored Room to see if anyone had turned in a lost phone. Surely Bobby would have seen it and grabbed it for safekeeping, right?

But what if he didn't? Hell, half his life was in that phone—all his contacts, his calendar, old texts, even his email. He had always intended to get around to password protecting the phone, as the wise Prunella had told him he should do when he first got it, but had never done so.

He got dressed again. He had no choice but to walk back to the Bored Room and hope that his phone was still there. If it wasn't, he was sure they'd let him use their phone to call Bobby.

Except you don't know his number. Who uses phone numbers anymore? You just press a name on a screen these days. Kevin sat down on the couch and put his head in his hands, feeling cut off and stupid.

Chapter Eighteen

Bobby sat at his computer, searching Craigslist for a hookup. Sometimes it was easier to find a partner through this online channel, where one could get just about anything one wanted if he or she looked hard enough, than to troll the online connection sites like Manhunt or Adam4Adam. Those sometimes took too long and had too many players who weren't really serious about hooking up. Craigslist had its problems, too, but if you found the right guy, you could email him your phone number and the game was on within minutes.

He glanced through the postings.

Navy Guy on Leave Looking for a Bottom—24—(Loop) pic
25 horny latino—25—(Lincoln Park)
cocksucker—38—(burbs)
Massage—30—(Lakeview) pic
Milking Monday nite crossdresser—m4m—(Skokie)
I Can Host A Top—50—(Oak Park)
Providing Oral Service Monday—m4m—53—(Blue Island)
older seeking older—m4m—60—(Gurnee)
Muscled Pecs—45—
slow fuck my mouth till you shoot—(westburbs/travel)
regular thing—24—(Des Plaines) pic

Looking for mutual play—34—(Evanston)
fetish, glove, latex—65—(Chicago) pic
into older—23—(Chicago)
Fuck your tight married ass—(Chicago)
Hosting a smooth bottom today—25—(Streeterville) pic
looking for a massage today—25—(lakeview) pic
Blow and Go!—47—(Andersonville) pic
Looking for FWB/Work Out Buddy—m4m—22—(South Loop) pic
Masculine/Muscular for same—m4m—44—(Tinley Mokena) pic
Suckfest for black bear—(Humboldt Park) pic
Hard Top looking!—36—(Uptown) pic
jo or Head now bi vgl!—25—(Belmont/Broadway)
Big Old Load For Your Butt—30—(Andersonville) pic
Married Men/Bi Men—m4m—41—(Rogers Park, Evanston, Lincolnwood)
cocksucker ready for dick—m4m—(northwest)
Masc wm looking for host nsa safe—27—(west chicago area. Oak brook trvl)
Excellent Monday j/o/head for you!—43—(Belmont/Sheridan)
Are you younger (30s) and prefer older (60s)?—62—(Chicago north)
Anon suck and go—m4m—35—(Lakeview)
I need a blowjob and men do it the best—48—(downtown) pic
Any WS/Piss Pig bottoms want to meet up?—53—(LSD) pic

There were plenty of prospects here, especially the Navy guy, the Latino, and Muscled Pecs. He already had default messages set up in his Gmail and a file of pictures at the ready that he could attach when he replied, so his system was maximized for efficiency. This was almost as easy as ordering a pizza. That is, if he ever ate pizza anymore. Now he shuddered at the thought of what all those carbs and fats would do to his six-pack.

He knew he should be pining for Kevin, wondering what his next move should be to win him over, but he needed sex now, and he hadn't yet cultivated Kevin to that point. Gone were the days when Bobby would moon, all dreamy-eyed, over some handsome hunk, thinking of shopping together at Whole Foods, walking their French bulldog puppy together, and joining other couples out for dinner and a play at the Goodman.

No, Bobby needed instant gratification, and now that the Internet was in full bloom, there was no reason to deny himself.

Oh sure, he wanted Kevin—and he knew he would have him—but he couldn't have him tonight, and Bobby needed cock *now*. He was not of the mindset that said anything good is worth waiting for.

Kevin *would* have to be worked on slowly. But once Bobby could convince him how wrong Caden was for him, it would be a quick slide into home base.

Bobby took the time to send out messages to the three he had winnowed out of the constantly growing list of hungry hounds on Craigslist and sat back, waiting for his email box to fill up with offers. It always did. Bobby shrugged, smiling. Who could blame them? He had great raw material to work with, right? And his photos, raw, nude, yet tasteful were alluring enough to knock any online competition right out of the field. Thank God he had met up with that photographer over in Wicker Park a couple of years ago. The guy had been so love struck, he took a whole series of hot photos of Bobby, thinking he was the one getting something out of the deal, when in truth it was the other way around.

Once Bobby had his digital photos safely saved to his computer's hard drive, he dumped the photographer.

As he was waiting, he heard the *swoosh* sound of a text being delivered. At first, he picked up his own phone, wondering if one of the guys on Craigslist to whom he had sent a message was an old fuck buddy and was now hitting him up directly. It was certainly within the realm of possibility. Bobby was no stranger to the embraces of most of the gay, and some supposedly straight, men in the Chicagoland area, as long as they were buff and cute.

But his phone's screen remained black.

It then dawned on him. He picked up Kevin's phone.

There was a text from Caden. Bobby grinned and read the short message: "*Are you there?*"

Bobby put the phone back down. He had a message from the Latino guy, who had sent a picture of his dick, which was thick as a beer can and measured—according to him—nine full inches. If the pic was real, Bobby doubted the guy was exaggerating. He had also sent a torso shot, revealing smooth, muscled café au lait skin, unmarred by the presence of even one hair. It was miles and miles of defined muscles. Bobby imagined laving every inch of it with his determined tongue.

"Yum!" Bobby said. He glanced over at the phone and thought he'd fuck with his pal Caden a little, before he got down to the serious business of having Mr. Latino over for some real fucking.

So he picked up the phone and replied to the text: "*Yup.*"

He then wrote a quick message to the Latino, sending him a pic of himself hard and another one of him with come all over his perfect stomach and chest. And just so the guy could see what he was in for, one of him on all fours on the bed, ass cheeks spread wide apart, revealing a perfectly bleached and shaved-clean asshole. Bobby fingered his hardening cock, just imagining the effect this would have on his soon-to-be Latin lover when he received the photos.

Caden interrupted when he texted back: *"I saw you tonight."*

What the hell could that mean? Bobby laughed—had Caden somehow seen him with Kevin? Could the universe have conspired to put Caden outside that café; what was it called? The Bored Room?

Oh, that would be too perfect! Getting Kevin away from Caden was going to be easier than he thought, especially if he could throw a little drama, hurt, and jealousy into the equation. But first, he had to be sure.

"What do you mean?"

Caden came back quickly. *"Don't. You know where I saw you and who you were with. Why didn't you tell me?"*

Bobby would have to play this cool. *"I don't know what you're talking about."*

"So is that how we're going to play this? I thought you had integrity."

Bobby laughed. Caden was upset. He didn't think the guy had the capacity for anger in him. He was usually laid back and easygoing to a fault. This was fun.

Bobby typed, *"??"*

"The Bored Room."

Bobby replied, "*That wasn't a date. We're just friends, honest.*"

"*You know Bobby is my best friend, don't you? Or at least I thought he was.*"

Bobby scratched at his face and checked his computer; Latino had responded along with Muscled Pecs, who inquired if Bobby was partying.

"*No. Your name never came up,*" Bobby responded, gleeful. Hadn't Oscar Wilde once said there was only one thing worse than being talked about, and that was *not* being talked about? The fact that Kevin hadn't even mentioned him—even though he had, endlessly—would really tear Caden up, Bobby thought.

"*I'm gonna call you. We need to talk.*"

And immediately, the cell phone began to ring. Bobby let it go to voice mail, knowing this action would frustrate and enrage his BFF even further. While he was waiting, he told the Latino to send more pics, but that he looked like he was going to get the green light for later tonight.

He responded to Muscled Pecs that he did not party and that if he wanted to keep his muscled pecs, he shouldn't either.

Caden texted: "*Are you going to pick up? Or isn't it convenient for you to talk right now? Is he there?*"

Bobby said, "*If he was here, would I be texting you? I don't feel like talking right now.*"

There was no response from Caden for several minutes. Then Bobby heard his own phone ring and looked down to see Caden's smiling face come up. He almost felt bad for a second. He hit the button to reject the call and send it to voice mail.

The Latino sent another batch of pics. This set had one of him in a tight T-shirt that showed off his broad shoulders and chest to good advantage. Finally, Bobby got a glimpse of the guy's face and just about swooned. He looked just like Ricky Martin, if Ricky Martin sported a neck tattoo and a faux hawk.

Bobby responded with his address in the next email.

Latino confirmed that he would be over within the hour.

Bobby needed to get in the shower.

Chapter Nineteen

Caden jogged along the vast lakefront trails that skirted the shores of Lake Michigan. It was early morning, and although there was a hint of pink and lavender in the eastern sky, the day's color palette seemed to consist mostly of gray. The bleakness matched his mood. Gray low-hanging clouds promised snow. The water of the lake, gently rolling, was a sea of gray. The concrete terraces that led down to the water were gray. Even the sand on the beaches looked gray in this just-after-dawn light.

He was running to see if he could improve his mood and inject some energy into his body. Often, for Caden, running was like coffee was for some people: a stimulant. But this morning, all he felt was cold. The temperature had dipped even farther during the night, a cold front moving in from the north. Caden guessed the current temperature hovered somewhere around freezing. In spite of his T-shirt, fleece, running tights, gloves, and skullcap, the wind whipping off the lake worked its way into his bones, chilling him to his very core.

But he kept going. In spite of the cold and the fact that his legs felt leaden, heavier somehow, he pushed himself onward, breathing quickly through his mouth, pumping his arms, and trying not to think.

But trying not to think about a thing was simply an invitation to the universe to make you concentrate on the very thing you wanted to avoid.

Caden had spent the previous night engaging in futility. First, there was the futility of the phone and then the computer. He called Kevin more times than he could count. He texted him. He finally resorted to emails, pleading with the guy to just talk to him.

All he got as a reward for his efforts was a wall of chilly silence.

Kevin had never before not answered his phone.

This caused Caden to imagine all sorts of things that could be keeping him from responding to a ringing phone, texts, and voice mail messages—and most of them centered on Kevin's odd connection to Bobby. As nauseous as it made him, Caden couldn't put a halt to the pornographic movie images that played and replayed in his mind on an endless loop—Bobby and Kevin in bed together; Kevin pounding Bobby doggy style from behind, on Bobby's face a smile of triumph and pleasure as Kevin worked his hips, sweating, groaning, gasping for air— ecstasy. Or Kevin naked, with his legs spread and Bobby kneeling between them, gleefully gobbling down his cock, tonguing his balls, and then lifting his legs to eat Kevin's asshole, all the while working Kevin's cock with one of his spit-lubed hands. Caden pictured geysers of come shooting out of both Kevin and the man he thought was his best friend.

All of it made him want to vomit.

Even worse, somehow, was when his mind went to the two of them in Kevin's bed, worn out, clinging to one another, in the contentment of a perfect afterglow. In those minutes, he would imagine their peace and contentment interrupted for a moment by Kevin's ringing cell phone. Kevin would pick it up, show the display to Bobby, and then toss the phone back on the nightstand.

Both men would then cling to each other, collapsing in laughter.

Long after midnight, Caden gave up on calling Kevin like some obsessive stalker. He had also, throughout the night, called Bobby's number and was treated to the same lack of response, which only bolstered Caden's suspicions and nausea-inducing fantasies.

Then he had gone through his second exercise in futility—trying to sleep. He had work in the morning and knew he would be no good to anyone if he couldn't make himself sleep for at least a couple of hours.

But it seemed he never did. To the best of his recollection, all he did all night was toss and turn, fret, and stare at the ceiling, at the dark shapes of his bedroom furniture, and the darkness, like a palpable presence, pressing against the glass of his bedroom window. Finally, he watched the gray light of dawn, like an intruder, creep into his room, giving gradual shape and definition to everything as the light filtered in, brightening, but dully.

So with a heavy head, heart, and limbs, Caden had sat up in his bed and decided to run. Running, at least, had never let him down, never betrayed him.

He lost count of the miles as he ran, simply heading farther north. As he ran along the edge of Hollywood Beach, also known informally as the gay beach or formally as Kathy Osterman Beach, he realized his subconscious may have had a destination in mind, but he pushed the thought away and continued going on legs that had been trained for marathons, trying to force any conscious thought right out of his brain.

But when he got much farther north, to Fargo Beach, he stopped for a moment, bending over, his hands on his knees, panting, and knew where his subconscious had led him. He had a decision to make.

Kevin lived just a few blocks to the west. Caden turned away from the water to look westward on Fargo Avenue, imagining Kevin's building where the street intersected with Ashland Avenue, the L tracks passing overhead.

Don't go. Don't put yourself through more heartache. You don't need the pain. Just turn around, run home, go to work. Going to Kevin's now will accomplish nothing and maybe even make things worse.

Even as he was thinking those thoughts, Caden was starting into a fast walk, then a jog, then finally almost a sprint—west on Fargo Avenue.

In fewer than five minutes, he stood outside Kevin's building, staring up at his second floor balcony and his dark windows. Was Bobby in there with him, right now? Oh God, if he was, Caden had never felt more excluded standing outside, shivering in the cold.

Common sense told him to turn away, to stroll over to Jarvis and hop on a southbound L train, warm up. Maybe he'd be tired enough when he got home to sleep.

He could call in sick.

But no. He had come here for a reason. He could no longer stand this limbo. He looked around and saw a guy about his own age, with prematurely gray hair, dressed sensibly in a pea coat and 180s, coming up the street toward him. The guy smiled at him, and Caden was unable to return it.

He was just waiting for the guy to pass by, for the coast to be clear.

Clear for what?

Caden wasn't sure, but he forced himself to march up to the little stoop, locate Kevin's name on the intercom and, hesitating for only a second, jab his finger against the buzzer. Again. And again.

If Kevin was inside sleeping (or whatever), this would certainly interrupt.

When Caden heard the bark of Kevin's mechanical voice coming through the intercom box, he knew what he wanted to say.

Are you sure? Yes.

Caden brought his mouth close to the speaker, and in a loud and as-calm-as-he-could-make-it voice, he said, "It's Caden. I just wanted to say..." He paused for a second.

Are you sure you want to do this? Positive?

"I just wanted to say..." He paused again, then let the words escape in a rush. "I never want to see or hear from you again."

He moved away, feeling the hot sting of tears at the corners of his eyes. Saying the words did not feel like a release, as he had expected, but like a jolt of electricity passing through him. Relief? More like regret.

He paused for a moment in front of the building, chest heaving, trying to hold back the tears. He knew he had done the right thing. So why did he feel so lousy?

When he heard the creak of the door opening above him, he looked up.

There was Kevin, staring down at him from his balcony, eyebrows furrowed in pain and confusion. He wore only his tatty plaid flannel bathrobe and shivered. "Caden?" He called down. "Caden, what's going on?"

Boy, you play the part well. If I didn't know better, I'd almost believe that confused look on your face. Almost.

Caden turned and began to run back toward the lakefront. Kevin's voice came down to him as he ran.

"Caden? Caden! Come back. Please come back so we can talk. C'mon, man!" Kevin said some other things, but the words were lost on the wind and garbled by Caden's quivering, sob-choked breath.

Chapter Twenty

Kevin watched as Caden ran down his street—looking more like he was dashing away from Kevin than out for a morning jog. Kevin's voice was hoarse from calling out to him. It was doing no good, anyway. Many morning commuters, on their way to the L or the bus on Sheridan Road, had looked up at the crazy man in the bathrobe, but not one of them was Caden, who refused to so much as turn his head.

Finally, with the cold feeling like an animal with razor-sharp teeth digging into his exposed skin, and the bare soles of his feet going numb, Kevin stepped back into the warmth of his apartment. The warmth offered little comfort, though, not after the frigid message he had just gotten from Caden. His mussed bed, where he had spent an uncomfortable night, did not look tempting in the least.

The cold and the shock of the man he thought he was falling in love with telling him he never wanted to see him again had awakened Kevin fully to the day, whether he liked it or not. He padded slowly into the kitchen, feeling numb and in a kind of shock, to put the coffee on. He wasn't hungry and didn't really want the coffee either, but thought the caffeine might make him feel a tiny bit more human.

He sat at the small table he used as a desk, set up in the corner of his dining room, and logged into his Gmail account, where he found several messages from Caden, all sent the night before.

Kevin had been too distracted by the loss of his cell last night (a trip to the Bored Room had been an exercise in futility—no one had seen the phone) to think about logging into his email or going online.

All of the messages from Caden were brief, and each one revolved around a common theme—why wasn't Kevin answering his phone? Why didn't he text him back? Respond to his voice mail?

Because I lost my phone, Caden! Is that what this morning was about? Because I didn't call you back last night? Jesus, I didn't know you were such a drama queen! Kevin shook his head. Sadly, he realized that perhaps Caden was using his not calling as an excuse to dump him, to ameliorate the shame of quitting Kevin simply because he looked different. Perhaps Caden took comfort in the fact that he wasn't being shallow if he could become infuriated at what he perceived as being ignored.

Kevin hit reply on one of the later messages, tired and irritated by all the rejection and hurt when he had done nothing wrong. He wrote: "I don't know what you're so upset about. Sorry I didn't call you back. I lost my phone. That's it—I left it somewhere. Believe me, it was nothing personal, although you sure as hell seemed to take it that way." Kevin hit send without giving it a second thought.

Maybe, he thought, getting up to get himself a mug of coffee (and damn it, he would have it with two sugars and half-and-half this morning—he deserved it)...*maybe I just saw things wrong when we were starting out. Maybe I idealized Caden, made him into what I wanted him to be rather than what he was. There could have been red flags all along, and I just didn't see them through the passion and happiness of our first few times together and then through the closeness of helping him cope with the very real possibility of losing his mom.*

Kevin didn't want to believe these thoughts, but how else could he explain away the person Caden had become since he returned to Chicago? Kevin didn't find it easy to swallow that Caden was having trouble accepting his new look. But it was a big change, and he could at least cut him some slack and give him some time to get used to it. But to just walk up to his apartment and scream into his intercom that he never wanted to see him again?

That was crazy.

And for what? Because he didn't call him back?

Kevin downed the rest of his coffee and headed into the bathroom to shower. He actually looked forward to the day, which would be spent mostly with animals. They, at least, were much easier to deal with.

*

Bobby awakened with an itchy crotch. Sleepily, he scratched at himself, then flipped back the sheets to look down at his nude body.

"Ah, shit." There, nestled into his trimmed auburn pubic hair, were a couple of black dots that Bobby did not believe were lint from his underwear. No, he knew immediately, because he was so familiar with the condition, that Pedro from the night before had left him a parting gift.

Crabs.

Cursing, Bobby got out of bed and padded to the bathroom. In the medicine cabinet, there was still some RID leftover from when he had last hosted these annoying little guests. He put a dollop of the stuff in his hand and rubbed it into his crotch, remembering the night before and how this was *so* not worth it. Pedro had barely gotten himself inside Bobby before he was moaning and cursing in Spanish, shooting his load in about thirty seconds flat. Bobby had wanted to look up into his dark-brown eyes and ask if anything had happened, but bit his tongue and pretended it was amazing.

Now, he was surprised they had been connected long enough for the crabs to have transferred. At least he had caught the condition early, and one treatment should be enough to "rid" himself completely of the charmless little critters.

He walked naked into the kitchen, set the timer on his microwave for ten minutes, and then went to the window to stare out at the pewter-colored sky.

Waking up to this irritation made Bobby think of Kevin as even more of a prize. In spite of his penchant for getting sex—and lots of it—with the hottest men in town, Bobby almost felt he was incapable of finding someone he could love and who would love him back.

Maybe Kevin was that person. He eyed his cell, still lying on his desk from last night. He would erase the texts and then head over to Kevin's later, playing the hero, and say he had picked it up last night when he left it on the table, which was the truth.

Kevin need never know about his little exchange with Caden.

After waiting the ten minutes, Bobby stepped under a just-below-scalding shower and scrubbed himself hard, hoping his efforts would leave him parasite free. As he turned under the hot spray, he thought about Kevin, about seeing him later. He would be so grateful to Bobby for finding his phone! Bobby knew that, these days, a good part of our lives were contained in the little devices, so returning Kevin's would make Bobby a kind of savior.

To thank him, maybe Kevin would propose taking him to dinner. And maybe dinner would lead to bed.

Bobby grew hard as he recalled how Kevin looked naked. Even though that time in the locker room had not afforded him a chance to see Kevin hard, his own imagination was more than willing to fill in the blanks and create an enormous, precome-dripping cock sprouting up from between Kevin's hairy and muscular thighs.

The image was too much. Bobby took himself in hand and, using the soap as lube, worked his cock slowly and then with increasing abandon, imagining Kevin inside him, riding him, slapping him, pissing on him, until Bobby shot his seed down the drain. By the end of it, the tip of his cock was burning from a combination of RID, soap, and his own relentless friction.

"Next time"—he panted, stooping to turn the shower off—"next time, it'll be the real thing. You just wait and see. Nobody can resist Bobby's charms."

Bobby stepped from the shower and rubbed a hand across the mirror opposite so he could take in the view. As always, he was slightly taken aback at the magnitude of his own beauty. His cock hung heavy and thick between his thighs, still half-engorged. It looked porn-star huge. His stomach was slick and well-defined, appearing as though he was secreting a cache of cobblestones beneath the lean, taut skin. He shook his head and couldn't imagine why he was still alone.

As he finished toweling off, he heard his landline ring. He wrapped the towel around his waist and hurried into the living room to quiet it. The landline sounding meant only one of two things—a telemarketer was calling or the doorman downstairs was letting him know he had a guest. That doorman was a study in discretion, never saying a word about the volume of gentleman callers showing up on Bobby's doorstep. Good thing he tipped the guy well at the holidays!

"Yes?"

"Mr. Price? There's a young man down here to see you. It's your friend, Caden."

"Send him up, Pete."

Bobby grinned. This was an unexpected windfall, but Caden's appearance here could play right into his plan of ensuring he had Kevin to himself. He simply had to remind himself to play it cool, to be mindful and not say anything that would entrap him later.

Knowing just what kind of picture he wanted to paint for Caden also assumed a risk that Caden would talk to Kevin and expose Bobby's duplicity.

He would have to be sure he made it so Kevin and Caden never spoke to one another again.

Making sure of *that*, with some of the things he had planned to say, would not be difficult. He smiled as he threw on his white robe and finger-combed his hair.

He hurried to answer Caden's knock.

When he opened the door, he had never seen his friend looking worse. *Good Lord, you don't deserve a man like Kevin, looking like you do. No, you should just stick with your fatties, who will appreciate you.* Caden's eyes were red. He was sweaty. And he stunk.

Bobby stepped back to admit Caden, resisting the urge to hold his nose. But the dude was rank. Bobby wasn't sure how someone could have sweat so much when it was so cold outside.

"God, man, you look like hell."

Caden gave him a pissed-off smirk in lieu of a smile. "Thanks."

"Seriously. And you smell bad too. You wanna take a shower?"

"No." Caden moved to sit on Bobby's black leather sofa. Alarms went off in Bobby's head, issuing warnings to grab a towel to put under Caden's ass, but the guy sat too quickly for him to react.

Caden looked up at him with eyes that seemed tired, older somehow.

Bobby decided he had been too harsh. He took a deep breath and shaped his face into what he thought would be perceived as an expression of concern. He sat down in a chair across from Caden, modulating his voice so it came out low and soft. "Seriously, though, are you okay?" He leaned forward, turning his mouth down in a sympathetic frown.

Caden's eyes were bright for a moment, as though he was about to cry, and then he got a hold of himself. *Thank goodness! I don't need to be worrying about snot on that couch. Not when I paid four grand for it!* Bobby reached out and patted Caden's hand.

"What's the matter?"

Caden looked up at him, his eyes narrowing. "You know what's the matter. For God's sake, isn't there anyone in this world who's willing to just have a simple and *honest* conversation with me?"

Bobby leaned back. *Tread carefully. Very carefully.* For drama, he gnawed on one of his fingernails and let several charged moments pass before he spoke. "You mean Kevin?" he asked quietly, making sure he met, and held, eye contact with Caden.

"So you're willing to be honest?"

Bobby allowed himself a sad smile, tinged with embarrassment. "We had coffee."

"Is that all?" Caden leaned back and crossed his arms over his chest. He eyed Bobby through slits.

Bobby, in turn, regarded the wall, the floor to ceiling windows behind Caden's head, the dining room table in a corner of the room. He allowed his gaze to go anywhere but Caden's eyes. He needed to play this exactly right.

"What do you mean?" The question came out of Bobby almost a squeak.

Caden sighed. "I thought you weren't going to play games. You were with him, weren't you? You guys fucked, huh? That's why you didn't answer last night." Caden laughed, but it was bitter. "That's why *he* didn't answer."

Bobby said nothing for a minute or two, then used the line caught, shamefaced men had used for centuries: "It just happened." With a sense of glee he didn't show, Bobby added, "We met for coffee; that's all. Then he asked me back to his place so we could talk more. I don't know how things went the way they did, but before I knew it, the guy was grabbing my dick and trying to pull my shirt over my head." Bobby shrugged. "Before we knew it, we were in bed."

Bobby could see the hurt immediately on Caden's face. He knew then that the poor guy was hoping he'd say something else. Hoping maybe even Bobby would lie. Bobby knew, suddenly, what the word "crestfallen" looked like. The definition sat right in front of him.

"I met him at the gym," Bobby began. "We flirted in the locker room. You know how it is. And then in the shower—I got hard; he got hard. We exchanged numbers."

"When was this?" Caden's voice was flat, dead.

"A few days ago." Bobby thought for a moment, then added, "Before you were even back in town."

Caden stared down at the polished hardwood floor.

This couldn't have gone better if Bobby had scripted it out in advance. He knew that by the time Caden left here today, he would never want to see Kevin again.

Then the field would be completely open for Bobby. He could play the sympathetic friend, the one with the great cocksucking technique and the tight hole. He knew how to comfort a man.

"We had a couple dates." Bobby stopped himself. "Wait a minute! You didn't think I knew, right off the bat, who he was? I didn't. I swear. I didn't actually know until you and I talked about him, and I realized who he was." Bobby held up his hands in a gesture of helplessness. "By then, it was too late. I fell for him."

Bobby hopped up and sat next to Caden on the couch. "Tell me you forgive me, Caden. You're my best friend, and the last thing in the world I want to do is hurt you. But you said yourself, the magic was gone when you got home. I thought it would be okay."

Caden just turned his head and stared at him, mouth open.

"It'll be fine. You'll find yourself a nice stocky type like you like, and we'll go on a double date. We'll look back at this and laugh."

Bobby then played his trump card. "Besides, I have a bone to pick with Mr. Kevin." Bobby laughed. "He gave me a little present last night."

"What are you talking about?" Caden spat.

Bobby got up and crossed to the kitchen where he left the bottle of RID earlier. He grabbed it from the counter and showed Caden. "Let's just say the shampoo I used today was *not* Paul Mitchell!" Bobby laughed, but Caden didn't join him.

Bobby sat back in the chair across from Caden. "I'm sorry, man. But the fact that he gave me a case of the crabs shows the guy had not exactly been true while you were out of town."

Caden said nothing for the longest time. Then he looked up at Bobby and said simply, "I hate you."

Bobby didn't have a chance to respond. Caden stood quickly and left, slamming the door behind him.

Bobby stared at the door, smiling. "Law of the jungle, baby. Law of the jungle," he whispered. "When it comes to men, all bets are off."

Chapter Twenty-One

Caden returned home from work that evening still feeling numb. After leaving Bobby's that morning, he had considered calling in sick—he was certainly heartsick—but relented, thinking that he'd be better off in the office, preoccupied with something other than the hot mess his own love life had become.

But the eight hours or so he spent in his cubicle had simply dragged. A change of venue could not make a broken heart feel better, even temporarily. So, instead of brooding at home, he had brooded at work, staring out his window at the view he had of the Tribune Tower and the Wrigley Building, barely seeing either of the beautiful buildings. Instead, he let his dark thoughts carry him away. *Maybe if I'd been more welcoming when I first saw Kevin, instead of being aghast at the weight he'd lost— and then uncertain—then he would have never been amenable to Bobby. He might never have fallen for his seductive charms.* And Caden was sure that's what it was. If the two of them had gotten together, it was Bobby doing the seducing. He was a master at it.

But what of the issue of giving Bobby crabs? Was that even true? If it was, then Kevin hadn't been faithful while Caden was away. But who knew if it was true? Bobby was with different men practically every night of the week, sometimes having more than one in a day. He could have gotten crabs any number of places, including the bathhouse, where it was not uncommon for Bobby to have five, six, or more encounters in an evening.

Now, back at home, Caden quickly undressed and tossed aside the idea of a run—not tonight. He was weary to his bones. He doubted he'd have even the energy to eat, which was a good thing, because he wasn't hungry anyway. He plopped down on a living room chair, shirt unbuttoned, and wondered if it would be too outrageous to simply crawl into bed, pull the covers over his head, and wait for the morrow to come.

He glanced down at his chest. "Oh shit." He had worn the crucifix Kevin had given him for so long, he had almost forgotten about it. It was like the cross and gold chain had become part of his own body.

Now, with things the way they stood, he had to give it back. No matter what a shit he thought Kevin was, nothing could erase Kevin's gesture before Caden had left for Pittsburgh. It would always be a sweet memory, wrapped in kindness, no matter how much present day reality had soured it.

Besides, it was a memento of Kevin's mother, and he had made it clear to Caden he would one day want it back.

Sure, Caden thought, he could be a pill and just throw the thing into the trash, but he wasn't that kind of man.

Tired as he was, he wanted this connection to Kevin to be out of his life, and that was enough to give him motivation to go over to Kevin's tonight and return the jewelry to him. He thought about putting it in a padded envelope and dropping it in the mail, but what if it got lost? Again, Caden was not the kind of person who could take a chance with something obviously so precious to another human being, even if that human being had hurt him deeply.

He changed into jeans and a hooded sweatshirt, his Asics, and forced himself to eat one of the power bars he kept in the pantry. It was an adequate enough supper after the day he'd had. Before he left, he popped open his laptop and scanned his email.

There was one from Kevin, sent that morning. Caden read the short message about Kevin losing his phone.

Caden slammed the laptop shut. *Good cover. Nice try, but I'm not buying it. I know different.*

Caden got up on legs that felt much older and headed for the door. The sooner he got this errand done, the sooner he could hide himself away in bed. Maybe he'd never come out.

*

Kevin was glad he was tired. It had been a twelve-hour day at work, what with the vet clinic getting backed up with several emergencies, and then, at the end of the day, the receipts would not balance, and Kevin didn't get out of the animal hospital until almost seven thirty.

Now, as he sat back on his couch, propping his feet up on the oak coffee table before him and wearily aiming the remote at his TV, he was grateful for the fatigue. He'd made himself a quick dinner of a can of chicken noodle soup and a container of yogurt and now wanted nothing more than to bury his head in the sand of a night of mindless TV. Scanning the on-screen guide, he saw that there were several *House Hunters* and *House Hunters International* on HGTV tonight, all in a row, and this was just the kind of thing to remove him from his own worries.

The last thing he wanted to do was dwell on Caden, or even Bobby, for that matter. He was too tired and too numb to deal with the drama either of those men would bring. No, bring on the drama of bickering couples trying to decide which of three houses they would settle into.

His plan, though, was not to be. He had barely begun an episode of *House Hunters* where a young lesbian couple was searching for the perfect rural home outside Asheville, North Carolina, when his buzzer sounded.

He paused the show, set the remote on the coffee table, and sat up. The metallic box's bark sounded more jarring than usual, perhaps because Kevin simply wanted to be alone tonight. In fact, with the way things had gone over the past few days, being alone for a very long time sounded like a great plan. He was even glad his cell phone was not around and he was effectively cut off from the outside world.

"What fresh hell is this?" Kevin mumbled, getting up reluctantly from his place on the couch. He glanced out the front window, but it was too dark to see who was standing outside.

He leaned on the intercom button, "Yes?"

"Hey, man, it's Bobby. I've got a surprise for you."

Kevin rolled his eyes, wondering if the surprise was eight inches long, five inches around, and cut. Normally, the idea of such a surprise might have been a temptation, but tonight it had all the appeal of a tuna fish cupcake. He was about to snap into the intercom, "Haven't you ever heard of calling first?" when he remembered he no longer had the means with which someone could extend that courtesy.

He felt he had no choice but to buzz him in, which is what he did, without further conversation. Kevin stood by his front door, waiting for the sound of Bobby's footfall on the stairs. When he heard him rounding the landing leading up to his front door, he opened the door.

And there was Bobby, three steps down and smiling up at him. Kevin had to admit the man had a killer smile that paired perfectly with his killer body. Maybe fate was maneuvering Bobby into his life to comfort him for the loss of Caden. Kevin suddenly wished he didn't look like such a slob—he was wearing a pair of old gray sweats and a faded black T-shirt that had seen too many washings, was now too big for him, and had a hole in one armpit. But he was going for comfort when he got dressed after he got home, not expecting company.

Apparently, though, Bobby did not agree with the self-assessment because his grin broadened when their eyes met. "Well, aren't you a sight for sore eyes?"

Kevin shook his head, paradoxically delighted with the compliment, yet on the other hand, in no mood for it and simply wanting to get back to *House Hunters*. "You're fuckin' with me, right?"

"Oh, don't tempt me. No, you just look so manly—like you couldn't care less what you look like. And I find that very hot, mister."

"Well, I'm glad. You wanna come in?"

Kevin stepped back to allow Bobby to come into the apartment. He smelled as good as he looked. Bobby pecked him on the mouth. "Good to see you again."

They stood near the front doorway, and Bobby peered into the living room. "Is it okay that I dropped by? Not interrupting anything, am I?"

Actually, you were. An evening of blessed oblivion, to be precise, something I very much need right at the moment. But Kevin said, "Not at all. You want anything? Beer? Water?"

"Nah." Bobby walked into the living room and made himself comfortable on the couch. "I love this show."

"Me too." Kevin sat on the opposite end of the couch, wishing now that Bobby was here in his living room he would go. At the risk of sounding rude or impatient, he said, "So...you said you had a surprise for me."

"Can't wait? You're gonna like this!"

Kevin supposed he was probably right and wouldn't have been stunned to see Bobby grab his own crotch to indicate the surprise. Although hooking up with the Adonis was certainly not out of the realm of possibility, especially with Caden looking more and more like a mistake fast fading into his past, tonight was not the night it was going to happen.

But Bobby did not pull out his own dick.

He pulled out, instead, Kevin's cell phone. He held it up like it was something of a prize, which it was.

"Oh, thank God!" Kevin snatched the phone out of Bobby's hand. "I thought I was going to have to replace this—and that's not the worst. Do you realize how much of my life is in here?"

Bobby grinned. He was obviously pleased with himself. "You left it at the Bored Room when we were there."

"Phew! You don't know what a relief this is."

"I would have called you, but I couldn't find a listing."

"I haven't had a landline in years."

"That seems to be the way of the world these days." Bobby scooted over closer. "You know, I wouldn't mind a little something to drink after all."

Kevin felt a lot more hospitable all of a sudden and actually glad Bobby had stopped by. "I can get you a beer, or I have a bottle of Syrah open if you'd prefer that."

Bobby waved his hand, dismissing the offer of alcohol. "I'll just have water—maybe some ice if it's not too much trouble."

"Sure. I think I'll grab a beer."

Kevin was in the kitchen, pouring water from a pitcher and adding ice to the glass when his buzzer sounded. This time, he laughed at the sound of it, calling out to Bobby. "It's fuckin' Grand Central station here tonight. Now, who can *this* be? I'm not expecting anyone."

Kevin moved, once more, to the intercom on the wall. "Who is it?" he called.

There was a pause that went on long enough for Kevin to begin to think someone had pressed the wrong button downstairs. Then a voice came through, softly, "It's Caden. Can I come up?"

Kevin looked over at Bobby, who, curiously, had sat up straighter, his smile gone. Did he look tense? Kevin cocked his head, a plea for understanding. He whispered, "It's the guy I told you about. I'm gonna buzz him in."

"No, don't!" Bobby shouted.

Kevin's eyebrows came together in confusion. He gave Bobby a weak smile. "Why on earth not?"

Bobby looked around desperately. What was with him, anyway? "Uh, I was hoping you and I could be alone tonight."

"That's not gonna happen, Bobby." He turned back to the intercom. "Come on up." He pressed the button to admit Caden.

He opened the door a crack so Caden could simply come in when he got to the top of the stairs. "What's going on with you?"

Bobby sat on the edge of the couch, clutching his hands together and pulling at his own fingers. "Nothing. I told you—I wanted to be alone with you." He tried to smile, but it came across to Kevin as just looking sick or sheepish. "Not for that! I know you need time." Bobby's breath, Kevin noticed, was coming a little quicker. "I just needed to talk to you about something—a personal matter."

Kevin smiled and tried to appear reassuring. "We can do that—right after I see what Caden wants." Kevin thought for a moment. "With the way things have been going between us lately, I doubt he'll want to stay long."

They both went silent as they heard the slam of the vestibule door downstairs and then the tread of footsteps on the staircase. Suddenly, Bobby stood. "I gotta go."

"Okay. Is everything all right?"

"We can talk about this later. Um, I think I know this Caden guy, and, um, it would be better if I didn't run into him. You have a back door, right?"

"Yeah, but—"

"I'll just head out that way. If you don't mind, I'd appreciate it if you'd not mention I was here."

And before Kevin could ask why, he heard Bobby moving quickly through the kitchen, the creak of the back door opening, and the slam of it as Bobby hurriedly closed it. Kevin wanted to call out, "You need a key to open the gate to get out of the backyard," but didn't have the chance, since Caden was coming in the front door at almost the very same moment.

Kevin turned to face him.

There he was. Caden. In spite of everything, Kevin's heart gave a little lurch when he saw him. His man. His beautiful man. Just because someone stopped loving one or their feelings toward one mysteriously and regretfully changed didn't mean you could turn off your own feelings like one turns off a light switch. Caden might not have had the movie-star good looks Bobby did, but he was *more* gorgeous in Kevin's eyes. There was a simplicity about him, a sense of kindness and nurturing that was absent in Bobby.

Kevin wondered if he'd ever be able to get over this man.

He wanted to gather him quickly in his arms, now that Caden was only a foot or so away from him. But he restrained himself. Tension still hung in the air between them like an invisible wall.

Caden looked toward the kitchen. The first words out of his mouth were. "Did I just hear the door slam?"

Kevin debated what he should say. Bobby had asked him not to mention that he'd been there. He looked to the back door and then back at Caden, a grin he realized appeared sheepish creeping across his face.

Caden frowned. "He was here, wasn't he?"

"I don't know what you're talking about."

Caden hurried through the dining room and into the kitchen at the back of the apartment. He peered through the glass of the door, finally opening it to look out into the night. The screech of metal against metal sounded as an L train rumbled southward. Caden closed the door, leaning against it with his arms folded across his chest. "Are you going to tell me the truth?"

"The truth about what?" Kevin said, knowing how dumb he sounded, worse, how duplicitous. Why was he covering for Bobby, anyway? What was any of this about?

Caden shook his head. "I would expect shit like this from him, but not from you. I had thought you were different." He sighed. "I guess it just goes to show how you can never really know a person." Caden laughed. "I suppose I shouldn't really say I knew you. We only fucked a couple of times."

Kevin winced as if Caden had dealt him a physical blow. It was—had always been—more than fucking.

Caden moved away from the door and edged by Kevin, as if he couldn't bear for their bodies to come into contact.

Kevin followed him into the living room. Caden surveyed the room, as if he were looking for evidence. He froze, and then moved to the coffee table. He snatched up Kevin's cell and held it out to him. "The phone you—" Caden made air quotes with his fingers. "—lost?"

"I did. I left it at a coffee shop." Kevin gnawed at his lower lip, wondering if it would do any good to come out and say that Bobby had just returned it to him. Why was he protecting Bobby, anyway? But right now, Caden looked so furious, so full of disdain, Kevin wondered if there were any words that could possibly lighten the moment, make the situation any better.

Kevin felt sick inside, paralyzed.

"You did not. We both know it."

"Why?" Kevin cried out. "Why do you think so little of me? What did I do?" Kevin felt very close to tears, but held them in. He had done nothing wrong.

"Who was here?" Caden insisted.

"It was a friend." Kevin gave up. Bobby may have had a reason for wanting Caden not to know he was there, but he didn't know what it was. And the cost of keeping that secret was simply too dear.

"Uh huh. What's his name? Bobby, by any chance?"

Kevin smiled. "Yeah, it's Bobby. We met at the gym."

"Unbelievable." Caden groped in his pocket, and for a wild, unreasonable moment, Kevin thought he was going to bring out a gun. But then he saw the glint of gold in his hand—his mother's crucifix. Caden spoke softly, "I knew you'd want this back. Thank you for letting me have it. It *was* a comfort." Caden set it on the dining room table. For a moment, he looked sad, and Kevin thought there was a chance that they could perhaps talk, smooth things over.

But then Caden sneered. "I'll go now. You can call Bobby back in, and you fellas can pick up where you left off. Far be it from me to interrupt."

Kevin opened his mouth to reply, but Caden held up his hand. "I don't want to hear it."

And with that, he was out the door. Nauseous, Kevin listened to his rapid footfalls down the stairs.

Kevin pressed his head against the door, having never felt more hopeless. The words to call Caden back stuck in his throat.

Kevin turned the deadbolt. He looked around his empty apartment, amazed that everything was still in place. The home actually appeared tidy. Kevin felt like it should reflect a tornado sweeping through—breaking ceramic, crushing wood, shredding fabric, scattering trash and feathers everywhere—or at least that's how he felt emotionally. It was like someone had sucker punched him in the gut.

And he had no idea why, or what he had done wrong.

He pulled out a chair at his dining room table, placing his head in his hands. After a while, he looked up, his gaze lighting on his mother's crucifix. He fingered it, still marveling at the warmth he felt when he touched the thing. He slid it back over his head and pressed the cross against his chest.

Suddenly, the memory of when he had gotten the crucifix came back. He had just gotten home from junior high school, and he knew something was wrong as soon as he walked in, as he always did, through the kitchen door. Mom was usually there when he got home from school, either working on dinner or doing a crossword puzzle in that day's edition of the newspaper, her reading glasses perched low on her nose.

Today, the kitchen was quiet and dim. The lights were off, and the day outside was a drizzly one, gray. Kevin had turned to his right and looked through the dining room and into the living room, where one of the lamps was lit.

He heard soft voices.

And something else—something he couldn't quite believe. Someone was crying.

He padded softly into the room and saw his father on the couch. His head was in his hands, and he was bent over, weeping, his shoulders shaking. He sucked in a great quivering breath and let it out in a sigh. Next to him, Kevin's Aunt Eleanor sat, her hand on Dad's shoulder, rubbing. She looked up as Kevin entered, and her lips turned up in a sad smile. Kevin noticed her eyes were red from crying too.

The scene was so unreal that, for a moment, Kevin was struck dumb. Finally, when he could get his breath and tongue to cooperate, he asked, "What's wrong? What happened?"

And a panicked thought jumped into his head: *Where's Mom*? A sense of dread rose up, knowing what he was about to hear before Aunt Eleanor spoke the words.

In a soft, crushed voice that wavered, his aunt said, "There was an accident out on the highway." She stopped. "I hate to have to tell you this, Kev, but it was your mom. She..." Her voice trailed off, her eyes scanning the room, landing anywhere but on Kevin's own eyes. Finally, she blew out a breath and said in a rush: "She was hurt bad. She didn't make it."

The words hit him like a jolt of electricity. But after the shock, there was only numbness.

His dad finally looked up. He shook his head and then held out his hand. "I know she would have wanted you to have this."

Kevin moved forward, still not believing any of this was real, and took the object clutched in his father's hand. It was his mom's crucifix.

He had stared down at it, thinking of it around his mother's neck.

Kevin shook his head, clearing it of the sad memory. He brought the cross to his lips and kissed it. He stared at the wall, thinking nothing for a long time until finally, a voice in his own head started talking to him.

You have to go after him. You have to make things right. See, people are precious. In the end, they're all we have. And our connections to them are so fragile—they're like the most tender plant shoots, needing nurturing, and without it, they can wither away to nothing.

And they can be gone in a flash.

You need to find Caden. Make him talk to you. Because you did nothing wrong and something is not adding up here. You need to make him see that love is possible.

Love is too valuable to toss away over a misunderstanding.

You need to at least try.

*

Bobby stood at the gate at the back of Kevin's yard, watching as people went by. He felt so stupid—trapped here in this apartment building backyard. One side of it was a high fence, and the other sides were bordered by high concrete walls above which were the L tracks. For security, he supposed, the only way in and out of the yard was through the residents' apartments or through the gate that he now clung to, which required a key to open.

He couldn't go back upstairs, not with Caden there. If he, Kevin, and Caden were all together in the same room, the truth might come up, his duplicity exposed. He couldn't let that happen, not if he had any hopes of making Kevin his own. He just hoped Kevin didn't say anything about him that could lead to embarrassing questions—questions that would upset his whole plan, shaky and impulsive as it was.

As he stood shivering in the dark, he felt alone, and it occurred to him that, for someone as promiscuous as he was, he felt alone a lot. He'd had an endless parade of hotties in and out of his bedroom, and he had been in and out of theirs (and some other places, too, like the backrooms of bars and bathhouses), yet here he was, all by himself in the cold. The loneliness was as familiar as an old friend, clinging to him and making him wonder, in spite of all his muscles, his chiseled features, thick hair, and perfect teeth, if he wasn't all that desirable.

Sure, plenty of guys wanted him for sex, but it seemed none of them wanted him for anything else.

Kevin, he thought, could change that.

If only Caden didn't screw it up for him.

Bobby looked down at the ground, rubbing the toe of his shoe into the grit on the concrete. When he looked up, he saw what he had been waiting for.

Caden.

Bobby stepped back against the brick wall, where he was hidden in the shadows, and observed his friend.

Caden stopped just within Bobby's line of vision. He had his hand pressed to his eyes as if he was holding back tears. Bobby felt a twinge of remorse but told himself that by taking Kevin away from Caden, he really wasn't hurting Caden. Caden liked fat guys; he was a classic chubby chaser. He would never be happy with the new and improved Kevin and would cast him aside anyway, for some bear in a flannel shirt and forty-waist jeans.

Kevin and Caden might be hurting now, Bobby told himself, but in the end, if he could get things to go his way, everyone would be happier, paired off the way they were supposed to be. Although Caden couldn't see it now, Bobby was actually doing him a favor, seeing to it that he ended up with someone he was truly attracted to.

He watched as Caden drew in a few deep breaths and then did something odd. He pulled his leg up behind him at the knee, then the other one. Then again.

What the fuck is he doing? Stretching?

That was exactly what Caden was doing. Bobby thought it wasn't so surprising. His friend was addicted to running, had been ever since he first met him. Hell, the guy had even done the Chicago marathon—twice.

Bobby could never understand it. Why run for fitness? It was so solitary. Your chances of meeting a sexy guy were slim. Not like at the gym, where there were hot men in spandex all around, pumping iron and, if you were lucky, pumping your butt later. He had even once told Caden he should join the gay running group, the Frontrunners, so he could meet other men who liked to run.

But Caden was having none of it. He told him he liked to run on his own, that it cleared his mind or some such shit. He had even made vague assertions to the effect that running was like meditation for him.

Bobby watched as Caden finished stretching and then sprang off at a brisk clip. The guy was actually going for a run. Bobby hoped it calmed him.

Right now, he had to get back to Kevin.

*

Kevin tried calling Caden's phone once more. And once more, it went directly to voice mail. He was beginning to think he'd just have to go over to Caden's apartment and demand to be let in.

As he was setting his phone on his coffee table, he heard someone rapping on the glass at the back door.

He shook his head. He had forgotten all about Bobby. He got up and went to the kitchen, where Bobby was staring in at him through the glass, a big, stupid grin plastered across his face.

Kevin was unable to muster a smile in return. He opened the back door. "What? Unable to leap tall iron gates in a single bound?"

"Not so much." Bobby came into the kitchen, rubbing his arms. "Man, it's getting cold out there."

"Why didn't you come back up sooner?"

"I don't know. I thought someone might come along."

"That's not the reason." Kevin turned and went into the living room, where he remained standing because he did not want Bobby to sit. He preferred that Bobby not get comfortable.

"What do you mean?"

"Why did you run out of here when you knew Caden was coming up?"

"I told you—we have a history."

"So?"

"And it just wouldn't be cool for him to find us here together."

Kevin's eyebrows moved toward one another quizzically. "Why? You and I barely know each other." None of this made sense. "How do you know Caden?" A thought crossed Kevin's mind, one that filled him with dread. "Is he your boyfriend?"

Bobby laughed—actually laughed for a long time, as if the idea was so absurd it really tickled him. "No! No, the guy is like a brother to me. We've been friends for years."

Kevin cocked his head. "So why? Why wouldn't you want to see him?" Kevin recalled Caden's anger, his asking if "he" had been here. What had Bobby said to Caden?

Bobby looked out the window, then examined one of the throw pillows on the couch. He moved toward the door. "Listen, I gotta go."

"You're not going to answer me?" Kevin moved in front of Bobby, blocking his path to the front door.

"There's nothing to tell, man. I don't know why I ran out of here. Maybe I was afraid Caden would get the wrong idea if I was here."

"Why would he get the wrong idea, Bobby?"

"I don't know! That dude's paranoid." Bobby shoved Kevin out of the way. "Ask him yourself. Maybe you can chase him down. I saw him going for a run a few minutes ago." And with those words, Bobby was out the door.

Kevin rushed out behind him and called down from the landing, "What do you mean? He went running from here?"

But Bobby's only answer was the slam of the front door below.

Kevin went back inside and regarded his smart phone once more, which, in its uselessness, currently seemed pretty stupid. Why bother trying to call Caden when he was out there running?

He wouldn't answer.

The way things stood, he might not answer if he was standing still.

And if Kevin showed up outside his building, would he let him in?

Kevin had to put things right, and there was only one way to do it—face-to-face. He began struggling out of his clothes and dropping them on the floor as he headed for his bedroom.

There he dressed quickly in a pair of running tights, long-sleeved T-shirt, knit gloves, cap, and his running shoes.

Caden loved the lakefront trails, and Kevin figured he had a fifty-fifty chance of finding him because he could only go either north or south once he got to the eastern end of Kevin's street, where it dead-ended at Lake Michigan.

Logic told him to go south. After all, that was the direction in which Caden lived.

Kevin made sure he had his keys and slipped his phone into the pocket of the fleece he pulled over his head. He headed out, praying logic would work in his favor tonight.

It sure as hell didn't seem to be working too well otherwise.

Chapter Twenty-Two

Caden ran as if his life depended on it. He ran as though his heart was not breaking, trying to outpace the sickness he felt when he thought of Kevin and his best friend alone together in Kevin's apartment. He imagined that Bobby had simply been waiting outside for him to leave, and that once Caden exited the building, he would scurry back up the stairs and into Kevin's waiting arms.

Caden realized he was running hard, running fast. Sweat poured from his hairline and trickled down his sides from his armpits. His lungs burned, bellowing in and out like some sort of furnace running at capacity. His heart hammered out an almost tribal rhythm. He had been a runner long enough that all of this felt good, pushing his body to its limits.

What was *not* working was that the physical challenges were not having the desired effect. He wanted to run so hard that he became a machine, aware only of his lungs, his heart, the muscles in his legs, and his arms pumping. He hoped making outrageous physical demands on his body would keep the heartache at bay.

But it wasn't.

Running was supposed to release endorphins in the brain, calming and producing a kind of euphoria.

That wasn't working either.

When he wasn't thinking of Bobby and Kevin together in Kevin's bed, he was thinking of Kevin and how, suddenly, it no longer bothered him that he was not his husky ideal.

He was Kevin, the man he had begun to fall in love with. Those same eyes, the same smile, the same sandy hair and hirsute body were all there, and now that Caden realized he had most likely lost the man, these things had all clicked into place as desirable.

What was it a wise person had once said? Something along the lines of never really appreciating something until it's gone?

He stopped for a moment, because the hitch in his breathing was not from running, but from being close to tears…again.

Kevin *was* gone.

Caden had been a fool, and Bobby—damn him!—had stepped in and snatched up his man before Caden even had a chance to think about it.

For Bobby, getting men had always been a competition. It had happened over and over again throughout the course of their friendship. Caden recalled how, on more than one occasion, he would find a guy he was getting along with at Sidetrack or some other watering hole, and he would leave him alone with Bobby to use the facilities or get another beer, and when he'd come back, they'd both be gone.

It wasn't that big of a deal, really, more of an irritant than an outrage, because before this, Bobby had never stolen anyone from him that he truly cared about.

He looked out at the black expanse of water that was Lake Michigan, letting the cold breeze lower the heat he felt in his face and waiting for his hammering heart to slow a bit before setting off again.

He knew one thing: he was not the kind of guy who would pull the kind of stunt Bobby most likely had. He would not try to "win" Kevin away from him if Kevin was, indeed, now with him. Kevin was a grown man and made his own choices. Love was not a competition, despite Bobby's pronouncements to the contrary.

Caden took a deep breath and bounced off on his heels again, heading south, toward home, where the comfort of a pint of Ben and Jerry's Coffee/Heath Bar Crunch awaited him, after a long bath.

*

Kevin's knees hurt. His hamstrings ached. His lungs felt like they were ready to give out—his breath burning as it wheezed in and out. His hair, under his cap, clung to his skull, so wet with sweat it felt as though he had just stepped out of the shower. He had been running for weeks now, but never before had he pushed himself like this.

But he was determined to find Caden, to catch up with him, and if that meant pushing himself beyond his limits, then, by God, he would do it.

Thwarted love, combined with adrenaline, could be a potent cocktail.

But part of him was simply dejected. He had no guarantee that Caden had done the logical thing and headed south. He could have just as easily have turned to the left at the lakefront, heading northward, Evanston-bound.

Bobby could have been talking out of his ass, and Caden might not have been running at all tonight—or if Bobby did see him running, he was merely sprinting to the L station a block south of Kevin's apartment.

Kevin had looked at every male he passed on the Lakefront Trail, peered at each face passing him by in the opposite direction. Twice, he thought he had spied Caden, and once he had even run up to a guy whose build and gait were identical to Caden's, crying out for him to "Wait up!" But when he caught up with the man, he saw that the face was not Caden's and was greeted with a look of suspicion.

So now, as he saw a guy in jeans stopped at the wall along the edge of Hollywood Beach, he told himself to not get too excited, that this might not be Caden. But he knew in his heart that it was. Wheezing and pumping his arms to close the distance between them, Kevin moaned aloud as the man he was pretty sure was Caden turned and began running again.

"Shit," Kevin spat out on a breath of what felt like the last of his air. He had a stitch in his side now. Caden was fast.

The thought crossed his mind that he could simply stop, collect himself, and allow his heart rate and respiration to return to normal levels. He could then walk—well, maybe limp—to Caden's Edgewater apartment and ring his buzzer. Hell, he could even splurge and hail a cab.

But such a plan depended on Caden being home and, if he was, his letting Kevin in.

That was not something he was willing to gamble on, so Kevin pushed on, trying to catch up with Caden and ignore the screaming pains in his body, which told him to slow down or stop.

He would catch his man.

He had to.

*

Out of the corner of his eye, Caden saw someone running up fast behind him. Too fast. As though the man were chasing him. Like most urban dwellers, and especially those in a city the size of Chicago, Caden had ample measures of good sense and paranoia, qualities that protected him.

He increased his pace without looking over his shoulder. Making eye contact with someone, if they meant you harm, was never a good idea. So he pretended to be blissfully unaware of the dark figure closing the gap behind him.

He told himself that, most likely, it was simply another runner, out as he was, for an evening jog. But the cold wind off the black void that was the water and this particularly dark part of the trail made him frightened.

The man was close enough now that Caden could hear him wheezing.

And then he stopped, gasped for air, and turned around.

Caden had heard his own name.

*

Kevin didn't think he'd had it in him to call after Caden. He simply didn't believe he had enough air in his lungs to maintain his pace and put breath behind the one word that might make Caden slow or stop.

So it was with a supreme effort of will that Kevin was able to call out—no, more like bark out—a single word: "Caden."

The name emerged as a wheeze, with barely any force behind it. Kevin knew if Caden didn't hear him, he was finished. He could not run fast enough to catch up with him. Not tonight.

Maybe, to be able to run fast enough to catch Caden, he would need years of training.

But Caden stopped.

And turned around.

Breathless, Kevin smiled and held up a hand. He was breathing so hard the smile was a real accomplishment. He did not yet have enough air in his lungs to voice even one more word. For several long moments, he simply stood and stared at Caden, so many words piling up in his brain, but not having enough air to say them. All he could manage for the present was panting like a dog.

He bent over to alleviate the pain in his side.

Caden drew closer, looking at him curiously. "What were you doing? Chasing me?"

Kevin wished his breathing would return to normal so he could speak. But that eventuality was still minutes away. So he simply pointed at Caden and nodded.

"Why?"

Kevin dared not shrug. He held up a finger indicating that Caden should hang on for a moment. He bent over even more, hands on his knees, trying with sheer force of will to slow his respiration, his heart rate, and the sweat streaming from every pore.

At last, his breathing slowed enough to allow him to speak. "I have to talk to you."

Caden smiled, and it was a beautiful sight to behold. Not only because his smile lit up his face, making him even more adorable and fetching, but also because it meant Caden was going to allow him to at least say something. He wouldn't turn away, sullen, and sprint off—*away.*

Kevin couldn't bear that, mainly because he just didn't have the energy any longer to go after him. His breathing was quick, almost normal, and the sweat had slowed to a trickle. But his face was hot, making the wind off the lake even more chilling. He moved closer to Caden. "I ran and ran and ran—all because I needed to catch up to you, just so I could talk to you." He sucked in a couple more deep lungfuls of cold air. "I was afraid you weren't on the trail or you went in another direction, and yet, here you are." Kevin cocked his head, smiling. If the love and relief weren't radiating off his face, then his skin had turned to stone.

Kevin was relieved to see Caden return his smile. He could tell that Caden was pleased he had chased after him. Maybe he was even flattered. Was that too much to hope for?

"What? What did you want to talk to me about?"

"Us. You. Me. We can't just leave things at an intercom *Dear John*, for God's sake. And I think you have the wrong idea about a whole lot of stuff."

Caden's smile vanished. "I don't know about that. I have eyes. I can read."

"What do you mean?"

"The texts you sent me the other night. Your not picking up your phone all night long. Bobby there with you. Bobby is a gorgeous guy. I don't blame you for sleeping with him." Caden looked out toward the water, which moved restlessly against the shore. "He's pretty irresistible. But I can't say it doesn't hurt."

"I never slept with Bobby."

Caden moved a little closer. He smiled, but the smile did not reach his eyes. He put a hand on Kevin's shoulder. "Please. Lying doesn't become you. That's not the guy you are. I know that much."

"But..."

"You don't have to pretend, Kevin. He told me. Bobby told me."

"Told you what?" Kevin knew the answer, but he didn't want to believe it. Bobby had seemed like a horndog, a total man slut, but he didn't seem like someone conniving and deceitful. Yet that's exactly what he was if he had told Caden they had slept together, when nothing could be further from the truth. Perhaps Caden had misunderstood? "Are you sure he said that? I mean, we did spend a little time together. I don't deny that. We had lunch; we saw a movie. I met him at my gym." Kevin smiled. "I didn't know you two were acquainted until an hour or two ago."

*

Caden couldn't look at Kevin. If he did, he might believe him, and he wasn't sure that was the right thing to do. He wanted to believe Kevin. He really did, but he'd had his heart slammed down and trod upon before by liars. Who hadn't?

Why would Bobby have told him all he had if it wasn't the truth? He was supposed to be his best friend.

Are you really so stupid? Bobby is all about being the best: the best looking, the best lover, the best cocksucker, the best power bottom, the most wanted. He would take Kevin—or any man—away from you in a heartbeat if he thought he had the chance, if he thought it gave him some kind of crazy edge, boosted his self-esteem a little more.

Still, Caden knew how men were. And how tempting and seductive Bobby could be. He had seen, time and time again, perfectly normal men make complete fools of themselves, all in an attempt to curry favor, to get a second glance, even, from the undeniably gorgeous

Bobby. If Bobby swooped in when Kevin was feeling low because Caden was less than thrilled at his new appearance, he might have been easy prey.

Caden couldn't blame him. At least his head couldn't blame him.

His heart—his gut—told him another story. The idea of Kevin with another man was nausea-inducing, and the thought of him with the man he once thought of as his best friend was intolerable.

Caden turned back to Kevin. The fight had gone out of him. He appraised him with new eyes. He saw— simply—that Kevin was still the same man. All at once, he could see the old Kevin, still somehow managing to be part of this new, leaner one. Why? Because the essence of a person doesn't change with his appearance. To the core, essentially, people are not a collection of blood, skin, bones, and muscle, but something harder to put one's finger on. The body is a shell, and it contains the fragile and ethereal spirit of the person.

It was Kevin's spirit, Caden realized all at once, that he had fallen in love with. Sure, when he was heavier, the beefy blond, as he had once thought of him, he had fallen in lust with him.

But later, it was the man's essential goodness, his kindness, that had made him want to stay around for longer.

"What are you thinking?" Kevin was shivering; the wind whipping off the water was icy and seemed to be getting worse. He bounced up and down, rubbing his arms.

Caden looked up to see a few snowflakes dancing lazily in the air.

"I was thinking we need to get someplace warm."

"You wanna go get coffee or somethin'? Maybe cocoa?" Kevin asked hopefully, and Caden was sure he was trying not to push.

Caden shook his head. "My place is just a few blocks west. Let's go there."

Kevin nodded, his smile broadening, and followed Caden as he started to jog west, over the grass and toward the underpass beneath Lake Shore Drive.

"Wait!" Kevin cried.

Caden turned.

"Can we just walk?"

Caden laughed. "Sure."

Chapter Twenty-Three

Kevin took a moment to survey Caden's place once they had gotten inside. In their short time together, before Caden's mom was taken ill, they had always met at Kevin's place—so he had never seen where Caden lived.

The little studio, a garden unit just below ground level but not quite a basement, was spartan, a reflection, in a way, of Caden's simplicity. There were hardwood floors that revealed not a speck of dust. A pulled-out but made-up futon sat in one corner of the room. A nightstand stood next to the futon, a reading lamp atop its walnut surface. There was a desk opposite the bed, and on that was Caden's computer. A small kitchen occupied another wall, and then a door led, presumably, to the bathroom. There was only one window in the place, and it had iron bars—a requisite for ground-floor urban living.

"Wow. You really keep things neat."

"It's not hard with a place this small—and when you're by yourself. Mom always taught me, everything in its place and a place for everything." Caden peeled off his fleece, and Kevin longed to take him in his arms, but it was not the time for that.

Not yet.

Not ever?

At least now, Kevin's heart rate and breathing had calmed back to normal. He noticed the return was happening faster and faster the more he ran. And it was blessedly warm in the studio apartment. Kevin stopped shivering, but he could not stop trembling—not entirely.

Because he sensed that a relationship hung in the balance here. Something precious could be gained. Or it could be lost. And Kevin had a strong sense that one or the other would happen tonight.

Caden interrupted his thoughts. "You want something warm? Tea? Coffee?" He moved to the kitchen and bent down to look in one of the cupboards. "I even have a bottle of Jack if you want that kind of warmth." He turned around, smiling, holding the black-labeled bottle aloft.

Kevin shook his head. "Ah...tempting as that is, I think I'll pass. Need a clear head. I'll just take a glass of water."

Once Caden had gotten their waters, there was really no place for them to sit other than on the futon together, so that's where they ended up, but Kevin noticed Caden took the opposite end.

Caden said, "I didn't really ask you back here to rehydrate or to talk about my obsessive-compulsive neatness."

"I didn't know that about you."

"There's a lot you don't know."

Kevin nodded; it was true. But he wanted to know all of it. The good and the bad, the happy and the sad, the delightful and the irritating—everything. He just hoped he had the chance.

They said nothing for a few moments, and Kevin got the feeling Caden was waiting for him to begin. So he did.

"Look. I think, from what you've said, there's been some confusion over what's gone on since you came back. And I don't know if you've gotten the true picture."

"You mean about Bobby?"

"I mean about Bobby." Kevin felt something inside him go dark, and a thought sprang, unbidden: *How can something so beautiful on the outside be so ugly on the inside?* Kevin asked, "I know he's your friend and everything, but could I ask you to just clue me in on what you think, what he's told you about us?"

"Why? So you can tailor your story to fit what he said?"

Kevin had to try hard to restrain himself from rolling his eyes. "No. So I can make sure you're not operating under false impressions."

"He told me that you came on to him at the gym—that you got hard in the shower looking at him. That's just for starters." Caden tried to smile but, within seconds, gave up on the effort.

Kevin had to decide whether he should try to deny these things one by one or just let Caden tell him everything. He was certain there was more, especially if Bobby had twisted his own behavior and feelings from the gym around to make them Kevin's. So all Kevin said was, "Go on."

And Caden told him everything: Bobby's sheepish admission that the two of them had slept together, how Kevin had even left him with a case of the crabs.

Kevin couldn't help it; he had to laugh out loud at the last part. "Crabs? I can assure you I have never had crabs. Not now. Not ever. Wanna check?" He wiggled his eyebrows at Caden.

"That's okay."

"What about the texts you sent me from the Bored Room?" Caden paused, took a sip of water. "I watched you and him that night...from outside. Watched the two of you. You looked like a couple on a date, laughing, heads pressed close." Caden looked away, and Kevin could see the memory hurt.

"We were just having coffee." Kevin scratched his head. "And I never texted you that night."

"Oh, come on." Caden walked over to his desk, picked up his phone, and began scrolling. "I have proof. Right here. So please don't lie."

Kevin took the phone, glanced down at the screen, and saw the conversation between himself and Caden. But he had never written these messages. In fact, glancing at the time told him they were sent long after he left the Bored Room, where he had left his phone behind.

With Bobby.

Kevin knew Bobby had been up to something, but seeing the in-your-face proof of it right now was a jolt. He liked to think better of people. This was out-and-out deception. He handed the phone back to Caden. "And you call this guy your friend?"

"Why?"

"Why, indeed." Kevin stood up, paced the room. "I'm not the one who's a liar, not now, and not then. I didn't write those texts. Bobby did."

"What?"

"I did have coffee with him that night. If it's any comfort to you, all I talked about was you. But you might be interested in knowing that I left my phone there on the table when I went home." He sat back down, close to Caden, making eye contact. "If you don't believe me, call the Bored Room. I went back there that night and tried to find it. There was a woman working there that night—I remember her because she was so funny and her name was Venus. She helped me look for it when I went back.

We turned the place upside down. She'd remember, if you need proof.

"Bobby was at my place tonight when you showed up because he was bringing back my phone. So, he sent the messages—not me."

"And that's why you wouldn't call me back…"

"Not wouldn't. Couldn't." Kevin eyed the phone, still in Caden's hand. "Go ahead. Call the Bored Room. I know they stay open late, and maybe Venus is working again tonight. If she isn't—leave a message for her to call you back. Really, I know she'll remember."

Caden stared down at the floor. He didn't speak for so long, Kevin was beginning to think he never would. And if he didn't speak, it must be because he didn't believe him.

But then Caden looked into his eyes. "I don't need to call. I know. I think I even knew before your offer of proof. It hurts to think Bobby would do this, but I'm not surprised. He's a sick puppy—and really, for all his hot looks, he really has very low self-esteem."

"Are you mad at him?"

"I feel sorry for him."

"Where does this leave us, then?"

Caden thought about the question for a long time. His epiphany on the lakefront came back to him—about a person being more than just an exterior. It came back with even more force because it made him think not so much this time of Kevin, but of Bobby, who underneath his sleek, charming, and "fucking gorgeous" exterior was really a sad little man who didn't know how to love himself.

And if he didn't know how to do that, no one would ever really love him.

It was sad, really.

But what wasn't sad was what he had right here before him—the start to something good and whole, something all the more precious because he had almost let it slip through his fingers, simply because he allowed himself to put too much emphasis on what was on the outside.

What a loss that would have been!

He laid his head on Kevin's shoulder. "I'm sorry," he whispered.

Kevin stroked his hair. "It's okay. You just need to put your trust in me. I promise—I'll never lie to you."

"No. It's not okay. I didn't trust you. I thought you were someone else, and I was too blind to see you were not and that, in fact, you—the man I love—were standing right in front of me. All the time." Caden's lips turned up in a rueful grin.

"Yes. I am. Right in front of you. Well, next to you. The question now is: What are you gonna do about it?"

"This." Caden leaned into Kevin, his lips and tongue seeking out Kevin's own, connecting. He pushed him back on the futon.

About the Author

Real Men. True Love.

Rick R. Reed draws inspiration from the lives of gay men to craft stories that quicken the heartbeat, engage emotions, and keep the pages turning. Although he dabbles in horror, dark suspense, and comedy, his attention always returns to the power of love. He's the award-winning and bestselling author of more than fifty works of published fiction and is forever at work on yet another book. Lambda Literary has called him: "A writer that doesn't disappoint..." You can find him at www.rickrreedreality.blogspot.com. Rick lives in Palm Springs, CA, with his beloved husband, Bruce, and their fierce Chihuahua/Shiba Inu mix, Kodi.

Email: rickrreedbooks@gmail.com

Facebook: www.facebook.com/rickrreedbooks

Twitter: @rickrreed

Other books by this author

Unraveling

Sky Full of Mysteries

The Perils of Intimacy

IM

Coming Soon from Rick R. Reed

Raining Men

BOBBY'S DREAM

Thunder rumbles. Rain hisses. Flashes of lightning—brilliant and blue white—rip across the sky.

I know I'm dreaming, yet something about this whole scenario seems as real as the nose on my face, the hair on my head, the dick swinging between my legs.

In addition to the natural sounds of the storm, there's another noise, and it makes me smile. Music. Rising. Percussion. Disco beats. And the powerful wail of Martha Wash and the Weather Girls singing "It's Raining Men."

I'm standing under some kind of awning—red, canvas—watching the rain pour down not in drops, but sheets. Blinding. The flashes of lightning are like a disco strobe light, revealing in flashes of blue and silver, a darkened cityscape. Night. But a netherworld cityscape, blue gray, unreal.

It's the music that makes me want to move out from under the awning. The music that has me smiling, my hips, head, and arms in synchronized rhythm with the beat.

Glorious!

Even the rain, a cold shock to my naked body, isn't enough to keep me from driving myself out into the downpour to dance to the song, which has long been a favorite of mine.

What a delicious notion—raining men! Men falling from the skies! More men than one can shake a stick at (or something that rhymes with stick, heh-heh).

I look up into the midnight-blue clouds, my mouth and eyes open to the water pouring down, and I see it: the first of the men.

I stare in wonder as he drops from the sky. A blond Adonis, smooth and muscled, allover tanned with a dick thick, long, and perfectly hard, pointing back up at the sky. He lands somewhere outside my vision, and I dance, spinning toward where I saw him fall, hoping to find him where he has landed so I can say hello, reach out and touch him.

But before I can make any progress, another man falls from the sky. This one is hirsute, bearded, husky but hard-muscled, putting me in mind of the actor Jeffrey Dean Morgan. He smiles. Before I can even smile back, other men tumble from the skies, and I want to laugh, cry out in jubilation at my good fortune.

It truly is raining men!

Hallelujah!

They start raining faster now—blonds, redheads, brunets, black, white, Asian, Latino (yum), lanky, beefy, short, tall—all the most gorgeous men I have ever seen. All naked.

All for me!

I raise my arms and shout, "Come to Papa!"

And they do.

The first body hits me hard, feeling more like a ton of concrete instead of the delicious marriage of sinew, skin, and bone that I have come to know and love as the male form. I collapse to the ground, wind knocked out of me, and look up at the man who has rained down on me. He seems to have no awareness that I am beneath him, and I scurry to get out from underneath the crushing weight threatening to suffocate me, pressing my bones into the wet concrete beneath my back.

I manage to get out just as another man drops from the sky, a hot African American, bald, and looking just like Taye Diggs. I scramble free of his path, but he lands on my leg anyway as I crawl through the rain-slicked street.

I hear my leg break with a sickening crack. It takes only seconds for the pain to radiate throughout my entire body.

I roll over, gasping, wincing, groaning, and look up to see an entire sea of naked men falling from the sky in ever-increasing velocity—all headed straight for me.

The music reaches a crescendo in time with my shrieks.

*

Bobby Nelson woke.

The sheets beneath him were twisted and damp with sweat. He gasped, trying to regulate his heartbeat, which was jackhammering so hard he expected to look down and see it lifting the skin off his chest. A cartoon heart.

The room was silent.

Where did the music go? Martha? Weather Girls?

Where was the rain? The thunder?

He breathed in deeply and exhaled slowly.

Calm.

Just a dream. A nightmare.

Where are all the men?

Finally, he grinned, turning over in his bed.

Why, there's one! Lying right next to me, looking at me with a concerned face, a handsome face. Even in a darkened bedroom, Bobby could still tell if they're hot or not. It was his specialty.

This one, with a mop of curly blond hair and pecs like Michael Phelps, was a ten.

His voice was husky, sleep-choked. "Dude. You were having a nightmare. You okay?"

He placed what was meant to be, Bobby was sure, a comforting hand on Bobby's chest. Bobby cringed a little, moving away.

This has never happened before.

I have no idea who he is.

Before Bobby could stop the words from tumbling out of his mouth, they came. "Who the fuck are you?"

Also Available from NineStar Press

Connect with NineStar Press

www.ninestarpress.com

www.facebook.com/ninestarpress

www.facebook.com/groups/NineStarNiche

www.twitter.com/ninestarpress

www.tumblr.com/blog/ninestarpress